SEARCHINC

DAVID SMITH

SEARCHING FOR AMBER

Cover artwork courtesy of Leesa Le May

Matador
9 Priory Business Park
Kibworth Beauchamp
Leicestershire LE8 0RX, UK
Tel: (+44) 116 279 2299
Fax: (+44) 116 279 2277
Email: books@troubador.co.uk
Web: www.troubador.co.uk/matador

ISBN 978 1783063 581 (Paperback)
978 1783063 598 (Hardback)

British Library Cataloguing in Publication Data.
A catalogue record for this book is available from the British Library.

Typeset by Troubador Publishing Ltd

Matador is an imprint of Troubador Publishing Ltd

To my mother and sister

CONTENTS

I	Dawn	1
II	Calypso	21
III	The Beguiling of Martin	33
IV	Peter Grimes	59
V	Amber's Return	87
VI	Sunday Morning	109
VII	The Depths of the Sea	141
VIII	The Water Nymphs	163
IX	Moonlight Crossing	175
X	Sam Crow	191
XI	Calypso's Return	219
XII	Storm	231
XIII	Passacaglia	247

I – Dawn

But soon there breathed a wind on me,
Nor sound nor motion made:
Its path was not upon the sea,
In ripple or in shade.

Samuel Taylor Coleridge, *The Rime of the Ancient Mariner*

Dawn – September 2nd 1979
Aldeburgh Beach

Under the fluid metal of a steel-blue sky, the body of a young woman strokes silently through the dawn waves. Her legs are extended, the icy water chilling her skin, her arms reaching for resolution in the graininess of the dawn. As she glides lazily through the current, she disturbs the balance of the channel, releasing a surge of rings, strong and certain. The greens and greys of the water's surface feel thick like sugar around her waist, her wash dragging a chain of fishing buoys from their jaded rest, allowing the wearied gulls no sleep. The project that she has pursued over the past months is near complete, but she is acutely conscious that her true search is as yet unfulfilled.

She reaches a platform around a hundred yards from the shore and looks back at the now familiar view. She scans the coast from the Martello Tower in the south, past the town buildings, towards the headlands at Thorpeness in the north, searching for a clue, any small clue, to the mystery that has yet eluded her. Frustrated, she dives again into the sea and vanishes. A minute, a minute and a half, two minutes go by, before her lean and lithe body breaches the surface of the frigid waters and she shouts into the sparkling air, panting with her desire for resolution. She repeats the cycle three times, each dive a little deeper and longer, each surface expulsion of breath more violent, before swimming back to the platform in a vigorous crawl. As deep as she dives, the depths of the sea hold their secrets still in private dignity.

She pulls herself partly up on to the decking; threading her fingers loosely through the strands of hemp, pulling the rope taut so that the muscles tighten around her neck and her stomach coils and unwinds in rapturous imitation of life. The platform has been bleached by the action of sun and waves. Her exploration is intended only for her own knowledge, her exercise for the solitary pleasure of exertion; the deck ensures no possibility of observation, no attention from passing strangers. This is her dawn sanctuary, precious moments of independence composed before the world has awoken, determination formed in her spiritual intercourse with the sea.

Now fully aboard the platform, she lies for a while in the cold air, satisfied and breathless, her boyish body shimmering in the low rays of the early sun, young and defiant, surveying the peaceful shoreline, searching for some further sign or signal to proceed. Then, still dissatisfied by what she sees, she slips back silently into the deep waters, breaking the surf that dances in the amber light, letting the cool mouths wash the last taste of night from her skin; her lungs full, her body flowing with vital intensity, her legs kicking until they have been swallowed again by the green mist of the underwater, until there is no sign of her body in the churning.

There is no sea like the Aldeburgh Sea – it talks to me.
Edward FitzGerald, author of *Rubaiyat of Omar Khayyam*

As she surfaces for the last time, she hears the seaside air rent by the demented shrieking of herring gulls following the first boats back to the shore. The hour is early still and the beach all but deserted, clothed in its early morning sheen, the gentle chugging of a generator and the lapping of the waves the only other sounds to disturb its slumber. It is still too early for the shallowness of human pleasures to defile the shingle's quiet permanence.

On firm ground once more she relaxes, allows her

exhausted limbs to recover their energy. She feels her gulping lungs rise and fall in the faint sun, feels the delicious tease of endorphins throbbing through her body. The gulls are still laughing insanely around her head, laughing perhaps at the prodigy of her daring, copying the blushing smile that has begun to crease her face. She laughs herself, a deeper laugh this time that proceeds from the intensity of her soul. She knows she can survive, knows for sure she can secure her own future, craft her own destiny, realises all this, here on this beach, in the sharpness of the morning light. She laughs aloud with the gulls at her discovery, breaking the melancholy of their quiet introspection.

Surely there is a new brightness to her eyes that carves beauty into an otherwise plain face, surprising the faintness of her slim frame with the intensity of their strong glare, lighting up her cheeks, high and proud and distinct. She feels the wind rise to dry her skin, holds her head against the breeze, squinting at the day's new brightness, her cheeks glowing like shining berries in the early morning sun, the gusts threshing her short, dark hair into shimmering ribbons around her face. Vivid thoughts colour the shingle, her mind drunk on new-pressed freedom, drunk on freedom's possibilities, numbed a little by its unbounded dimensions, by the sea's redemption.

Later, Jade lies stretched out on a towel on the beach, studying the silver rings on her fingers, the sheen of drying moisture on her faintly tanned skin, the ripples of tone-shadow around her ribs. Thoughts pass through her mind like quicksilver, grains of new ideas bright as magnesium. She is brave shining fortune, newly crafted on this bitter shore; she feels torn between humility and delight. She is determined and her ambition plain for there is a knowing smile written across her face.

The wind drives the first clouds across the sun's pale disc and she feels the chill begin to penetrate her skin; pulls a towel around her to stop shivering. She packs her costume tightly into her bag and pulls on canvas jeans, a scarf and a deep blue cardigan, threads the thick laces carefully back through her drill boots and hangs them over her shoulder. The pebbles are wet and new between her toes, the fresh breeze cool like the sea, carrying the tincture of seaweed and fish. The anonymity of her clothes distorting even more the smallness of her figure.

Externally, she has about her the purpose of one much older; the confidence of knowledge, a firmness of intent that signals much more to come. She is highly logical, allowing her to look past extraneous detail and perceive clearly that which others might overlook. She has a personal depth and dimension that few know intimately, but many admire. And she is her own worst critic, always wanting to do better, always striving towards the next thing, driven on by a desire to achieve for someone she has never known. For despite this outward bravado, Jade knows that inside her heart, she is still plagued by uncertainty. Her inner doubts nag her as always and she must shroud them jealously with her fiery independence, a contradiction and duality of character that belongs to one in love with hope for the future but held back by a depth of sadness, of past disappointment.

She has lived in Aldeburgh now for two months, researching and taking photographs. The idea for her project came from a chance encounter and then a deeper, but unconsummated relationship with a man, Martin, who has continued throughout to bemuse and confound her. His scars of boyhood had become hers by adoption and she had been increasingly intrigued by the contrast between the seasonal frivolity of this festival town and the grim reality of poverty and tragedy amongst the local fishing community with whom he had grown up.

As a foundling child herself, brought up by adoptive parents, her life so far had always been a struggle between her own ambition and the emptiness that came from lack of knowledge of her natural family. Often in the past she had craved for the reassurance of a parent's guiding words, for the knowledge of unconditional love and support that comes from a mother and father. But now, at this moment of transition to womanhood, perhaps, this need for a reassuring arm had developed into the need to reach and touch the firmness of a lover's face for reassurance. Such rapid change in mind and body and clarity of intent is confusing and daunting.

The shredded scenery flapping around her dances in the rising wind, moving with the giddiness of an incomplete plot. She re-runs her earlier thoughts in her mind to confirm her own understanding of the next stages of her plan. Between hers and the profile of any child there is virtually nothing; but she is already attractive, desired, exciting. She brushes the silk of her scarf away from her eyes, takes her faithful camera from the denim bag lying by her side, lifts it and begins to work methodically again, as if physically stretching the pebble ridges of the beach like calico with her lens. In this way, she records for the last time the first moments of new life in the town, the prologue of the busying day.

Originally she found this primitive seascape lacking in inspiration, uninteresting, boring even, compared to the energy of the city, the buzz of college and friends. She had dismissed the indistinct colours of the shoreline that bleach to nothing under the influence of tides, the scorched and blasted heath, the watery marshland, the steady motion captured in stillness, rhythm in silence, preferring to record in the precision of black and white. But today even Technicolor photographs would be hardly sufficient to capture her newfound conceit, the mean scale of the seaside town no match for the exuberance of her soaring imagination.

She is aware of two figures approaching her from the north; early walkers, she can barely make out their outline against the surf and the morning sun. As they approach, one is revealed as a middle-aged man, the other a young girl, holding a pink-faced doll close to her chest, meandering loosely along the beach. She is in steady conversation; he walks silently, not returning her gentle chatter; related certainly, but walking distantly, she tripping through the sand in her own private game of hopscotch, he following more deliberately the gentle curvature of the shoreline, picking through the seaweed-stained stones as if he fears mines on a battlefield.

She recognises him of course. She has seen him before wandering the beach to the north of the town with his distinctive hat and old-fashioned jacket, sometimes walking his dogs. He even has a bit part in the story that she is weaving of this town's history in the 1950s. He is rarely seen in the town itself, living like a hermit in the great house up the coast. His family had owned and developed the Thorpeness holiday village but he was now the last survivor. Each time she had seen him before, he had always been alone and so she is intrigued by the sight of the young girl now skipping behind him. Maybe a niece, she wonders as she knows he is a bachelor. In the relative movement of these two figures, she sees two lives entwined, but somehow separated; two souls walking independent paths, playing with hidden language. She imagines their familial relation is saddened or broken by some unspoken history, but she is a little surprised by feelings of jealousy of the young girl's protector, something she herself lacks.

Their attention is caught by something amongst the driftwood. Jade watches as the little girl stoops to help a seabird that has become trapped in a patch of black pitch defiling the shoreline jetsam. For a while the girl struggles urgently to wash the oil-stained wings with brine trapped in the pools by the water's edge. Her eyes are soon full of tears, but her guardian's eyes are already far off, drawn too readily by the glistening waves. From her vantage point, Jade calmly adjusts aperture and exposure to capture those two figures. Her actions are analytical and precise, measuring the light reflected on the surface of the water, the little girl's frustrated face and the tired shadows passing across that of her guardian. Although she is concentrating on technique, a verse is already in her mind, simple thoughts, like thrift in the wind. The poignancy of the moment captured in her lens. She feels a wave of sadness catch her by surprise, melancholy turning in the smoothness of the stones as they tease her toes underfoot.

Eyes so red, eyes so red,
salt roses in an ash-limed bed.

Jade finishes the first roll of film and reloads, then puts down her camera and continues to watch them, feeling a curious empathy with the girl's urgent administration to the seabird. She sees in her busy demeanour something of her own obstinacy and determination, elements of her own wilfulness. She feels even a little enraged at the way the man is ignoring the girl's efforts. She believes strongly in observation, working beyond visual expression or outward appearance. She won't interfere, but like an actress researching a character she will train her lens to reveal secrets, capturing the careful consideration of a face; a motion, unspoken thoughts and unwritten words. She had once heard a great actress describe her technique – how to speak the lines so that the words themselves reveal characterisation, rather than impose your own view on the subtlety of the author's lines. She had adopted this method in her own photography, but sometimes little things like this girl's tears can still break through the emotional detachment.

She wishes to go over and speak to the girl, but knows she should not if she wants to find the right moment to capture on film. From an early age she has nurtured this ability of detachment, unsentimental, clinical, playing games with the casual knowledge of personality. In this way she exaggerates the dichotomy between the man and his charge – the young girl desperate to save life, her tears mimicking the bird's distress, the man weary, detached from the tragedy, every so often stealing a glance at the emptiness of the sea. This is the nature of her idea of art – to breathe the exotic into the commonplace, make themes dance through light and tone, grain and exposure. To succeed she must cut forensically under the skin to uncover without artifice the raw emotions of pain and joy and love that lie beneath.

Now that he is closer she realises he is not so old as she first thought, probably only in his mid-forties, about the same age as her father would be, she thinks. She knows nothing at all of her father except that she had imagined him to be handsome like this man. He appears exhausted by the girl's concentration. She watches as he falters and seeks the convenient support of a lobster basket, almost breaking the slats with the unbalanced force of his fall, removing his hat to wipe his brow. She sees clear signs of the man's weariness all over his body – in his frown, in the weight of his shoulders, in the sombre colour of his corduroy jacket, his narrow tie and straight, greying hair. Her irritation turns to sympathy. The young girl does not notice his tiredness, and continues her futile resuscitation, oblivious to his heavy sighs, defiantly breathing her precious balm into the poor bird's darkened breast, unaware of the man's frown as he extends his legs in the morning stiffness. Has he almost given up, she asks herself; has he almost conceded defeat? Why, she wonders. What has caused this indolence?

The young girl is suddenly bored. She releases the gull in a flapping of wings and skips off lightly down the sand, singing to herself a familiar rhyme of childlike repetition.

Lavender's blue, dilly, dilly,
Lavender's green
When I am king, dilly, dilly,
You shall be queen.

As she skips, the little girl continues to search the shoreline for new interest. Her face carries the unmarked innocence of childhood, hair wild and unbound in the wind. Her attention seems fickle and pretty, betraying the mercurial focus of the only child; her expensive floral pinafore dragging in the water as if it were cheap cloth, bright red sandals already caked in sand. Jade remembers how much like this she was once: she had owned a pair of red Clarks sandals like those, a long-gone image of her own remembered youth, a fragment of gauze stretched across her own brow. Fey, wilful, caring for all God's fallen creatures, a child inspired by nature, unlimited by the pretensions of adulthood, challenging every rule, every limitation on her own invention.

Even later, as a young girl, wandering the streets of her home town with the other children, dressed in simple cotton shorts and T-shirt like a poet's sprite, Jade would chase the demons of convention, smear paint and river-mud over her sun-baked arms, whoop along with the boys' boisterous war games, all feminine decoration exiled, bewitching them all, deferring to none. She was proud to be one of the boys but acting always as their superior.

Naturally, she had later succumbed to rebellion, descended into the darkness of teenage cynicism, swung violently from sprite to goblin, brooding, dark and rebellious. She had felt at that time consciously as if she had been entering a tunnel, watching helplessly as the economic recession gathered around them, almost remorseless in its progress, tarnishing the bright ridges of her increasing academic achievements with the reality of their increasing lack of money. In response she had gone out of her way to earn her own living, create her own independence, taking part-time jobs, serving in teashops at the weekend, quickly throwing off the innocence of childhood. As she had created her own income, she increasingly rejected the urgings of her adoptive parents to settle down and find a nice young man. As her inexhaustible ambition had grown, she had wantonly destroyed and wasted much she had touched, like a malevolent Midas, breeding her own young woman in her angry thoughts, confounding the expectation of others.

She bore heavily the orphan's curse. She knew virtually nothing of her parents, having been adopted as a young baby, her story that of a foundling left on a doorstep with no history to her name. All she had was a locket with a tiny photo of her mother, standing next to another woman who held a baby in her arms, with the faceless shadow of a man to her side – her father perhaps and maybe an aunt or sister? She had been given it by her guardians on her sixteenth birthday; the only known link to her past. The photo was one of those posed shots taken by a seaside photographer against the painted background of Manning & Sons amusements – donkey rides, candy floss and on the back in tiny pencil it was inscribed simply, 'Me with Sam and Sarah at Felixstowe'. She had no idea even of her mother's name and there were no other clues as to who Sam and Sarah were, whether Sam was the child or the faceless man or whether she, Jade, was even the child. Often she had wondered if she could ever track them down, but there was so little to go on. She had shown the photograph around Felixstowe and asked the police, but nobody recognised them. It was just one of a million holiday snaps taken by the seaside photographers in the late 1950s. There was nothing unique, nothing to identify them by. This, then, was the source of the sadness and disappointment that she still felt in her heart despite academic and increasing artistic success. She was bereft of a mother's arms, having to forge her own way in the world through her own mettle. Her adoptive parents, though well-meaning, had no vision for her beyond marriage into the local community, no basis on which to advise or appreciate the possibilities of her potential. But that sadness, that hole in her heart, had also hardened her so that her will took over her and steered her away from showing outward gloom to the world.

Of course in researching her project and Martin's fishing family, she had often gone back to this photograph and wondered if she could find out more about her own history. Her adoptive parents had both passed away in the last few years and although she had searched their possessions carefully, there was nothing else, not even a letter. So it seemed as they had always claimed, that they really knew nothing more about her origins, and if it was any different, they had certainly taken that truth to their graves.

Throughout her teenage years, she had watched them quickly grow old as the comfortable retirement they had planned after their former lives as domestic servants rapidly turned into increasing financial problems, as their savings and small pensions were eaten away by rising inflation. As they aged, each day they lost something of their vitality, a little less of life shining through their stern expressions, their spirit was haemorrhaging from their souls. Their skin became thin and waxen in the artificial light of the terraced cottage, where they spent most of their time in front of the TV screen – near-beauty hardened and faded by the metallic atmosphere and the sterile sun. She did not feel great affection for them, just thanks for giving her a home but this was always mixed with resentment – she knew this was an arrangement that in some way they now regretted. They had had no children themselves and were not prepared for the tensions of living with a strong-minded adolescent. In retrospect, it was a wonder she had survived those desolate years, the rebellious arguments, without descending into drugs or worse. She constantly sought the strange, the new, and the taste of grim determination sometimes to shock but sometimes just to strengthen her own resolve to continue, her own hopeful idealism. Yes, she had played a little with fire, but never too close to burn herself.

Despite the lack of any physical link to her mother apart from the locket, each passing year strengthened her own mental conviction that she would one day discover more; each year she felt she understood in her heart, from her own experiences, more about the woman in the picture, more about the truth her adoptive parents had been unable or unwilling to reveal to her. She imagined for her mother a series of histories or tragedies that had led to her abandoning her child. With each personal success she had seen the sepia reflection of her likely mother mirrored in the darkness of her own doubts. She felt therefore that she knew who she was, even if she did not know her name. She had transplanted her own cares and worries on her mother's memory. This self-created knowledge had become courage, a memory of a nameless home, of the bitter cycle, of the names of others in her unknown family who had continued to shuffle towards that nameless inferno. Unknowing and unknown, without intervention they would be drawn, colourless, by unerring patterns of history, but history could be broken and fate could be created and she could discover those connections for herself.

Ancient shores, future smiles,
Generations linked on one desolate stage.

Despite all of this subtle insecurity, she was intent on

moving forward; she would not let melancholy consume her. On that she was fully determined. Now that, at last, she had begun to taste the sweetness of success, with every hard-won success she wanted more, determined to triumph partly for the memory of her mother and partly to prove something to all those who had no faith in her ability and talents, who dismissed her work as trivial and wished that she get a proper job.

She looks back at the couple on the beach. The lost expression on the man's face plays again on her mind; it holds some cautious anguish, a distance she cannot quite measure. He is handsome enough, maybe he was once brave also, she thinks, but now he seems so deep in another place that his former pride is divorced from common activity, abstracted from the daily struggle of life. His countenance is disquieting, like the face of someone who has lived too long away from the world's shallowness, someone unable to maintain a desire for life at this level, anticipating already a higher existence. She sees also in his face frail traces of beauty, the still-sharp darkness of his eyes, and the creased radiance of his paper-like skin, stretched sun-torn over high, bony cheeks; his hair quietly turning silver, framing the faded handsome features like a negative.

Yes, there was something grand and romantic about him, or at least that was how she imagined it. This was the imposed truth for which she now searched with the precision of her lens.

She rises and walks a little further along the beach, kicking its coarse reefs with her toes, feeling the wind caress her hair like a watchful lover. She feels alive and excited by such moments, the ability to orchestrate passion through her own artistry, to feel in her stomach the delicacy of her own creation. Was she recording or creating, probably a little of both, in the lyricism of her photographic story-telling?

As she comes closer to them, she sees that he holds a book close to his chest: a small, leather-bound volume. She watches him turn the stiff paper and write carefully in the margins of the closely printed pages, his shoulders arched over his work as if wishing no one to see. She wonders for a moment if it could be a diary, but cannot see in him the patience for mere personal history – too painful surely for a man who shuns outward lustre and dresses so shabbily.

She immediately feels an uncontrollable desire to read those words written with such secrecy, to know his innermost thoughts, his soul's voice. Maybe she could invent a candid religion just for him, a driven spirit; a man seeking his own god, defining his own doctrine, bringing his own conscience to peace in the face of adversity. As she watches his hands move across the pages she notices for the first time the ring on his third finger, almost the only embellishment about his person – heavy, dull silver, unpolished except for the wearing of his skin, a dark amber stone stained like blood in its centre. She feels herself drawn into his story, empathy melting her normal professional detachment.

Strands of the same yarn;
Innocents to plead the case.

The wind rises again, blowing objects around the beach, filling the lazy flags that line the coastguard shed with restlessness. The gulls wheel and clack and coo in their stations. Above them, the Crag Path is still empty, too early yet for any but the hardiest tourist and devoid even of morning joggers. But beyond its narrow barrier she hears the early morning noises of clinking bottles, of engines starting, of footsteps on the upper lanes, the quickening passage of time as the men and women of the town seek their workplaces. One of the fishing boats is returning already, its bright red hull dragged up the shingle cliffs by a yellow land tug. It is exactly 7.23. She smiles.

Through the summer she has allowed herself to become a small part of this place. But like her the town has a split personality, which is the source of her project. She still feels uncomfortable with the contrast between the rich villas and smart hotels that line the shoreline and high street and the mean alleys and ugly, squat fishing cottages beyond; the contrast between summer gaiety and the spine-numbing bitterness of the east winds that blow day and night, seemingly without respite throughout the winter months. She has collected all these contrasting images in the collection of stills for her intended photographic exhibition. Perhaps at last in this man she has a fine and new hero for her imagination, for her portfolio of imagery.

From the bench where she now sits she can watch the man privately as his eyes finally close in on sleep, hidden by heavy lids, the hairs on his cheeks rising slowly with each tentative breath. He wears his loneliness openly, the dark and hollow clothes shouting solitude. She decides she will invent for him a place where maybe he can find peace and love, while he snoozes in the smallness of the morning sun. Despite his drab appearance, she does not condemn him. There are few things about him that she could dislike and a few that could demand affection. Even those that would tell his history are mostly anonymous, common things. Shoes, trousers, jacket, so little evidence of any former history about him, save for the book and that solitary jewel on his finger, and the fine lines around his eyes and brow.

While he naps, the little girl continues to play with her doll by the shoreline, finding delight in every shell and stone. She chases the waves in their lapping frequency; shrieking with delight as the water wets her feet.

Jade studies his hands further. They are delicate, not a worker's hands, with thin wrists and long fingers like a musician. The ring and its amber stone, so clearly a sign of emotion, perhaps even of loss. Someone once loved in youth maybe, darkening a lifetime. She sighs inwardly at this unknown story, feels an urge to reach over to him, put an arm around his shoulders, wipe his brow, blow a daughter's kiss across the small space that separates them, call him *father*, her warmth bringing her whole emotion into his body, projecting the passion of her own gender into his dreams. She feels a girl's affection for this man who was the same age as her father, who maybe had felt such loss so long, holding on to the final flames of passion without distraction. The remnants of two people completely in love with each other, like the words written in his book, drawn in long lines across his brow, thorough and deep. 'Don't walk away without a word. We have time, but you have to choose,' she whispers. Yes, she believes him to be a brave man, braver still for loving once maybe? Was he her mother's secret lover? Fanciful, she knows, but why not?

She looks again to the east towards the vast expanse of water that falls from the sky. Sometimes when she looks at the sea and sets her mind adrift in its indigo streams, times and places begin to twist together in the driftwood, fragments of amber sparkle in the sand, the reassurance of a distant light soothes and fine details, once forgotten, are freed again to roam the glistening shore.

Despite the town's small quaintness, there is something daring about this seascape, something unstructured but majestic, that has caught her, which has suited her art. The three bands of colour that form her images; the foreground, featureless, bleached, graded, like a stage where summer children sink their toes into clawing swamps and night lovers lie twisting in the moisture from the shingle. Next, in depth, is the glaucous cruelty of the sea, more powerful than the other fields, more brutal than any man's power. Finally there is the sky of nothing – no moon, no stars, just grey violence; swirls of midnight blue, devoid of light, flame or passion. It all has a potency of its own that she has learned to capture expertly in her camera.

Her thoughts drift further into nonsense, into naive longing, uncontrolled meaning, allowing herself the luxury of momentary infatuation, so that her heart beats faster. She looks a last time at the man's face, still handsome, yet bruised. She wants to brush the rough stubble with her cheek and kiss him. Don't give up, she thinks; don't slip away from the day without a word. Stay while we have time, while we have our dark sides, our torment; let's wander this forsaken shore together. She shivers and shakes herself back to rationality, feels guilt at these silly musings, carried in the silence, in the intimacy of a shroud.

Maybe she has spent too many of her own recent hours unhealthily candled, awake through night's seven shadows, ripping through the fabric of long dreams, sensing the false dawn of the sun, without a lover to embrace. Maybe it's time she found someone to brave the future with. She had had hopes for Martin, but then again he was another mystery that remained for her untapped.

She realises these sentimental thoughts are distracting her from the serious purpose of the morning. The September wind has drilled through her clothes and she begins to shiver further in its dry smile, perhaps also sensing the coldness of her own thoughts. She steals his image one last time, thinks about asking him for permission to use the shots, and then thinks better of it – these should probably remain her private images. She turns around to the south and walks further down the beach, absently tracing her feet with the lens as she drags furrows through the wet-scented pebbles. She leaves the man and his ingénue, thinks no more thoughts of them and walks up the steps, across Crabbe

Street onto the unsteady pavement of the High Street. Each photograph she has taken is now locked in her camera like strangers together, illicit treasure, powerfully combined in her own imagination.

II – Calypso

And she wrapped the hero in a cloud
of her hair, and she howled across the arid
waves where no one could hear:
'Not to be! Not to be! More than nothing
but less than dread, not ever to be again.

Giovanni Pascoli, *Calypso*

Late morning – September 2nd 1979
The Calypso Café

As usual at this time, she enters the fisherman's café. The sound of the early morning blares rudely from the counter – a DJ talking inanely over a Chris Rea song she happens to recognise and like.

She repeats the lyrics to herself, smiling at the thought. Although it is still early, she can smell the faint glad aroma of bacon and fried eggs and tea on the brew. She has not eaten and feels the hunger from her early start rising in her belly.

She takes her customary seat next to the window, from where she can observe the rough faces of the fishermen just back from sea falling through the door. She holds a cup of bland milky coffee in her hands, warming her chilled fingers, staring blankly through the window, listening to the men's fish-tainted boasts from the dark depths within, etching private smiley faces with her fingers into the condensation of the paint-flecked panes as she waits for her breakfast to be cooked. The radio bristles with electronic gaiety. The floor is wet and muddy from the fishermen's boots. The lazy curls of their tobacco remind her pleasantly of college, of stale pasties eaten in the earthiness of the student bar, of dark caverns of intimacy, spiced with musk and stale beer.

Here she is again amongst men, breathing the smells of men, as they stand sweating their labour through their brine-stained shirts, smearing fish-oil into their matted hair. She watches the milk dissolve in fatty droplets into the brown liquid, and then reappear to her as a picture in her mind.

Worn faces breathing faithless air, lungs filled with the black chlorophyll of diesel and shag. The forgotten margins of men reclaimed from this desolate coast. This is a man's world, but she knows she can hold her own, match them for rudeness and strength and loyalty.

Recently, she has spent many mornings amongst these unsung heroes, watching as they emerge from their night sea world, fascinated by their ravaged faces and the screams of the gulls fighting over overflowing fish bins. They are the rejected working products of the cold, cheerless side of this little town, the underclass that the tourists do not notice except when they want fresh fish for dinner, recognised but unheralded by the musical elite. She is interested by this perverse contrast, knows that the town's reputation, even its soul, has been built on their endeavours but at the same time the money from that success has pushed them to its margins. She had read in a newspaper that it was Mr Britten that made this place, but what good had it done them? She also now knows that what she wants personally in life is far from this place, far away from the vinegar stinging her eyes, from the promenade battered by east coast gales, from the rust-stained sea piled up in waves against the groynes. What she wants are days of clarity and delight, the perfection of her own achievement, but this place has its uses for now, and has suited her purpose well. Her first solo project brief is almost fulfilled and her mood begins to swing back towards euphoria.

Jade is distracted from these thoughts by the figure of a woman in her mid-thirties leaning her bike against the wall of the hotel opposite her. She studies the movement of the woman's hair in the wind, the reddish curls flapping loosely in the breeze. Her clothes are heavy and unfashionable, her cheeks flour-white, as if powdered by the salt air. She pulls her coat closely around her body and searches with her sea-green eyes, as if waiting for someone to return. Maybe the man and her child, muses Jade. Maybe she is waiting for him to lean with her on the rail, put his arm around her shoulder, for love, for protection, for consolation. She is crying. Jade ponders whether there really is any connection between this woman's tears and the loneliness of the man on the beach and his young friend. Maybe she should introduce them, perhaps that is it, a poignant theme for the documentary she should create with her photographs: a reunion, a famous kiss. She catches fragments of their imagined conversation in the wind, listens to their voices. The woman repeats incessantly how good it is to see him again. His grunts of acknowledgement are without humour. They shelter together; huddled under a dark sky, rain the colour of bloaters. Her words to him seem silent but unshuttered, her dark green eyes pleading with a voice the shadow of silk. The distraction of the child tugs between them. The woman breathes hotly on his neck, a passion to which he does not respond. There is now no doubt in her mind that they must have slept together, or that he loves her as much as her open passion reveals.

Her thoughts drift to her own earliest experiences of love. Of course there were many who were part of that journey. She was passionate. Prolific but not promiscuous, using her feminine guile to manipulate the Felixstowe town boys to her advantage. Leading them on just so far, until she had them trapped, impossibly smitten, reeling in her surly wake. She would drive them on with the hint of her body, but was always careful to commit only so much flesh as was needed, as if measuring the promise. Despite her boyish body, nothing escaped her, no secret of womanhood, establishing her claim and then driving mercilessly to her own end. She pitied their mothers clinging to the hope that they would marry well, even during the darkest phases. First boys and then young working men, she consumed and rejected them, shattering maternal dreams of long engagements. She was a prize, clever but a strange one, and knew her own mind too strongly for most.

I believe in life and love and the right to dream.

Where are they all now, she wonders, now that she needs someone to hug, someone to lean on.

She looks back into the gloom of the café, into the stew of smoke and perspiration, searches for a likely candidate. There is an undoubted attraction to these rough men, straightforward, giving her the eye as if she is common property. They had become familiar but not too familiar friends – she had maintained professional distance despite plenty of grunted offers. Their gestures, their unsubtle stares would make most women uncomfortable, but she feels secure in their company. She knows that they would not push. In fact, she probably knows by now all their wives and daughters. She certainly knows their basic honesty. She is sure if she had felt the urge to go further, she would not disappoint or be disappointed. She continues to flirt with their eyes but that for now is all.

Earlier that summer she had cut her hair into a boyish bob to avoid any confusion over intent and it was a while since she had known any man in that way. She was in a period of self-imposed abstinence, not wishing any distraction from her immediate goal of completing her project in time for the planned exhibition as part of next year's festival.

After leaving school with a decent set of exam results she had spent a couple of years at college, studying art but unsure what she really wanted to do next. There, she had mixed mostly with the moneyed southern accents, a much more dangerous breed than the town boys of childhood, not respecting restraint or convention. She shared a flat with two other girlfriends, who both fawned on these strutting middle-class peacocks. Louise was stern and attractive although not classically pretty, with round, over-sized eyes like a doe in heat; pleasing short blonde hair and a broad, winning smile. She was athletic, winning trophies in a host of sports, but tended to move with awkward gawkiness as if her body was uncomfortable in controlled motion. Always neat and well-groomed, she dressed habitually in home county dark green plaid and pearls, her vaguely upper-class speech always full of self-assured talk of boyfriends and dogs.

Sally, on the other hand, was the uncultured, yellowed northern pearl, natural brown locks dyed blonde and dragged into odd curls, still wearing her dressing gown at 11 in the morning, eyes girlish and blue; fearing pregnancy every month until her period came with dull monotony. Her speech was full of *hecks* and *reets* and delivered at breathless speed with a wicked sense of humour. She struggled with clothing and fashion, never seeming to get the right combinations, but they loved her for it and she was funny and full of touching vulnerability and warmth. Jade secretly felt they were happiest together as girls, the visiting boyfriends often an unwanted intrusion.

The digs they shared were so small they often collided in their morning haste – coffee, toast, cigarette smoke lingering in the living room, underwear dripping in the bathroom, a collection of trophies and gifts from their eager suitors stacked precariously in the hall. Whatever Jade wanted, these friends would oblige. From casual girl talk to strange animalistic rituals performed over incense in the darkness of night, three witches manicuring and preening. In long conversations, they would metaphorically grind their suitors' bones at midnight parties and into the early morning, long before the first pallid hopes of day, dancing near-naked in the rain-washed streets. It was all too cute. There was not much work done and they rapidly fell behind in their respective studies. It had lasted two terms before the college threatened to throw them all out.

She remembers that occasion vividly, the set face of her tutor, red and angry, frowning darkly at her across the desk.

'I think you know why you're here...' The words lost in more redness, anger rimming his collar, nervousness sending his fingers tapping, and the crack of gravity in his voice. Outside the room, before the interview, the tension of the moment had screamed at her in the intense static of fluorescent light and she had felt her stomach tighten with worry. But once inside, she relaxed, saw he was more nervous than she, saw past his unyielding eyes, avoiding contact, clanking voice, clawing fumes of masculinity... She heard the mild threats and feigned disinterest. She felt a will weaker than hers trying to force her where she would not go. Secretly she tore at his face, but openly she was polite and flirted. What else could she say or do? She smiled innocently as he rose and shook his head briefly before leaving to discuss her fate with his colleagues. What did she think of as she was waiting in that room; what she was going to have for tea, what to take on as her next project? And, of course, they relented; she had done enough to survive.

It woke her up a bit and she worked harder from then on, but she was, however, no changeling: she would not yield to their strictures, not to any man, not to any petty convention. Screw them all! Yes, maybe she would – one by one. Why not? They clearly all fancied her after all.

After graduation, she was still undecided what to do and needed money. She had tried for a while to be the responsible career woman. She got an administrative job with a city bank, but the loss of the freedom offered by college life hit her morale badly. She hated the daily obscenity of the rushing of Tube trains, the despairing whisper of the wind between the tall buildings, the mongrel trees stirring blindly in the fragile lanes. She had replaced the breadth of the coastal sky with forests carpeted with asphalt, greenery banished to tiny allotment squares and cracks between uneven pavements. However, she was well-paid and partying hard with her new friends. There were lots like her too – pretty faces, sucked dry, bent into frowns by the paucity of language, children of odourless smiles. The girls brandishing Oxford Street names, the boys tattooed, sharp, huddled in tribal groups. Soap-scrubbed young faces with collars buttoned and fixed with gold. Thoughts lost to the world, suffocated by the pace of life, by the acquisition of the material. They were content with, and wanted more of this, but she wasn't and didn't. She saw only the fine line between a yawn and a scream, not a life for her. Not yet, anyway.

So she started to live out a separate life at night, adopted a stage name, joined a band as a singer and danced along to something Celtic and wild rather than the sad punk that filled so many pubs. She rebranded herself Calypso, the new shape of her name building to a peak, then diving deep into the valley. She loved the way it sounded on the back of her throat, she loved the boldness of the shape written on paper, soft and cursive. She was a poet, not a hyena. She knew of course she was in danger of wasting her life, she knew that she could do much better. It was a dangerous world full of dangerous men, who often did not know where the line was drawn. Fortunately, the next spring, before it was too late, she found a job as a pool photographer at a magazine edited by a friend of Louise's. She grabbed it and did not look back.

In the greasy café she gasps at the close passion of these memories as she watches the woman through the window. She is preparing to leave and suddenly their glances meet in the infinity of reflection. Jade turns away, embarrassed. Clearly the woman knows she has been watched and frowns. Jade self-consciously brushes her hair from her forehead, removes strands unblemished by sweat and hard labour. She feels again that empty, hungry feeling in her belly. She is on a journey with a destination, maybe a journey that would lead to the brink of the abyss, but a journey of her own. That earlier life in the bank had threatened to squeeze every breath from her body. The scream was ever closer. She was lucky to get out alive and sane. Now she had the chance she was going to grab everything she could get. For her, this project in Virginia Woolf's 'miserable, dull sea-village' had been the perfect opportunity, the opening up of new opportunity.

She pays and leaves the café to low wolf-whistles. They know her well by now, that she can give as good as she gets. She shoots them a stare that freezes like only the coldest day; deliberately runs her hand provocatively through her hair, brushes her hands down her firm waist and hips, offering a glimpse but no hope of redemption. They are the salt of the earth, pitiful in their narrow bashfulness, but she leaves them now to squirm. If only they knew… If only there was a real man among them, she thinks, she wouldn't disappoint but she feels the source of their hesitation, the barrier of education. Outside the door she coughs the last breath of smoke from her lungs, and pulls out a yellow oilskin coat from her bag.

> *I saw a fisherman mending his nets one summery, autumn day, sitting quietly absorbed among the people of the resort. So poor – he seemed to have the riches of time. Children rushed about in flower-garden colours; people picnicked, paddled, dived, swam, played with dogs. He stood within and beyond it all, plying his patience.*
> Adrian Bell, *The Power of Patience*

The high street is still virtually deserted. With her coat close to her body, she walks past the steady face of Barclays Bank, past rows of chemists and grocers, past the tea and tourist shops, filled with unwanted summer junk, souvenirs that slowly gather dust on glass shelves – lurid pink rock candy, ugly dolls, and china dogs. She notices everything but does not pass judgement; the season almost over, some of the shops already boarded up against winter storms. She passes the seedy penny arcade inhabited only by a gang of pale spotted youths, hears the electronic jingles and occasional chink of a coin but mostly the sullen bored voices, the practised pouts, watching her without watching.

She is beyond the main shops now and passes the travellers packing up the children's fairground on an open piece of ground. She is saddened by the finality of her summer season, the air no longer oily and electric, the smell of fish and chips absent, the grass spread only with rotting festoons of candy floss from the last bank holiday of summer, the lazy click of the little roller-coaster grating only against the steely sky. A few young kids chase sweet wrappers amongst the dripping rides. She pays to ride the Ferris wheel, the only customer. From the top she can see the whole of the coastline spread out before her, falling shadows caught in its great span, the clouds yellow like tar paper against the uncertain blue of the sky. She hears the boom of a flare somewhere out to sea, lifts her hand to her brow, straining to see against the glistening sun. In her mind she forms the next stages of her own plan.

III – The Beguiling of Martin

Yes! Then he wept, and to his mind there came
Much of his conduct, and he felt the shame,
How he had oft the good old man reviled,
And never paid the duty of a child;
How, when the father in his Bible read,
He in contempt and anger left the shed:
'It is the word of life,' the parent cried;
'This is the life itself,' the boy replied.

George Crabbe, *The Borough (letter XXII)*

SATURDAY AFTERNOON – JULY 1976
FELIXSTOWE SEA FRONT

Jade had met Martin for the first time a couple of years ago in Felixstowe. She remembered the events almost as clearly as if it were yesterday.

It was a Saturday. She was working the summer season, saving every penny she could for next year's college fees. The Felsto sports bar was across from the leisure centre, where she worked mornings as a lifeguard. The bar was full of a mix of locals and crew from the container ships, scavenging some repetition of a recent sporting triumph, recalling how the enemy had been stalked and cornered, individual boasts of bravado, and the spoils of victory. The stench of male in that place was overpowering, rarely were there many female customers during the day. It was their world, not hers but it was another job, bar work and for a student it paid OK. The propositions which came regularly were easy to deflect and mostly they were more interested in the bubbly bleached blondes who served alongside her behind the bar.

At the end of her afternoon shift she had walked out into the strong sun, her head still fizzing from a quick vodka and lime shared with the staff. She was not a big drinker, and the combination of the alcohol and the intensity of the light stunned her eyes, made her feel even more light-headed. The streets were glistening in the east coast sun, burnished by the light of recently fallen rain, the tarmac sharp as steel in the late sun's rays. Across the road there were a few forlorn-looking children playing chase around the boating lake. A friend had offered her a lift but she felt she needed some air and so she decided to walk home alone. After all, she had lived in this town most of her life, what harm could she come to?

She walked slowly for a while along the prom, past the groynes and the first beach huts towards the Spa Pavilion and Cliff Gardens. At the old Grand Hotel buildings she turned up Bent Lane onto the steeper climb to Hamilton Road, passing the little row of shops to her right. At the bank, she remembered crossing the street on her usual route and heading into the lane that ran behind the Methodist church. She also remembered the voice that called to her from a doorway; she had seen the tramp there before, ruined, whiskered and shapeless, holding out his shaking hand for coins. Usually she gave him a few pennies and was on the point of walking past but then changed her mind, guiltily fumbling for change. She felt none and pulled out the Queen – smiling, beguiling she thought – the product of her week's industry. She could smell the raw alcohol on his breath, the whiskers around his mouth stained yellow with chewing tobacco. She dropped the note into his palm. That was enough to buy fish and chips for a whole family. Of course she knew in her heart he'd likely spend it on more drink. She didn't much care – she was free, it was her decision and she felt good about this random act of generosity.

'God bless you, miss. You're an angel.'

She walked on a little more lightly now. Her head was throbbing again and there was a hook of a song spinning in her mind from the jukebox in the bar. Suddenly she was gripped by nausea and she felt uncertain of her feet and bearings, the euphoria of her escape from the bar sinking into unease amid the deserted backstreets. The rain had started again, beating down in sheaves on the grey pavement. In the distance, she could hear sirens, probably another chip shop fire, she thought. She turned up the collar of her yellow raincoat against the drizzle and walked into the small, open space behind the Salvation Army. She had been through there a hundred times; there were no cars, just a couple of lads younger than she loitering in the shadow of a doorway. She didn't recognise them; they didn't look local. Immediately she could feel the menace on the hairs at the back of her neck and felt a sudden rush of panic. She couldn't avoid them, realised there was nobody around to hear if she cried out, too late to turn round now. So she took a deep breath and looked straight ahead, continuing across the waste ground, pretending confidence; hoping they would not notice her. But of course they did. 'Hey, darling! Want something?' shouted one. She continued to walk without looking at them. 'Hey, don't ignore me! I'm talking to you. It's good stuff.'

Their cold-hearted laughter was rattling quickly behind her. There was a shout and she sensed a darker edge to their voices – the corner of the old Felix Hotel buildings opposite cast ill-defined shadows against the road. She increased her pace, no longer dodging the puddles, not daring to look back; the imminent threat clearing her mind as her shoes clacked along the road. Behind her she heard a shout, 'Go, get her!' and could hear the sound of a dog barking, then running quickly towards her. She turned round and put her hands up to her face just as the dog pounced and pulled her to the ground in a horrible snarling mess of teeth and saliva. Fear gripped her throat but fortunately the snarling beast seemed more intent on dragging her bag than attacking her. 'I said do you want some stuff?' the youth repeated as he ran up and pulled the beast off her.

In panic, she tried to reach into her pocket, but the kid saw her intention and kicked the spray out of her hand then hit her across the face. She felt a fist and then a kick. The blow was hard and she could feel pain and blood seeping from her nose, down onto her lips; warm, thick stickiness dribbling between her teeth, the smell of pubs and venom on their breath. 'Slag, you lot don't mean shit to me!' he said.

He hit her again, and as she struggled to protect her face, the other lad also began to kick her in the side. She shouted out and although she could clearly hear the horns and traffic and the sirens, the chippie going up in fire like a tinderbox in far-off streets, the sounds magnified by the pain, she feared herself too far from help and in all sorts of trouble. Her life swam before her. The kid kicked her again and she felt something sharp in his shoe pierce into her skin and automatically curled up into a ball, yelling now at the top of her voice for them to get off. Then she heard a click like that of a flick knife, a tearing of paper, the sharp prick of a needle in her side. That was the moment when she thought she was going to die.

That was two years ago. Standing now on the peaceful beach looking over the gentle lapping of the waves, Jade remembers those moments of terror, the intense rain, lightning flashing somewhere in the sky. There was a shout, a voice rolling like thunder, deep and resonant. She remembers the silhouette of another man stumbling through the wilderness of masonry and rubble towards them. Her attackers saw the approaching figure and made a last grab for her purse, but she was quicker. The one with the dog kicked her one last time in the face and she felt her brow filling with blood. Before she fainted, she saw for a moment the face of her angel, blurred and red, and then felt and saw and heard no more.

In the tiny flat where her rescuer has taken her, a wan-looking female face stares blankly at her; skinny and pallid, long, lifeless hair parted at the middle. There is a fuming calor gas heater in the corner, a child crying angrily in the next room. The furniture is cheap and sparse; the room smells of boiled cabbage and gripe water. The girl leaves the room briefly to attend the child and then returns with it in her arms, her face still unmoved. Moans and smells emanate from within the echoing bowels of the building, alarming and intimidating.

'Martin, I'm working tonight so she can stay here if she likes,' the girl says in flat tones, her accent tight and grim. 'That club again?' he asks, his tone animated by Jade's appearance in his downcast world. 'I thought I told you to quit? It's no place for a kid.'

'We need the money for the rent – I can leave her with my sister...'

'I just don't want you going there, I told you.'

She turns away and swears under her breath.

Listening to them argue, Jade is suddenly overwhelmed by nausea. She rises from her seat, but immediately falls back again, feeling faint, unable to support herself unaided. Without a word, the man rises and offers her a hand. She allows him to pull her up and then puts her arm around his strong waist, glimpsing over to the other girl to make sure this level of intimacy is alright with her. The girl seems to understand her question and shrugs disinterestedly.

Jade stays standing for a second as her head steadies, propped up against his chest, her eyes closed, nursing her bleeding, throbbing head, wishing she was home in her digs, wishing she hadn't got up that morning, wishing she could just rewind the tape and start the whole day again. She hears his voice more impatient this time and takes her hands from her eyes to look up at the green-washed walls, her legs ready to collapse again.

'It's OK... you're OK,' he says softly, catching her and helping her back to her feet. They pass through a door together into a small, damp kitchen. Shadowed and sun-starved, paint flaking from the facings of the old cupboards, dusty curtains half-drawn at a tight window looking out over roofs and a dirty yard, washing-up upturned on the dull, stainless-steel draining board, a collection of jam jars and dead-looking plants on the window sill. He sits her down on a stool, rolls up his sleeves and collects the jumble of washing up on to the draining board so that the tap can flow unimpeded.

She vomits inelegantly into the sink. He grunts, washes it away, gives her a glass of water to rinse her mouth, and then without a word, wets a cloth and begins to clean off the slabs of blood that have dried on her brow. She winces but smiles at him encouragingly. Now that her stomach is empty and her head is no longer throbbing so badly, she feels better. She notices how thick his forearms are against her slight frame, feels his chest against her back, the closeness of his breath on her neck, a shudder of excitement she doesn't expect... While he works, she glances round at the sorry squalor, the walls peeling with damp near the ceiling, the ancient wiring, the only decoration an ugly pot plant, a carved painted cross. Nappies are airing on a clothes-horse in front of a chipped and fuming boiler. A jumble of pans and stained plates are stacked on the draining board. When he reaches the wound she winces again, but he continues, holding her head roughly with strong fingers and applying some iodine cream. 'I don't know, it's not that deep, but maybe you ought to get it properly checked out,' he says.

She moans again and shakes her head. 'No need, I'll be OK.'

'Where else does it hurt?'

She points down at her side. He indicates to her to loosen her blouse, which she does slowly, with some pain. Already the bruising from the kicks she has received is beginning to show on the skin above her ribs. She is conscious of, but comfortable with her semi-nakedness reflected in his eyes. After he has bathed her again with the cool water, he carefully inspects her skin but finds only superficial cuts around the bruising and a single puncture mark that is not too deep. He rubs the cream gently into her bruised side and back and applies a plaster to the wound. Still they remain silent, asking no questions, she content to feel the soothing of the sponge on her hot flesh. She is not sure she wants him to stop. 'You'll do for now,' he says at last. She re-buttons the stained blouse slowly and doubtfully, hoping he has not noticed the untidy state of her underwear and thanks him. They sit again in silence while he boils water in an old battered kettle, spoons two pinches of PG Tips into a dark brown teapot.

She remembers how tentatively he'd held her, as if knowing she might fall again, but not wanting to get too intimate. It had been the perfect opportunity but there was nothing sensual in how his hands had touched her, just another chore to get on with. She hadn't known what to say. If only she had known, had given him even a word of encouragement, would he have acted? It seemed to her at the time that he was like a saint in the making, vulnerable but brave – any other man would have taken advantage of that situation.

Sunk back in the chair she looked at him more closely. He was strongly built but his face was tired and drawn, the freckles spreading outrageously from his nose across school-boy cheeks, his expression dulled, she assumed, from lack of sleep due to the baby cries. His hair fell in shanks on to the skin of his neck, deep-toned from a lifetime of sun. He had a rough beard of red and she could see tattoos beneath his thin cotton shirt. In contrast to the bulk of his body, his eyes were dark, dancing and beautiful, looking right through into the darkness of her heart. She found that she had to look away from the intensity of his gaze. Yes, her angel was a rough diamond but beautiful.

He had gone out for a while to fetch fish and chips for all of them while she recovered, drinking more tea, listening to the radio, breathing in the dank air. The other girl had stayed behind so that she was not alone in the flat. She didn't say much but watched the TV in sullen silence. Jade wondered if they were really a couple; she wasn't sure, there was a lack of touching despite the baby, and the girl seemed oblivious to her company. Her few questions were met with monosyllables or a shake of the head. She found out enough, though: they were cousins, not lovers, sharing digs to save rent. She worked in a men's club as a dancer. He worked in a local shipyard, was a loner, no girlfriend, and largely kept himself to himself. Jade did not enquire about the baby's father, but she could guess from the girl's answers that he had done a runner – probably one of the punters from the club. The kitchen grew chilled but she did not wish to leave. She had felt suddenly at home, comfortable and safe for a while. This was real life, not the artificiality of student digs. She was still shaking a little from the attack although she was curiously unable to remember exactly what had happened. She wondered if she had indeed been drugged.

Martin had returned around nine and the sallow girl had gone out to her job, presumably in one of the seamen's clubs. She knew there were lots of them down by the docks, but it wasn't somewhere she had ever ventured. Jade and Martin sat watching TV, sometimes in silence, sometimes in quiet conversation, breathing together the same air, sharing the same moment. In the gloom she had not fully understood the anxiety running like a flaw from his lips, the sallowness of his cheeks, the frown betraying more of life than she imagined. There was more than knowing here: the loss of innocence more than fear, a butterfly struggling for the sun.

Later, after declining the offer of his cousin's bed for the night, she stumbles back with him through the dark streets, past the balconies of newly terrifying buildings, walking in silence, the frailty of her bones balanced precariously against his strong frame, till they reach her digs, where her legs finally cave beneath her and she passes out again.

What lies beyond?
Blackest cherries,
smooth,
polished,
swollen.

At what point does the chemistry begin?
At what point are words superfluous?
At what point is ambiguity resolved?
When is action enough?

He picks her up as if she is weightless and carries her in his strong arms up the stairs. Holds her in one arm while he fumbles in her bag for a key and after finding one turns the key in the lock. The door opens. She groans and comes round.

'OK, we're here but I'm still not sure I should leave you alone,' he whispers on the empty landing, concerned not to disturb the other occupants of the bedsits.

'No, thank you it's fine, I'll be fine now.'

'I'm really not sure. I don't want you passing out again. Let me at least make you some tea.'

She rests reclined on the sofa while he disappears into her kitchen this time. Hearing the sound of the kettle filling and the slamming of cupboards, she shouts instructions to him on where to find things. Her head is throbbing again; she just wants to sleep, to return to her cotton carapace, to her Habitat-covered duvet. He returns after a few minutes with two mugs and some toast then sits down heavily in the armchair the other side of the fire. Her room reflects her student finances – a basic, but comfortable bedsit. The bookshelves on the wall are full of course books and papers. He lights the gas fire with a taper and switches on the radio. She does not possess a TV.

'So, you are an artist, then?'

'I'm sorry?'

'An artist, I saw the drawings,' he says, pushing the toast towards her. She realises he must have seen her sketchbooks on the kitchen table.

He looks at her, his face motionless, frowning, waiting impatiently for an answer. His voice is rough but strangely gentle, with a clear Suffolk burr. She notices again that his ruffled hair has a slight reddish tint to it; his eyes are hazel, the irises ringed with the deepest brown, and his skin covered in freckles. She nods and then tells him again that he can leave now if he wants, really she will be alright. She doesn't actually want him to leave, but she needs to sleep; she is almost too tired to think straight.

That was two years ago. Jade leaves the little fairground and walks out along the sea wall to the South of the town, past the Old Fort Greene Mill, towards the remains of Slaughden Quay. The waves have risen along with the wind and are beginning to crash against the shingle banks that form the town's southern defence. She watches three teenage boys fishing from the beach, their dark green umbrellas almost lost against the vast emerald wash of the ocean. The rain is coming down hard now, but she continues walking, heading for the Martello Tower where the salt marshes start.

One time in her first year at college, before she met Martin, she had found the words of another heart, hidden, presumably forgotten, behind a picture frame, inscribed in shy blue biro on the folds of a pocket book. A work of such gasping passion she had hesitated to read for fear of intrusion, feeling complicity in the intensity of betrayal the verses recorded. She had returned the pages, discreetly, anonymously, to their hiding place, regretting perhaps the breaking of a confidence, but that first taste of another's obsession had awoken in her the desire for her own deeper artistry.

In the ensuing months she had sought out in her mind the anonymous author of that prose, despairing of tenderness, hungry to share her agony. She had taken those short verses and embellished and decorated, created for herself a story of a jilted lover, an edifice of tragedy. And through this exercise she had learnt how to love and to hate with her own words. Now, if she shuts her eyes and lets her mind settle on the patterns of light that float across her lids, she can create stories from pure light. She can act and perform and love in her shyness; slip between the flow and drift, orchestrating the structure of a dream. It is a dream of forgetting, a dream of obsession, and part of the artistry of her photography.

That first evening two years ago, after Martin had left her alone in her digs and she was sure the door had closed behind him; she had staggered to the kitchen and retrieved the drawing pad. It was open at a group of charcoal gesture poses she had made in her college life class. There, so he had already seen her naked intent. She sat on the painted chair, took up her pencil and laid the pad on her knees, drawing out the rough structure of his face from memory, shading the interplay of light and dark values of the surface of his torso.

Although she had never needed to try too hard with men, Jade was at heart a romantic. Usually she favoured a deliberate sensual pattern to her relationships, the slow build-up and the intimacy of pursuit, an enigmatic phrase, a smile, an engineered touch or embrace. With her fellow students too often it had been different and quick – too much to drink, sweaty parties, loud music, the hot tongue in her head that soon seemed to render everything else redundant. Yes, of course she was not a virgin; she had known bodies intimately, fully even, so that it was almost as if there was nothing else left to know. But so often it remained a purely physical act – warmth without tenderness, fleeting stimulation lacking in fulfilment. Often in those circumstances her lovers soon became friends out of boredom with sex but this was not to deny her potential for a deeper faith in a relationship or for greater tenderness.

So, in the quiet of her digs, she had worked quickly, imagining him standing there, staring out of the window, frozen in space, never once looking into her searching eyes. She had drawn the tones of his skin, the gloss of the white pad turning to sepia in the candlelight, accentuating the dark strength of his hair. She had drawn his remembered form as if tracing the 3D curves of reflected light that grace the half-tones and highlights of her own dormant flesh.

Her pencil threaded fine lines of lead deftly through the thick straightness of his hair, through the strong curvature of his shoulders, finding darker shades for the valleys at the confluence of his limbs. She had worked quickly, firmly stroking the undercut that separated the core of his stomach from the utter darkness of the night, transposing reflected light with the deepest rejection of light. In her drawing, he was peaceful but inert and sexless in the depths of her thought. When she had finished, it was as if she had dragged him back from a dream. She had held the drawing to the light and kissed his face.

'Thank you again, my strange angel, my love.'

In the following weeks, in the early morning wanderings of her mind, in the calm moments before her alarm sounded and she needed to rise to work, she had quietly and comprehensively seduced him in this imaginary romance. And then in the evenings, she had returned from the busyness of college to stand on tiptoe in front of her tiny kitchen window, straining to see the face of the moon above the harshness of the street lights, hoping maybe to see him as he passed on his journey home. She knew he was becoming an obsession of memory, but she could cope with that – it had no bearing on the real world, not unless she acted on that obsession. She re-enacted the brief moments of their first meeting in her mind. Her arms stretched in an imaginary embrace around his manly hips, nestling her bruised and bandaged brow in the halo of his hair. She realises she has gone too long without such embraces, but was he someone she could afford to connect with, lost as he seemed in his own sadness?

She breathes slightly, feeling his imagined warmth beneath the fabric of her gown. Quietly his shadow kisses the nape of her neck and she shudders and blows the stars back into the sky. 'Are you happy?' she whispers, as he takes her into his arms again and lifts her gently this time onto the metal bed.

There is a thin shadow that cuts the moments that fly between the sleep of dreaming and the sleep of waking. There are seven shades to the shadow and the shade that falls at the arrival of dawn is the deepest and darkest. She fantasises that he sits in a low wooden chair in the corner of her room, watching her, while she continues to sleep, her pillows floating on garlands of wild flowers. Perhaps he has tried to draw her too while she sleeps. The stilted movement of his pencil following her contours in the same way as his hand had earlier slipped so assuredly over the fragile topography of her unresisting frame. And as he has drawn, the final bonds are broken and she has begun to break free, drifting through the cascades and pools that sparkle in the margins of the day, breathing the living water of unpolluted sleep.

What to do with such obsession?

The stranger in her dreams has caused her to cough and breaks the tension of the half-completed pose. He rises from the chair and covers her with a blanket, kissing her exposed shoulder. At the window, watching for a while as the morning rises, anonymous and insipid over the confusion of rooftops, she imagines him no longer ashamed by their nakedness in this disinterested world.

After the next term, her girlfriends come to visit her in Felixstowe and on the Saturday morning, she wakes after an evening drinking too much wine. Her girlfriends are both asleep on the floor of her bedroom, curled up in blankets she has laid on the floorboards to keep out the cold air. In the grey morning light she feels confusion and dismay. Did she really expect to see his cold and shivering form in the dressing table mirror, rather than the sleeping form of her friends? She is angry with herself for thinking of him like this. In her dream, she had been faced with a choice and withdrawn a little from his body, conscious of the chasm that lay between them. His troubled face staring at the form of her body; his expression sad, but not bitter – a hopeful kind of sad, one that with time she could conquer. She had watched their shadows for a while, reflected in the cracked and tarnished mirror. It was so long since she had felt that complexity of knowing amongst the casual affection of strangers, indifferent to tenderness, finding common cause only in the compulsion of desire. In the stark reckoning of dawn she felt the ache of craving and famished emotion, a hunger of spirit and guilt. By thinking of him in this way, was it possible even that she had now broken him, as a child breaks the wings of a butterfly by holding it too tightly? Had she broken the very gentleness of grace with the frantic selfishness of her lust? Had she broken the trust of her guardian angel?

So in weaker moments as she lies awake, stretches her arms to feel again for the dreamed-of brow of her handsome yet-to-be lover, her eyelids flickering over the watery beads of tears and guileless expectation that has trapped him, her breasts rising and falling in the shallow ebb of his not-so innocent breath. She has reverted to three parts a child again, wrapped in sheets of dewy splendour, fey carapace of airy mist, the lost confidence of her adult progress. She has fallen for a self-created image of him and she hates her selfish curiosity, knows she must act rather than lapse into sentimental lethargy.

'What are we going to do with you, gal?' asks Sally, seeing the longing in her eyes.

That first evening after Martin had left her and Jade had awoken for the second time, she had lifted her head to see the silhouette that she had dreamt was standing against the net curtains and realised his image had already departed into the heartless gloom. She had found her sketch against her cheek and understood and cried, because it was beautiful and he was beautiful. Then the bodily pain had returned and she imagined his shadow at the window, tired beyond caring of that town, watching over her, its small mind his solitude.

But two years have passed. Her blood is blacker now, her mind clearer. She is walking across the narrow spit of land between the town and the tower.

> *When the Landmark Trust acquired the Martello Tower in 1971, it was in a very dangerous state. Vandals and the elements had between them done their best to destroy it. A whole section of the moat had been washed away, allowing the sea to reach the base of the tower. A large coping stone had been dislodged from the parapet, allowing water to penetrate the wall, and loosen the outer brick skin which had fallen off in a large area. The main floor inside the building had been ripped out, and the 1930s concrete penthouse was cracked and derelict.*

> *'To the best of my knowledge, their effectiveness was never put to the test.'*
> W.G. Sebald, *The Rings of Saturn*

As Jade reaches the Martello Tower, she crosses the wooden footbridge suspended by its rope and is greeted by the local trust guide she has arranged to meet. They pass into the central chambers that span the four towers arranged in quatrefoil and ascend the internal spiral steps leading to the platform above. The whitewashed stairwell smells steeply of seabirds. The steps below her feet are covered with grit and straw that has fallen from the roof so that she is aware always of the danger of falling. She emerges out into the howling wind and hears immediately the crash of the sea raging against the beach below. The guide explains to her how the superstructure that would have been there in the 1950s was removed by the trust a few years ago, having become dangerous. They had also repaired the coping stones and railings for safety.

From the flagstone gun platform, Jade can see out beyond the beach into the very depths of the sea. She watches the whitecaps racing through the surge. She watches the darkness of the clouds gathering on the horizon presaging a storm. To the north, beyond the narrow spit of shingle the streets of the town cling to the margins between ocean and heath; to the west the estuary spreads out in a vast waterland of mud and reed and salt flats, pricked by bright triangles of sail and sheep in the fields beyond. And if she strains her eyes, she can also see the distant forms that walk beyond the beds of the marshes to the south, the giant architecture of docklands and shipyard cranes that were perhaps still home to Martin's workplace.

She wonders still about her obsession; there was something about him that haunted her then and even now. There were plenty of other eligible men at college, but she could not get him out of her mind. She had decided she would track him down at work and see what hand fate dealt her.

After some basic research on local shipyards, she found him eventually working in one of the shipwright's sheds at Pin Mill, pulling his broad shoulders along the great lengths of timber that were to form the frame of a yacht. She watched him secretly for a while, focused solely on him and the tools that he drew along the wood, shaping the spine of the boat with careful precision, the grace of his movement mesmerising, seductive, sensual.

On that first visit she had spoken to the foreman first, weaving a tale about a photojournalism project. The foreman seemed doubtful but she had a pretty smile. She had stood with him by the office door on the mezzanine above the shop floor, watching the men's industry, listening to the sounds echoing through the sheds. There were others working with him, of course – carpenters, electricians, and two men caulking the planking of a pleasure-cruiser. She was fascinated by the gradation of tone thrown by the shadows of the high loft skylights, passing across the stacks of timber that lined the walls. There was grime and sawdust everywhere, the stifling aroma of varnish and paint mixed with the sweet resin smell of new wood and the vapour from the steam-box where the curved sections were shaped. She breathed the strong smells in the shed, struggling to imagine how men could work in the close heat of this atmosphere – everywhere the stench of their industry, the sickening clench of glue, the ripe sweat of unwashed bodies. She realised then that it was the same odour she had smelt on his body as he supported her back to her room.

She must have observed him for half an hour, as his body passed again and again over the white lumber, studying the movement of the muscles at the back of his neck as they tensed and strained at the completion of each stoke. Always the same steady concentration, as if thinking of nothing else. He was oblivious to her gaze, oblivious even to the cheery banter of his colleagues. There was some sort of wall between him and the world, as it fixed into the structure of his cage. The foreman showed her other examples of his work as she prized out of him the scant details of Martin's life, always under the pretence of a journalist's story, a photographer's cover.

She learned from the foreman only a little more than she already knew – that he had started there as an apprentice, didn't smoke, didn't drink; a small bedsit shared with his cousin, did not socialise much, and kept himself to himself. He was a hard worker and studious, spent his time away from work learning what he could about his trade, from books borrowed from the office. The foreman understood he had no close family left and had sought an apprenticeship there rather than go to sea with the fishing boat crews in his home town up the coast. For some reason he would not reveal, he seemed afraid of the open sea but still so inextricably attached to it that he chose instead to work on the boats in the estuary as a chippie, rather than give up ships altogether. She was greedy for this background, hungry for knowledge of him, for discovery; working her feminine charms for all their worth. The foreman offered to take her over to speak with him, but she declined. That would be too direct an approach; her immediate purpose was already fulfilled. She made an excuse about needing to get back to her office and left quickly.

On the second visit she was more daring. She had dressed provocatively in a low-cut sateen shirt and tight jeans. As she descended to the shop floor, kicking her court shoes through the sawdust, she was aware that she drew open-mouthed stares from the dull youths who worked the lathes.

He recognised her of course and consented to talk to her without much enthusiasm – he was clearly not happy for his work to be interrupted in this way. During the interview, her journalist's formal questions were answered mainly by monosyllabic grunts and nods, as if no world existed outside the steady progress of his blade along the wood, as if their earlier meeting had been but a memory he had confined to the past.

She tried everything she could think of to get him talking, asked about his home town, where he had learned his craft. Nothing seemed to work and she began to worry that she was just annoying him. Every so often he glanced over to his sneering and winking workmates and seemed more concerned about the ribbing he might get later than her questions. She took some background shots and noticed that he winced as if the flash appeared to irritate him as well.

'Should I stop?'

'I'm sorry, I don't mean to be rude but we have a lot of work on this week.' That was his longest sentence, almost a speech.

She suggested a drink later. He consented under his breath – she guessed to get rid of her – looking back constantly at his colleagues to see if they had heard. There was not even the hint of eagerness in his words, his thick coastal accent betrayed by the straining of his vowels. He took a red handkerchief and mopped his brow and the back of his neck. Moisture glistened like frost on his perfect deep-tanned skin. She wondered what she would do next, given his lack of reaction and realised that he had suggested the solution himself in their first meeting. She recalled his words, *Are you an artist, then?* In the pub later, he had at least been a little friendlier. When she made the proposition, he seemed doubtful at first, but at the mention of money her offer was reluctantly accepted.

As the appointed hour approaches, she waits in increasing anticipation, her knees trembling slightly in the dimly lit room. At last, exactly on time, the stairs to the studio she has borrowed from her former tutor betray the heavy approaching steps of her visitor. He knocks and she unlocks the bright red door, lets it swing open on rusty hinges. She sees his tentative form blocking the light from the hallway; sees how he screws up his nose. 'Turpentine,' she explains, 'but you should be used to that.'

Now that he has arrived, she begins to relax and starts the artistic process efficiently. Like a sculptor, she views the rough dimensions of his body from different angles, sizes up his torso like a block of granite, the angles of his head. Forms float analytically in her mind, genderless topography. She has taken precautions to maintain her artistic distance, careful to respect his unspoken wishes. Her denim dungarees, worn and unflattering, are buckled anonymously over a striped vest. She wears virtually no make-up but there are stains of paint on her cheek, her dark hair pulled back tightly into a rough knot, so as not to intimidate. Still, he seems embarrassed, avoiding her eyes. She moves without touching, like a dancer, beckoning him to move this way and that. The room smells deeply of art, the floor cluttered with rags and sheets, walls flapping untidily with unfinished projects. She hands him a bottle of oil, his glance questioning. 'Sharpens the skin tones,' she smiles and sweeps back an unruly swain of hair from her cheek.

He watches her for a few minutes as she moves equipment into place, adjusts the arcs of light that fall on the backcloth. Her fingers work the barrels of lenses and shutters dexterously without thought. She notices his shadow fall across the floor, looks up at him expectantly. 'Sorry, I was just…' his words falling feebly on the polarised light.

'OK, it's time for you to get ready.'

'Everything?'

'All the way.'

She points to an adjacent room. He enters and removes his work clothes, rubs the oil into his work-tightened shoulders, sweating nervously amongst the shelves of paints and brushes. She calls him back and he wraps a gown around his body, swallows hard, his hands nervously threading the belt through its straps.

'I'm nearly ready for you. Don't worry; you'll be fine once we get going.'

He stares into the middle distance, admiring the evidence of her industry on the walls around him. Five pounds for four sessions, he thinks, five pounds towards the endless bills. That was all, a day's wages in the boatyard. It wasn't his thing but all the same, it's money for old rope. He's not ashamed of his body, in fact it's not modesty that really concerns him, more the unexpected interest of this pretty woman that he feels is an unapproachable distance from his own world. What does she want, and is she just playing with him?

She moves behind the Nikon and signals for him to take his position. She stares through the lens, checking the light, adjusting filters. She walks back to him and moves his body like a surgeon, contorting the muscles, the great pads of his shoulders, adjusting the way the light falls on the planes of his torso. Suddenly he feels like meat hanging on a butcher's hook, like a doll she is playing with.

'Just let me know if you begin to feel uncomfortable, I will be as quick as I can. Your shoulders are very tense – just relax and think of somewhere nice you've always wanted to go.' She takes the first shots and sees that he does indeed begin to relax, almost a smile across his doubtful face. Twenty minutes later and she is satisfied at last. She takes her final shots and signals that he can replace the robe.

'Tea?'

They drink, she pays him, and few further words pass between them, the first contract fulfilled.

In a corner of her mind, she had wondered again at his quietness. No jokes, no nervous banter. It was almost as if this was something normal for him, part of his job. She frowns more as the images are born later in the shallows of her developing tray. She has captured him perfectly, his features handsome but troubled. But the photographs bear an unintended darkness, pathos breaking through the grain of the image. She has captured more than she expected of his soul.

In the boatyard, she had watched how he had felt the form of the timber in his hand, expertly divined the grain through its growth, cut mortises that fitted each other in their individual complexity. Now he would return once more to the boatyard, anonymous and private but at the same time captured forever in these heroic images. He had become just a little immortal. She realised though as she reviewed the negatives that he still showed no real connection to her, no affection, no relationship except that between artist and model, except the private transaction of art, except imagined beauty. To this extent she was no further forward in her quest.

After that first session, she developed a new fantasy about him. That she would crack the dark intensity. That she would find the thing that ate him. Maybe she had been too enthusiastic, too gushing; maybe she had frightened him off. She was confident enough in her own looks to know that she was attractive; comfortable in her own skin, even if not looking for a long-term relationship. Virtually any other man would have made a pass at her in that situation, just for the sake of ego. There was something deeper going on. She wasn't going to be defeated by such a challenge; in fact she was now more determined than ever that she would discover why it was that he was lost in his own sorrow.

The second session passed by uneventfully but by the third he had begun to open up.

'I'm not sure why I am saying this, but I feel I know you.

I can tell you things that I haven't told anybody else, no one,' he said.

Some hope, she thought but worth her trying. What do they say about films, the love interest is there mainly to get the hero to tell us his story? Well, she was trying as hard as she could.

So during the following month before college resumed they had continued the weekly sessions. Each time it became less about art and more about them as she had continued her careful interrogation, starting with his childhood.

As a boy he had lived about as close to the sea as you could get; a life lived like a dream, played out in a landscape of his own. In that regard his life was in some ways parallel to her story but in brutal reality so much more painful than her childhood experience. The more that she delved, the more he reluctantly allowed the storybook to open a little and for her to enter. As he talked, there was a still indifference in his voice that created in her a feeling of compassion but also a tension, a distance. She could not break this distance merely with words. The ritual storytelling was the nearest she could approach – serious, scholarly and ultimately psychological deconstruction. She would have to possess him, but how?

IV – Peter Grimes

Old Peter Grimes made fishing his employ,
His wife he cabin'd with him and his boy,
And seem'd that life laborious to enjoy:
To town came quiet Peter with his fish,
And had of all a civil word and wish.

George Crabbe, *The Borough (Letter XXII)*

Early morning – Winter 1953
Aldeburgh

'What is your earliest memory?'

'I remember the hob-nail boots tramping the streets at four in the morning.'

Salt-steeped, weary from the sea
In boots and oilskins, they appear
More present, anchored and alive.
Katrina Porteous, *Longshore Drift*

He describes this childhood world to her as they float together, contained but separate within their interconnected worlds.

I loved a woman once, and she loved me.

They come in waves, emerging like rabbits from their cottages into the darkness of the night. They shuffle in groups towards the fishing huts, their bodies stiff from sleep, dragging ropes and tackle along the cobbles, breathing heavily in the night. When they reach the boats, the men stand grimly, saying little, smoking and staring at the sea, listening to the stays whispering in the wind, their feet stirring the shingle. They are strangers to daylight, longing for battle, dreading its consequences. The air chilled and fresh like sherbet. Salt stains their lungs. Such early sunless mornings were his heritage.

If he listens closely he can still hear the creak of his father's footsteps in his mind, the frozen cough rasping in the air, the heavy sounds of starched overalls and the crack of leather hardened by sea water. He can hear his mother's voice straining anxiously in the parlour.

He tells her how he would carry the little stool to the window ledge, pull himself to the sill so that his nose became frozen to the frosted pane, watching the breath of the men outside glimmering like little fires in the air, his lungs full of coal tar from the vaporiser. From his lookout, he could just see the icy sea, the torches floating around the braziers, count the hunched forms gathering on the shingle, rubbing their hands against the bite of the wind, the gales tearing the words from their mouths. This was their daily parade – each man, each jacket, each piece of tackle, known intimately and anonymously. He tells her of the wives and children, the shoreline stories, the tales of hardship and violence, his childhood longing for the time when he might join them, his mind intoxicated by the smell of fish and salt, jealous of their comradeship.

In his childhood room, shared with his sister, he would draw the blanket close around his body against the cold, shivering in the dampness, the burning oats filling the house with fragrant smells. He heard his mother's sweet gentle voice speaking patiently, insistent that his father left home with warm food in his belly. Boots in the hall, the rough sound of their parting embrace, the door squeaking wearily on its rusted hinges before it slammed shut. And then emptiness, silence, no sound remaining except the gulls restless on their night perches and the sea, as always, rocking against the shingle. Silence as his adored mother creeps back to bed and the peace of waiting descends like the last cut before dawn.

He would stay for as long as he could at his lookout, watching his father's brave shadow move with the others in the street, strange and foreign in that cold gloom. Coxswain, warrior, worshipped – his only boyhood dream to join him on the boat, in battle with the sea. If the air was still, or from the east, and the sea calm, he would hear the curt orders, the shouts and jokes between the men, the sound of chains and winches as twenty of them turned the capstan, releasing the heavy keels down the beach. One day he knew he would be there, too; that day could not come too soon. He watched the tiny dull-coloured shapes, arks of wood with dark sails, the green and red lights of the masts, the false moon on the waters from the cabin glow, blown on the restless waves, riding with them until they were gone; the sails painted ink on damask, the last lights driven into the glow of a false dawn. Only then, when the dull drone of the diesel engines had faded into the blue-grey sea and the only sounds left were the constant rolling of the waves on the shingle and the excited cries of the gulls, would he return the stool to its place below the night table, creep back into the security of his sister's bed, feigning sleep, safe in her arms in the night air until his mother's voice called them down to breakfast.

Those were his earliest memories, dreams far from the reality of day. Memories of a place left behind, that was no more, which had been destroyed, which had been all but erased from his mind.

> *We've always lived on the edge, boy:*
> *Small boats, lines and nets.*
> *We've always fished as the old men fished,*
> *And the old men showed the sea respect;*
> *For they'd wait for the fish in their season,*
> *Shootin' a dozen an' two.*
> *I'll tell you, there's just one skipper out there,*
> *And that's not you.*
> Katrina Porteous, *Longshore Drift*

Another time he tells her about his family. He tells of his memories of his mother, Ellen, fretting over his father's evening meal; his sister, Amber, crowding around his father's legs, hoping to catch the smell of the sea on his clothes. Peter, his father, was small, bearded and quiet away from the majesty of the ocean, uttering hardly a word as he returned each night. Preferring music to words, he would hum a little as he shook off his clothes and sat steaming in front of the hearth, never joining the others drinking gin at the Blue Boar, preferring instead the comfort of his family's company. He would smoke quietly, while his wife and daughter sang over their mending. His father could not read, but knew everything there was to know about the sea; had not learned to navigate by charts, but could draw a map from memory of every creek and shoal for twenty miles. This was an education in boats that Peter had learnt from his father, which Martin would one day learn from him too. His mother would take them regularly to the Union Chapel, but his father's religion was hard work – there was no time for indulgence. Martin worshipped him, they all did. He was adored.

His mother was beautiful. She heard him repeat this often. He remembered her eyes as a depth of green, matched only by the intensity of the sea, pools of jade that reassured, like water lapping the breakwater on a winter's day, or a cat's gentle purring. At the sink, her hands felt soft on his face like milk, unlike his father's, which were sore and ridged from the ropes. She was well-educated, from a better-off family of merchants and ship-owners, the Garretts, but had married for love, much to the indignation of both her family and the rest of the town. Her ancestors had been suffragists and pioneers of women's rights. She had inherited the same strength of spirit and independence. He enjoyed her protection, her favouritism, sought sanctuary in her apron, hiding at times there from his father's gruffness. It was she that had fed them, educated them as best she could, and filled the long hours that hung open before his father returned with cheerfulness. She was skilled in needlework and when she had finished mending shirts and socks for the family, she sewed and knitted to supplement their income with patterns torn out of *Woman's Own*. He still had a jersey from that time with an anchor on it. Embroidery in those days was a luxury but he had understood nothing of the meaning of industry in the innocence of childhood. He knew only that she loved them and sang to them in a voice his father said had come to him from the sea. Walking in the wind on the shore, telling a tide by the seaweed it left on the beach, a south wind by the stench of mud on its wings from the marshes.

These earliest days were stretched out like new canvas in his mind now, becoming open to hers too.

There was a strict hierarchy among the women, depending on their husband's position in the boat. His mother had that honour as the coxswain's wife, but was considered by her peers too young for such responsibility; they were also suspicious of her background. She had not taken her ordained place. In the long wait for the boats to return, while the older women talked, mended clothes, swapped stories, prepared the tables for the catch, she had preferred to sit with Martin and his sister, making it her duty to watch over the younger children. He was huddled in that pretended education, hearing the stories of countries far away. Watching the old men repair the damaged nets, the boys sew wind-shredded sailcloth and prepare the bait. He lay there silent, amidst the song and the smoke, breathing in the rich tradition.

Two years ago then, through their meandering conversations, his birthright, his world, had taken on some meaning for Jade. It had given her the idea for her first solo project – contrasting the experience of the underclass that worked almost unnoticed with the sea with the glitterati that composed and painted and wrote about it for the better-known festival. And over this last summer, as she had charted in her photographs the story of these brave but forgotten working fishermen, she had also corroborated Martin's own story where she could by interviewing many of the older folk in the town. Now she felt she had a truer picture about what his childhood had really been like and the mystery of the man only deepened with the knowledge of his tragedies.

Martin's childhood afternoons were broken by the return of the boats. As soon as the lookout sights the sails, there is an instant transition, the winches cranked, the air filled with rust and oil, the whole crew manning the great capstan wheels. The women watch as the keels are dragged up the beach onto their overnight cradles. Watch as the strange brown and silver shapes are unloaded from their steaming boxes – dogfish, skate, cod and herring, stranger unnamed forms still drawn from the deeper waters; caught on long lines or small drift nets. The stench of the fish a powerful memory in all their lungs, treasure from the depths of the sea.

'But what became of your sister?' Jade asks impatiently one time.

He is reticent and at first tells her only that she was beautiful, too. She had inherited her mother's singing voice and independence, the colour of her eyes, her pretty face, wide and beguiling. Her hair however was burnt amber in contrast to her mother's lighter locks and fine as silk. Until she was twelve, she was Martin's constant companion.

There is a family scrapbook that Martin now shares with her, full of grainy pictures of relatives and ancestors carefully pasted into the pages. It was an exciting period for the town, he says, with the festival starting and many famous visitors in the summer. There are some postcards pasted in the book, a few seaside images of Aldeburgh *the quaint little watering-place* described by Wilkie Collins in his novel, *No Name*, and the coast – the carnival floats, the model boat pond, the summer tourists, shots of the fishing boats and the Martello Tower with its strange superstructure. But most importantly there are a precious few scraps of letters from Amber to her mother before she disappeared for good in 1959. She reads them and is saddened by the painful separation they reveal.

'There don't seem to be any pictures of Amber here Martin?' she says.

'I know, but only she could tell you where they've gone,' he tells her strangely.

He seems to have in his memory a vision of his sister that is only half-human, a child of the sea his mother said, like exotic flotsam delivered to them on the tide. Bright and wild, she had imagined for him a world of creatures and sea spirits. She saw in every natural object a meaning or a gift, breathing joy into their every activity. Playing with the doctor's dog Snook on the beach, dressing the same as the boys, rough cotton shirts, thick woollen jumper, rolled-up canvas breeches, refusing any bows and pinafores. Her hair was long and wild, rather than the plaits and braids that were still the fashion. She drew admiring glances from the older boys, and the other girls were jealous of her natural grace and intelligence. They were naive, as she loved her way through life, acting out the theatre of her mind. It seemed the entire world was her creation. He shows Jade a story from a book that his mother and sister used to read from, one of his sister's favourites:

On this peninsula, the sole inhabitants are an old fisherman and his wife, and their adopted daughter, Undine, a beautiful and fairy-like creature of eighteen; extravagantly wild and perverse, yet amiable and artless of temperament. The old couple had rejoiced, some years before, when they had been blessed late in life with a child of their own. But the child, playing, one day, by the water's edge, fell in suddenly, and at once disappeared. In the depth of their grief for her loss, they were astonished and delighted, one summer's evening, with the appearance in their hut of little Undine, who was dripping with water, and who could give no very distinct account of herself – her language being of a singular nature, and her discourse turning upon such subjects as 'golden castles' and 'crystal domes'. She had remained with the fisherman and his wife ever since, and they had come to look upon her as their own.

She was one of the race of water-spirits – a race who differ, personally, from mankind, only in a greater beauty, and in the circumstance of possessing no soul. The words of Undine, divulging her secret Ariel-like to Huldbrand, speak as briefly as we could, and far more eloquently – 'Both we, and the beings I have mentioned as inhabiting the other elements, vanish into air at death, and go out of existence, spirit and body, so that no vestige of us remains; and when you hereafter awake to a purer state of being, we shall remain where sand, and sparks, and wind and waves remain. We of course have no souls. The clement moves us, and, again, is obedient to our will, while we live, though it scatters us like dust when we die; and as we have nothing to trouble us, we are as merry as nightingales, little gold-fishes, and other pretty children of nature. But all beings aspire to rise in the scale of existence higher than they are.'

Baron de la Motte Fouque, *Undine: A Miniature Romance*

At night, after Ellen had put away her sewing machine and knitting patterns, she often read to them from books like this one bought in bundles from the Salvation Army for a shilling or occasionally as unwanted stock from the new bookseller in the town.

A town that lacks a bookshop isn't always a town that wants one.
Penelope Fitzgerald, *The Bookshop*

His father had granted her this one extravagance, for he too loved to hear her reading voice. She read from Everyman editions of famous storybooks – *Hiawatha* and *Moby Dick* were his favourites – tracts on self-education, fables, and adventure fantasies. He learnt the three Rs on his mother's knee and before he reached five, he could describe the wonders of the world as if he had visited each one himself. By seven he knew every detail of the modern marvels of science from the black and white images in the *Children's Treasury* they possessed. His sister let him shade the illustrations with cheap colours from her paintbox while she sang to the creatures on the shore. She was truly the happiness of his beginnings.

'They say that Jimmy Flynn's brother fancies you, Amber.' 'Really?' she says, blushing. 'But I could never marry a fisherman's son!' They laugh and he asks her to tell him the story again – her favourite; about the prince, the fisherman's daughter and the evil wizard who set her three impossible tasks to win the prince's heart.

'So why did Amber and your mother fall out?'
'Only she can tell you,' he repeats.

Jade decides to change her tack. She takes him back to the day in Felixstowe when he had rescued her as her lifeblood ebbed away, after she had been mugged. 'That was a moment then when I thought I was going to die,' she says. 'I think you saved my life.'

Had she really been dying? Would she have died? Can an angel with a marble face ever die?

Jade contrasts their life fortunes in her mind. Her own ambition is clear; she is a young woman in full flood, searching for a destiny, aching to be noticed by the world, to make a name for herself, cultivating a smile, flirting with life, creating her own journey. Yes, she has her own childhood tragedy, but it was long ago, before her memories began. The careful image of her mother that she has developed and protected is both without evidence and unchallengeable. There is nothing to search for as she has nowhere to begin and if there is a hole in her heart, it is more immediate, more about love and companionship, someone to share her journey, to love and protect, to enrich and support.

Martin is handsome and strong, desirable to the world, but hidden, a life trapped completely in a crust of despair, punctured by disappointments, fragile and unconfident. She knows that he is capable of far more, she knows already that he has a skill and a passion, but no ambition, no direction. There is a bitterness borne of triple tragedy: the loss of his father, his sister and his mother. These are anchors to his heart that will not let him move on, but which he will also not break away from. She can see hope for redemption; she can see a route to solve his depression, but this will take an extraordinary woman and a commitment to the search. She is still not sure if she is the one.

However, she will give it a go for she is determined to break through, wrapping his life like a ribbon around her fingers, stretching discovery to her own ends. Can alabaster ever crack? Can the face of an angel ever shed a tear?

Tortured sands, cream applied like a salve, torment, the click of the trigger, the pistol cocked, and a shout. We all have our dark side; all carry the seeds of our own destruction.

'What are you doing now?'
'I'm writing down your dreams for you.'

There were times when Jade stayed up all night, writing until dawn, shutting her ears, flying with the owls, breathing the lilac mists of scented asphalt.

Once, in love, they danced together in the sand.

After the final of the four photo sessions, they talk in the darkness, into the depths of the night in the intimacy of her shroud. It is as if she is a suburban Ophelia, reaching out with besotted love to her tragic prince across the night, his dreams ripped beneath by the rose-tipped shoals of doubt, knowing that he has such great sadness of his own. Like Ophelia in *Hamlet*, she is rejected by this troubled soul. Unlike her she will struggle on and avoid insanity. And in that dark studio his knees tremble in a new fear that she will really discover him, that his heart will let slip some secret in his gaze and he will, at last, discover things he had rather kept hidden.

She spreads fingers over his face, over that inert topography, so that he can feel the heat of another's breath in the ridges and hollows of his nose and cheeks. She watches his dark eyes shine briefly with colour, brows beginning to frown away the deepest shadows of despair. And for an instant she thinks she can see a way through his pain, to restore this spirit, broken and bleeding.

Did you know there were times that I stayed up all night to wait for you? I was patient, stranded on the other side, dancing till dawn in the starlight.

Above all from that early childhood, Martin recalls guiltless days. Hours spent searching the high-water flotsam for nodules of the reddish-bronze stone they called treasure – tangled like tar in the seaweed. There is a story that love resides in amber. Not the garish love of gold, too cultured and precious for such simple lives, but a deeper love, a quality of affection seen through the depths of an unpolished stone. Resin trapped in the flaws and pockets of complex inner surfaces, tears dropped and cooled in the restless body of the sea.

They would search together, Martin and his sister, crawling along the shore, running in the shimmering sun, faces lit by the fragile light. Her smile was home to his infant heart, her arms the ready protection of sun-warmth, brown and knowing in their safety.

The coastline was their desert, the marsh and heath their landscape, the stage of their endless roaming. Their footprints were shoeless in the shingle's formation, mountains and inlets of miniature geography. He tells how she used to lie staring at the sun, her legs a crutch for the sky, cotton breeches bluer than air, gems of chestnut crystal sparkling across her cheeks. Her laughter twinkled in the air.

Sometimes, when the hotness was delicious enough, they would kick off their shoes and leap into the margins of the ocean, breaking the power of a thousand-mile wave with the sturdiness of their legs, standing against the surge until the brine dried in glistening white marks around their shins. In this ready sink they washed the stones, tasted their saltiness with skin and red tongues – turned the coolness of their form in eager mouths.

His sister told him tales of another family, of imagined caverns and halls of sea kale, ancestors who swam in unnatural skins in the darkest lines of the sea bed. Crusty rooms covered in gemstones, serene profanity. Smooth and light in the palm, protecting the secrets of its inner glow from untrained eyes. Roughness hiding inner beauty – that is his story too, Jade believes.

Vulcan climbed the last hill by the light of a beautiful sunset. There lay Owlbarrow on the slope below them; it glowed

like a fairy city in the heart of a coal fire, beside the flame-coloured sea.
Kathleen Hale, *Orlando – A Seaside Holiday*

In the evening, they would lie together on the bone-parched shingle and feel its radiant warmth on their bellies, grinding chalk into their hair, roasting slowly on the coals until the heat was gone, counting treasure until the first stars came. She named each star from her father's instruction, until the sky took on its robe of silver above its darker mantle.

He recalls to her the glow in his sister's cheeks and the emerald in her eyes and tells her that love was there. Yes, they would search for amber in the last light of day, their words dropping like a marsh harrier from level to level. Did a brother ever love a sister so?

So, in the final darkness of that studio, he opens up to her at last and Jade carefully gleans the rest of the story, fills out the early memory of a child's undisturbed gladness before the onset of those triple tragedies. The unbroken pattern could not last; of course, there was no protection from the harshness of life.

The fierce winter of 1953 destroyed their innocent fortune. Throughout the east coast, many lives were lost in the flooding of January 31st: 38 at Felixstowe, 58 at Canvey, 37 at Jaywick. Days, even weeks passed when the weather closed in and the boats lay idle and the fear of hunger stalked the streets. Their cottage in the last of Slaughden village was washed away. His father was struck down with an illness that left him exhausted and weak, and threatened suffering and poverty. Many had told her since of the heavy faces on those winter nights. Faces that seemed to grow suddenly tired, as if exhausted by the struggle, aging by the hour in the shadows of the evening fires, faces that seemed to know already their time was almost spent. The long, warm days of summer were like a far-off dream. Jade had seen the memory of it on the faces of those survivors she had interviewed over the last few months.

But even as the worst was upon them, relief had come, temporarily. The late spring of that year had brought better weather, his father's spirits had recovered, they had found new lodgings and soon the nets were full and the streets smelt again of tar and fish and salt-stained sailcloth. In the summer, the day-trippers returned, pretty girls strolled the promenade and suffering was soon forgotten – relief and thanksgiving amongst the salt-splashed cottages. A normality of sorts had returned to the routine and structure of the town. The rhythm of the catch dictated by the sea – the early morning departure, the shouts of the men, the holiness of the women, the long hours of waiting before the epiphany of the return. But that season proved to be the calm before the final storm. They were unprepared for the events that would lead their world to forever change, to race to destruction.

Jade stares down from her elevated vantage point on the platform of the Martello Tower at the long spit of land stretching before her to the north, and in her mind's eye can imagine the scene that late summer, the fires burning and the whole working population of the town down on the shingle. The evening, hot and languid, a period of plenty after the winter's hardship, gulls are squabbling greedily over rich scraps, children playing merrily amongst the huts. The first autumn stars still hidden in the deep indigo sky.

'It was my sixth birthday. August 26th, 1953, I sat with my father watching the crew box the fish.'

His mother and sister were twisting wool, watching the older girls as they giggled and flirted with the strong-armed trawler crews from the boats tied up at the quay. Someone had brought a barrel down to the beach and the men passed the thick warm liquid around the circles in rough-slatted pails. Somebody else had brought a fiddle and started up with 'Lillibulero' and then Uncle Ned started to sing 'Old Joe Has Gone Fishing' and the others joined in. The summer sky clear and cloudless, the shadows long from the setting sun, the crackle of wood burning in the braziers, baked potatoes, and homemade fish and chips. There was a grainy stillness to the wind. The centre of the town was full of hundreds of people, making their way up towards a music concert in the parish church, but away from this throng at the far end of the beach was their own private playground, empty after the holidaymakers had returned to their hotels and B&Bs.

Around nine-thirty, the lookout whistled. Everyone knew the signal, the signal for strangers. At first there was silence, then a whisper. One by one they turned their heads to the North, some standing to see better, feeling the tension of the moment. Soon they all stared towards the town beach to a place where two shapes had appeared. 'Revenue!' someone cried and there was a scramble to cover the ale. The crowd jerked and hushed, and then there was silence as the two shapes strolled casually towards them.

The two young men appeared to Martin to be straight out of a storybook, dressed almost identically, dark slacks and white shirts, sleeves rolled up above the elbows. The taller one carried a jacket over his shoulder, the other wore a Panama; both carried musical instrument cases. Their appearance in the late evening sun was like that of two young matinee idols, features sharp like silver nitrate gods against the metal of the sea, cutting the air with their swagger.

His father scowled as they approached. He recognised them first – identified them as the two Ogilvie brothers from the big house up the coast. A sigh of collective relief and the crews went back to singing and drinking. His sister smiled at him, everything was alright then.

But the two lads did not stop, did not seem to want to respect the unwritten rule of separation between the town and the great estate. There was casualness to their gait, which suggested they had no purpose, a freedom from responsibility lightened their stride. They appeared unaware of the conventions of class separation within the town.

They walked right into the midst of the revelry, watched closely by a group of girls who had been flirting with the trawler workers. The girls attempted disinterest, brushing out their hair, pouting imagined cigarette smoke into the wind, but each of them followed the two strangers with the focus of hawks, their attention fickle and redirected. The two lads stopped by the boats. The taller laid down his jacket carefully on the prow of a tender, all the while puffing rings of blue tobacco into the air, surveying the beach with the air of one who did not need to try too hard. Martin's sister released him from her protection.

He ran to join the other boys, dodging to and fro between the smacks, their faces red from the game, backs burnt raw by the wind and the sun. While they ran around the interlopers, they heard strange words carried on the wind, eloquent and exotic to their ears.

'Hey, mister, got a light?' shouted one of the friends. How he always longed to be brave like his friend, Jimmy Flynn.

The elder of the two lads lifted a silver Zippo in the air, so that the solid metal glinted in Jimmy's face. He raised his eyebrows in an unspoken question and Jimmy nodded. Slowly, the young man took aim and threw the object high in the air towards him, but when it returned to earth and Jimmy caught it, he found it was only a pebble and they laughed at him, as if he would have expected otherwise. Then the younger of the two boys stooped and took another stone and bowled it towards his brother, who skilfully hit it full middle with his instrument case so that it flew high into the air. They marvelled in silent admiration at the shot. The stone landed by Martin's feet.

There was a struggle, but he had it. The others pushed him forward.

'Hey, kid, want to play?' the lad asked. Martin shook his head, struggling to resist the tears welling in his eyes.

'Cat got your tongue?'

He shook his head again. The others laughed. At this moment he longed only to run back to his sister's side, but there was no escape from the eyes of the gathering crowd.

Seeing the pain in his eyes, his sister pulled him away, gazing intensely at the young men as she wiped the salt-tears from Martin's cheeks. She stared at them in silent defiance, but unmoved, they carried on with their game, the elder one taking his pipe from his mouth and resuming his guard. This time his brother bowled and he hit the pebble right out over the boats into the sea. 'Six!' he shouted and grabbed Martin again, holding him high in the air, turning on his heels, aping victory at the other boys. Martin felt he would fall, sobbed uncontrollably in his arms.

'Leave 'im be, you should be ashamed a'yerselfs!' shouted Amber and tried to pull him down from the boy's shoulder, grabbing at his shirt. There was a small tearing sound and her fingernails met his chest, drawing blood.

'Whoa, little lady!'

Her defiant stare subsided to alarm. The boy lowered his arm to feel the scratch, holding Martin firmly with his other arm, head down above the shingle, so that he could hardly breathe. Martin felt he was going to choke and screamed. The boy lowered him gently down to the sand and his ears filled with the hot jeers of the other boys' laughter. His sister grabbed him, causing the lad to lose his balance and fall to the ground. A voice shouted to them to behave. Others lifted their heads from their tasks.

'I didn't mean…' Amber attempted to say.

'No harm meant or done, just a scratch – it's an old shirt.'

The boy got up and brushed himself off, while Martin watched from the safety of a boat. 'Here, little man, buy yourself and your sister some chocolate.' The boy threw a shilling towards him. Martin caught it and ran like the wind.

The two brothers head back towards the north. The younger boys follow at a distance, until they are far from the town, halfway to The Meare, around a mile from the town beach.

Every so often as they walk, one or other brother bends down to examine a piece of driftwood or toss a pebble into the darkness of the sea. Martin and the boys run and fight through the dunes, like Indian trackers, hiding behind clumps of furze. They follow until they have reached the outskirts of Thorpeness.

Here, they will go no further. Here, the path goes inland towards the great house that stands in the woods. They have all heard stories of the sting of the groundsman's belt. It is quite dark, and the wind is beginning to grow. Martin feels the goose bumps form on his back in its cold breath. In the distance behind them, the lights of the little town seem smaller than ever in comparison to the vastness of the ocean, and he can feel the tears welling up again in his eyes. He knows he is far from home, longs for the security of his bed.

'Last one home's a sissy,' says Jimmy.

They run home, silent as wolves. The fireflies dance around their ears, the sound of the crickets thick in the long grass. Behind them, Martin thinks he can hear a girl sing, in a voice clear and translucent like the sea, but when he looks back there is nothing except the wind and the waves and a few washed-up carcasses on the beach. His father gives him such a beating when he gets in, late. Amber, of course, is already curled up in her bed.

A month later, many small boats are caught by an

unexpected change in the wind. His father's boat is amongst them. Today, as she stands on the platform of the tower, Jade can imagine it all.

The sprat boats had taken the early morning tide. They had been fishing all morning and the nets were full. Suddenly the wind had veered sharply to the southeast, and begun to drive them out onto the banks. Those that had gone north had seen earlier that a gale was brewing and beached as soon as they had got in their nets, but Peter and his crew had been fishing around a mile south of the town, near to a series of treacherous shoals. It was around noon, they too were heading towards the beach and had passed the outer shoal, the crew struggling against the growing mountain of steel-grey waves, pulling desperately at the sheets.

She imagined the scene as the ropes wrestled their arms until they were almost separated from their bodies. Peter shouting orders, yelling defiantly at the wind, his words torn with contempt from his mouth as soon as they were spoken, and his instructions lashed back with torment around his brow. He strains at the tiller, changed in a moment from mariner to warrior, but he is weakened by earlier months of illness. As they begin to cross the inner shoal, they are overwhelmed by a great wave breaking over the quarter of their boat that more or less knocks her head in. Then just as the boat is luffing and before Peter can recover the helm, a second great wave strikes her on her broadside and curls right over her; they are forced over on to the starboard side, her mast and sail partly in the water.

They are about 150 yards from the shore, being driven by the wind and tide. With the sail in the water, the boat cannot right itself, but also cannot sink. They struggle with the tackle, both the mizzen and foresheets flapping around them. Human strength is thrown back at them with disdain. Heavy rain now begins to flail their backs with anger while lightning teases the horizon, the great wind howling relentlessly around the halyards. Peter takes his knife and cuts the sheets himself in an attempt to right the boat. The foresail is free and it falls fully into the waves with a thud, flapping violently around the deck. Now he can see the lights of the shore ahead, blurred and distant through the clouds of rain. He lets off the distress flare.

Alone on the shore, alert as always, waiting for the lights in the distance, the lookout sees the flare, runs to raise the alarm. In the town, they have seen the danger, now they all join the struggle.

Black and blue, thrashed and mauled, his back slammed repeatedly by rolling gear, Peter shins back towards the tiller. His mind is full of blood and pain, the bone of his hand gaping through a cut half an inch wide. He smells the mood amongst the crew, the raw fear of men who have spent a lifetime at sea yet still fear the fury of the waves more than anything else. Ropes and sails and net are all intertwined, whipping sorely at their backs. Again and again the waves break, each greater than the last, unrelenting. There is a bang as they hit the shingle bank, a bolt of lightning goes off just above them, and their fragile cradle begins to break apart. Some of the men start to climb out along the sail. Peter hears the mast crack under their weight and the boat starts to roll on its bottom. Instinctively, he ducks in time to save his head but his shoulder takes the full force of the boom. He screams in agony as his arm is wrenched out of its socket. He shouts to the rest of the crew to jump. Some clear the boat and make for the shore, but the backwash makes it difficult to swim. The boat rolls and slides bottom up into the shingle. Peter is trapped beneath the boat, gasping under 13 tons of gear and timber.

After the alarm is raised, all rush to the beach. In ten minutes the lifeboat is launched, but the wind is on-shore from the southeast, the tide in three-part flood and the waves so desperately strong that they struggle to make progress along the shore.

'Pull, lads, pull!'

The hull of the rescue boat cuts through the waves. The women shout from the shore. They pull to reach the wreck, straining against the anger of the sea, but it takes too long to reach the shattered craft. They wear brave faces, grim expressions that tell all in their determination. No time for cowards. There are desperate exertions before the men in the water can be reached.

Suddenly the wind dies, and a rope is secured. All are aboard except Peter, who has stayed with his boat till the last crew member is clear. His body is washed from under the vessel as she is lifted by a last heavy wave before settling down again permanently on the shingle. At that moment he would have been washed out to sea if the gunwale of the boat, as she went down again, had not closed on his lifebelt. When finally they reach him, they find him lashed by the flailing sheets to the wreck, his body crushed, an arm hanging useless in his sleeve, his spirit near exhausted by the struggle.

Throughout the drama, Martin watches with Amber from their bedroom window, his nose pressed up against the glass, eyes full of far-off lights, waiting and waiting. His sister's arms hang around his shoulders as they pray with all their hearts for their father's safe return, not appreciating the intensity of the danger.

The lifeboat crew brings Peter's body back to shore, where Ellen is waiting. But his strength is gone, a lifetime of struggle washed over the rail. He dies quietly as he has lived in her arms. In the darkness of that afternoon as Martin and his sister wait in silence, listening in fear to the wind, three lives are left shattered, a fourth lost forever.

One rescuer told the reporters how he had seen an angel rise from the waves and watch over them as they struggled to secure the rope, a flash of lightning reflected on the sea maybe, but to that man glory in the confusion of wind and rain.

Martin still keeps the clippings in a little leather tobacco pouch they took from his father's shirt. Peter was buried in the church with full honours. Of all of them it was his sister who had cried loudest. It was she who did not let go of his voice.

As he tells her this, Jade lifts her hand to Martin's face and strokes the hair away from his brow. She feels the veil between them move, the barrier lifting.

After the disaster, Martin and his sister had quickly slipped from youthful light into darkness. The bonds that tied them so closely unravelled without their father's presence. How quickly the last light of that fateful summer was forgotten.

For weeks and months his sister wandered the shoreline alone, moaning at the wind, her voice shrill and breathless. Her screams carried far into the North Sea, her grief mocked by the wind. One night they found her, collapsed and exhausted on the beach, her body soaked by rain, unable to speak through shouting at the sea. She developed a fever; some feared she too would die. Even when the fever subsided for a time she did not speak, would not be consoled, not even by their mother. They said she would never be the same again, her brain affected by the fever. Nobody could control her anger – raging incomprehensibly until she could speak no more.

The townspeople cared for them as best they could, but gradually their sympathy turned to reality; there was little margin for charity amongst such a poor community. His mother took a job in the greengrocers and helped with the fish gutting in the evening. She was brave and bore her loss with a dignity remarked on by all. Only at her deathbed years later did Martin finally understand how she had privately disintegrated, her eyes red and sore from the salt, her once soft hands callused by manual work. Her heart had been broken by that wreck as surely as her husband's life.

Eventually his sister did regain her voice, but it was no longer the childish voice that had sung to him on the beach. Now it was strained and dark and grown-up. Her words to him became matter-of-fact. She became passive, severe, as if she were punishing herself for some imagined fault that had led to their father's loss. He was almost unable to communicate with her.

She became sullen and withdrawn, no longer mixing with the other children and fishing families. Worst of all, she no longer wished to wander the shoreline with him, preferring her own company. At that age he could not understand how deeply she felt betrayed. For her the sea had been a friend, now it had destroyed everything she loved. At the time her coldness to him seemed like rejection, beyond the comprehension of his tender years. She dressed in grey, wearing throughout that longest winter a coarse coat given her by one of the rescuers, ignoring everyone else's stares, letting her hair grow ragged; she looked five years older than her true age. She took to cycling the river dykes and remoter beaches, speaking to herself in a sharp, chiding language of her own invention. Martin was excluded from this new world she was building. Gradually she retreated into solitude.

This mourning period lasted nine months and then just as quickly was over. One evening the next summer she returned home after dark and the hated coat was gone, in its place a dress of plainest cloth cut around her slender arms and in her hair a garland of sea pea and yellow poppies. Summer had returned overnight, she had become a woman: she had found love again.

After Martin has confided all this to her, Jade knows that she must somehow get him to the end of this story and help him find his sister, if she is still alive. She sees in his story a parallel to her own, but one where she can make progress. But she also sees the ghost, the look in his eyes: the terror has returned.

'Martin, I want to help you find your sister. Is there anything else you can remember?'

'There is something else I cannot forget.'

'Hush, you be quiet, Martin.'

It was pitch-dark. Jimmy led them through the black sheds that lie on the ridge of shingle, past the winch lines and lobster cages. They moved like Indian braves through the debris, barefoot, holding on to each other for fear of losing the way, shadowed by a drifting gull. In the wind, far off, they can hear the sound of voices, the smell of pipe smoke, and the signs of boozy celebration unmistakable. They felt the danger of adventure. Jimmy doused his hurricane lamp, no lights now, not even stars; the night dark and overcast, the beginnings of another storm. 'I seen 'em doing it, I tell you. Over there, behind that tarp,' he whispers. Like trackers, the great Hiawatha and his braves, feeling the ground with their toes, moving like the wind through the trees. No light to guide them, not even the stars; just the strange churring trill of a nightjar on a post by the boatsheds. They were blood brothers, on the trail.

They could hear hushed voices, giggles, the brush of clothing, a moan from the shadows. The moon revealed by those fickle clouds. Jimmy's hand rises to the sky for silence. They await his signal to advance, holding their breaths until their lungs ache. Jimmy returns. 'They're in there,' he whispers.

On naked stomachs they creep forward, sand filling every crevice in their skin. They reach the beached trawler and peer out over the gunwale. Cramp grips their legs and the smell of drink and cheap cologne drifts into their throats. They are witnesses to the ritual writhing of familiar limbs. Recognition dawns like nausea, disgust fills Martin's stomach.

Martin tells Jade that he thinks his mother knew the worst, but what could she do? Amber could not be controlled. From then on, his sister led a secret life. She disappeared for long periods and told them nothing about what she was doing. He knew, however, that she often went visiting the Ogilvie boys up the coast on her bike and came back with all sorts of strange ideas. And then when she was sixteen she left them completely, just after the older Ogilvie brother was killed in a fall from the tower. His death was never fully explained, and she left suddenly without even a word or a goodbye note. Everyone assumed her heart was broken again. A few letters followed, one mentioned a child, but within a year Martin's mother was dead. As an orphan Martin was taken in by his uncle and had heard no more of Amber since.

When he was old enough they offered him a place on his uncle's boat, but Martin had lost the stomach to go to sea and instead got a position in the shipyard. He started work as a shipwright's apprentice but spent his evenings studying books on carpentry on his landlady's kitchen table. By the age of twenty-two, he had built the greater part of several craft now berthed along the river.

In a corner of her mind, Jade wonders at the quiet anger of this man. For a few weeks she has tried to capture him, the image and the object, but he is like a chewed lemon, bitter and exhausted. On occasions after the photo sessions, the two of them had shared her room on Sunday afternoons listening to records, but only one was alive, the other merely existing in a dark cloud around her sun. She planned little things to amuse him – read him poetry, spread her oils over the petrified muscles of his back, but his essence seeped through her fingers, unyielding to his touch. And then one day she found him by chance on a park bench, tears in his eyes, and she knew it was all useless, he was unreachable.

Once you danced,
On the sand, in the sun,
Moving with joy,
so sweet, so simple.
and we lay and watched the rising stars,
and danced by that shimmering sea.

V – Amber's Return

'I know this is difficult, but please understand. I have to leave. I can't stand the name-calling, the stares. I'll be back soon. Look after Martin, I'll write…'

'Did you get my letter? I wish you'd write back. I met someone, Crow, we're in Felixstowe, moving on with his band every few days.'

'It's only weeks now, I feel the kicks more and more. Sarah, my friend, will take care of me – she has a boy of her own. Love you…'

'I checked in Woodbridge, there was nothing, no letter. She has your eyes – deep green like jade, a little wisp of dark hair. I don't know when I can write again, Crow don't like it. I wish you'd write. I think of you both in my prayers.'

'We're in Dunmow for the fair – there's no flitch this year. Baby's sick. This cold is bad, I know, but Sarah's helping. Crow's out a lot, I wish he wouldn't drink so. Please forgive me. If only…'

Late evening – October 1958
A deserted attic, Coggeshall

The crash that awakens Amber might have been in a dream, except for the smoke that now penetrates the air. She shivers in the darkness. The building feels chilled, the earthen smell of mould long established amongst the plaster walls. She gathers the blanket more tightly around her, her baby daughter moaning gently in her arms. She can now see the wisps of wood smoke rising in tiny columns through the cracks between the floorboards, caught by the candlelight. Through the cracks, she sees lights, lanterns probably. She coughs from the fumes, realises they have returned.

There are voices then laughter downstairs, the voices muffled, as if cloaked. She presses her head against the floor. She can hear Sarah's laugh, Crow's rasping voice. A black fear enters into her to hear his voice again. She imagines the nauseous smell of his alcohol-stained breath. She edges forward on her stomach, towards a place where the boards have split. Through the smoke-haze she can see the downstairs room, smell the drink on their breaths like ripening apples. One figure, dim in the half-light, holding a lamp, the other bent over the hearth, heavily clothed against the cold, clutching a bottle wrapped in plain brown paper.

'Hurry, Crow, I'm freezing.'

From the damp attic she watches them as they embrace, strangely alienated from their coarse passion, an observer, uninvolved. The woman bends over the man, rubbing her cheek over his head, pulling her hands through his body, grabbing hold of the open bottle and throwing a dash of alcohol into the fire.

There is a burst of flame, the liquid splatters and its spirit aroma rises with the smoke. The sound of a dance band crawls from the radio. She watches them clasp each other in drunken contortions, sees briefly his eyes in the torchlight, full of lust. She edges closer to the hole, both frightened and fascinated, feels her lungs ache from the breath that she dare not exhale. Her limbs are rigid against the floorboards, straw playing around her nostrils, sawdust like grit in her mouth.

Below her the two figures continue to rock breathlessly, the woman with her hands balanced against her chair. Amber moves away from the gap but realises she has moved too far, splintering the wood, her movement unmistakable. The man's voice seizes the downstairs room, strangling the woman's laughter.

'That bitch is up there watching us.'

Her heart is pounding now. All around her she feels the chill of a century's damp poverty. The sharp wood smoke stings her eyes. There is fear in her mind, the memory of his sweaty breath in her nostrils. How has she come to this situation?

'Amber, is that you, up there' he shouts. 'Bugger her! Help me up, woman.'

'Crow, come back, she's only a kid, don't hurt her again!'

Crow's body climbs the ladder and she sees his head emerge through the hatchway. He holds a poker, its steely certainty glinting in the gloom of the attic. The girl turns to hide her face. The auburn hair that she had earlier worked into plaits hangs around her eyes, her cheeks flaming like burnished copper. She pulls her child closer to her breast – a mother's protective instinct. In the gloom of the attic she sees little except the shadow of his body, much larger than her own, crawling towards her, cramped by the low eaves.

He shouts her name again, brings the iron down harmlessly on a beam. The dead sound splits the disruption of the loft around her. She senses his approaching mouth, ugly, drunken and enraged, breathing fumes of fire. His trousers rip, snagged on a rusty nail and he curses as he is prevented from moving further. The glow of the lantern reveals his face clearly for the first time. She looks into the blackness of his eyes.

'Come here, you little bitch!' he shouts, grasping towards her, his voice cold and evil, every wrinkle and pore of his skin dripping poison.

The flame, innocent like a feeble sun in the attic, casts ochre shadows over the straw, disclosing her frail shape cowering in the corner. She knows this voice, has learned to fear it, and recognises with weariness the precursor of violence towards her. Already she owns the scars of its wrath, the weals of its tongue. Like a great pig he rolls across the floor to free himself, his words and movements exaggerated by the alcohol, the careless stench of urine on his clothes. The poker descends again to the floor, sending shards of splinters into the air, his nostrils red with hatred and drink.

'I thought I told you to be gone when we got back?'

His eyes search her arms. She sees what he sees. Moments before the handle of the poker descends on her shoulder, nearly smashing her nose, she pushes the baby behind her body. Crow grabs for the child. She screams, in fear for its life as much as her own; blood begins to creep down her arm. She had never questioned him, never expected mercy. She had felt some blind loyalty, vestiges of earlier adoration, misplaced respect, love maybe, but she knows now that his heart is completely black, completely without redemption. Rising, she kicks hard at his groin, pushing him off-balance with her feet. She knows she can stay and suffer no longer if her child is threatened. He grabs her and she shrieks as all three roll struggling towards the hatch.

The lamp falls from Crow's hands, shatters on the

boards and flames begin to lick the grim oil. He tries to rise, but she is too quick for him and thrusts the point of the steel shaft into his shoulder so that he reels back into the straw. She has crossed the bridge now, knows she must complete her actions or suffer terribly. She hits him again full across the face, emboldened by despair, strikes him again and again with raw anger, a deep hatred, her body shaking now with emotion. She does not remember mercy, does not stop until his face has disappeared into a mass of blood, each stroke empowered with the fury of past hurt and pain. From below she hears Sarah screaming for her to stop.

There is no time to collect her belongings; she just grabs the child and a small bag. She knows she must flee, leave him to moan in the straw. She scrambles through the hatch, pulling the ladder away as soon as her feet find the ground. Above her he rages blindly, there is a further explosion as the loft rushes with flame. Crow's body falls through the air towards her, his clothes on fire.

'I'll kill you, you bitch, if it's the last thing I do!'

As she runs towards the release of the night air, she sees Sarah's shocked face frozen in the doorway, feels pity and love for this woman who reminds her so much of herself, someone gentle, lost, enslaved to his power. But now she must run and keep running, she cannot afford to falter for a second. Out into the night air, the barn in uproar behind her, Crow's voice shouting, Sarah screaming, the sound of a rabbit gun emptied into the night. 'Escape, Sarah, or you will bear him alone now,' she pants. She can stay no longer.

Beyond the lights, beyond the screaming, she runs. She continues out past the gate, down the slick black road, over the stile, into the fields towards dark asylum. Already she is breathless, but dare not drop her pace, running first along the river until she reaches the Abbey Farm and then ascends the old drover's path, climbing quickly through thick grass into a wilder scrub of bracken and hawthorn that clings to her clothing. The night is dark and there are no stars to betray her, but even though she knows he won't be able to follow in this darkness, she dares not stop.

The path is not steep but she struggles with the mud and rain and the weight of the child. She is driven to keep going, desperate to reach the top, twisting her rain-heavy body through the maze of tracks, unfamiliar in the darkness, the rolling storm approaching, the woodland lit by flashes of intense electric light, the child cradled close to her body.

A flash and then a crack, and then the next flash and thunder explodes almost directly overhead. Suddenly, the rain is released with dreadful force, curtain-black, dark-sheeting blasts. For a moment she is disoriented, unsure of her direction, which way to head in the half-hidden and unfamiliar landscape of woven paths. Peculiar tentative forms stare through the mist, ghostly shapes of stunted trees almost alive in the lightning. The rain is now beating hard on her back.

I am wind, my wailing cry.
I am thunder, my fearsome anger.
I am rain, my dreadful song.

She carries on up the path and at last reaches the saddle of ground at the top of the slope. The wind lashes her freezing limbs so that she can barely crawl. In the darkness, she enters the shelter of a roofless old barn and collapses, drenched, in its stony placenta, the storm raging all around, her child crying in her arms.

In these moments of time, half-frozen by the lightning, she watches the sparkle of the droplets beading the child's face, the little eyes closed tight against the night. She sobs, kissing its cheek, 'We'll be safe now,' she whispers. The storm rolls on, subsides and they are left together in stillness.

Sleep comes to her quickly and mercifully, its inky cradle protecting her against the sheets of night. She sleeps deeply but awakens early in the grey whisper of dawn to her child's hungry cries. She opens her shirt to feed the child, feels the pull at her breast, the intimacy of mother and child, the comfort of one who depends on her, the only one left to her now. In the dull light she realises the chilling significance of the place the paths have led her to, recognises the old blue farm diesel pump, the sign 'not for resale'. The site of her earlier seduction, a place Crow habitually brought his conquests.

Yes, she had loved him. He was handsome, violent, damaged, damaging – a pitiful, complex man. She had once been hungry for him, drawn on by his swagger and musician's charm, imagining in him the devoted lover, allowing him to seduce her while already heavy with child, in her blind desire to be loved, and her soul like others trodden and soon lost within his lust. His fidelity was as short-lived as the gaps between his drinking. It was her foolish weakness to have loved him. How dearly she had paid for that blind love.

She realises now that long ago she should have left that cold and burdened place, broken free of his suffocating fingers, his petty adultery. Tired of forgiving, tired of putting up with him, the months that Crow beat the heart from her, she thinks of Sarah, left to deal alone with his rage. She understands it was only Sarah's companionship that had made her stay.

The memory of him makes her aware again of danger, the proximity of wrath. The stained beauty of the ancient woodland is spread before her in the early sun, but she has no time for Nature's glory. She has hardly any money, no possessions and she dare not return to collect them from that terrifying attic; she has no choice but to continue running. She has no plan, knowing now only fear.

It was a year since she had run away from her own home, a year since childhood had ended for good, a year since her darling Ralph had fallen from the tower. She had been an innocent, knowing nothing of the world, no clue to the wickedness of those who would try to break her. She had said no goodbyes, left even before the first gulls stirred. Started from the very shoreline where her father drew his last breath; the sea iron-ugly, rushing to shore in angry crests, disfigured and tormented by the relentless wind. She can still hear the ringing of tragedy, forever feel the roar of gales and rushing seas.

She was not the first to leave that place. Others had gone before her, childhood friends. Most of them went to Felixstowe or even Ipswich in search of work, dreaming of riches, a world apart from fish and rope and salt. She had the same plan, but the reality was far bitterer, she knew that now, but like most she had not returned. Perhaps she should now. She did not know. Wasn't it enough to hope?

At daybreak, she walks tentatively along the field hedges, around the outskirts of the village, crossing the river and the old Roman road before taking the back lanes northwards, out past the old tile kilns along Robin's Brook towards the deer park at Marks Hall and then out towards the Colnes. She spends the second night in the cold October air, shivering in a ditch by the railway line at Mount Bures, an abandoned Massey Ferguson harvester and the rattling of the steam locomotive *Kilverstone Hall* their only evening companions.

For the next two days, she holds to the arable margins of the landscape, avoiding population, legs weakening every hour, following roughly the downstream course of the Stour. Her only company is the occasional robin flitting along the hedgerows between the hogweed. She gorges on blackberries and sloes twisted on the spiky blackthorn.

A 'cokadrille', given to Richard I after the siege of Acre, escaped from his menagerie before being killed by Sir George Marney at 'Bloody Meadow'.

At Wormingford she enters the village cautiously to buy food in the post office with the last of her money, shelters briefly from a rainstorm in the church with its strange dragon window and then scrambles on through brambles, elder and nettles, across two stiles and a dirt track into a wild garden of roses and orchards surrounding a series of old mill ponds. She watches from behind an unexpected stand of bamboo as an elderly artist paints the leafless trees by the banks of the ponds and his friend writes beside him. A woman approaches, his wife maybe, calling them in for tea – Christine, they call her. John is his name.

I was a poet but I longed to be a painter like the rest of them.
Ronald Blythe

They seem kind and she longs to talk with them but is afraid to stop, too scared to seek help, avoiding contact with the world. Heavy paths lead on through endless fields, the furrows sprinkled with tired shoots, the flat uplands ridged with windswept oaks. The third night is spent more comfortably in the animal warmth of a cattle barn near Nayland. She eats morsels of food the farmer has left in wooden troughs for the pigs across the stream, cradles and feeds the child with all the love left in her body. She continues northeast, past Stoke and Shelley, a vague route in her head from their earlier travels, navigating by the sun as her father had taught her, reaching the outskirts of a small town around dusk and waiting until the darkness gives her cover.

Her hunger now has reached a point where she knows that to survive; she must brave the consequences of discovery.

She approaches the first houses of the village and wraps the child tightly to her breast as she passes through the kissing gate off the common and edges carefully into the deserted streets, watching for any other person, cheating the rain for a while in the porch of the massive parish church.

Through the keyhole of the oak door, she can just see the glint of gold on the altar; the play of light from the stained glass, the decorated chancel walls and candle flames falling on rich tapestries and carpets. She hears a lone deep voice inside reciting Evensong to no one, surrounded by empty box pews and stone pillars. She remembers times when she was happy in such a place, when she still knew happiness, when her faith meant something to her. After he has finished, she follows the priest home and begs food for her child at his door, her pride laid bare by necessity. After he has fed her, she asks him, 'What is the name of this place?'

'Hadleigh. This is Lord Guthrum's church,' he tells her. 'He was the founder of the Danelaw.'

Out of pity and kindness he allows her to sleep in the house and takes her the next morning in his car to a nearby village, leaving her with the Welsh rector and his wife in their elegant Victorian vicarage. They too feed her and tend to the child and wash her clothes, while she sleeps off her journey and her exhaustion in a bed of unimagined luxury.

She stays under their kind hospitality, recovering, for a day or two. They urge her to go to a women's hostel in Ipswich and offer to ring ahead and take her, but she declines, tells them she is going home and then hitches a lift with a farmer into Woodbridge, sheltering for the night in a shack by the old tide mill.

> *It makes one wonder. The young are different. The past is boring and shabby to them.*
> Ronald Blythe, *Akenfield*

The next day, she is up early again with the dawn, eager to make progress, crosses the Deben by the ferry, bribing the young ferryman with a kiss, watching the speedboats and dinghies out on the river. She continues on, following a more easterly path heading into the chase of rolling heathland and pine forest around Rendlesham. At one point, she is almost surprised by a young policeman, whistling, as he rides his bike through the forest path and she jumps into the sea of bracken to avoid him seeing her. She rests for a while at a little house called Acorn Cottage, just past a large fire-watching tower, looking on hungrily as two bare-legged children, one with pigtails and the other a flop of blonde hair, eat a picnic of biscuits from an old tin box, her stomach rumbling just from the sight of the food. Later, a passing forester gives her a ride to the edge of Tunstall Forest in his jeep, so that by late afternoon she has reached a ridge where she can finally see her goal; the familiar twisting Curlew River, distant and neat, its whole form slipping beneath her. She hears the high-pitched whistle of redwing in the air. By now she is weary almost beyond standing, her boots clogged with the clinging mud of the forest paths, her clothes draped around her body, wet and heavy.

> *A few miles from here a frost-stiffened wood waits and keeps watch above a mere; the overhanging banks a maze of tree-roots mirrored in its surface. At night there, something uncanny happens: the water burns.*
> Anonymous, *Beowulf*

What strength she has left comes only from her desire to protect at all costs her child. She has a growing fever and feels light-headed with hunger once more – the baby's cries ever more piercing and desperate, but she has hardly any milk left to give her. Exhausted, she lies down under an old Scots pine seeking the mercy of sleep, imagining in the distance the familiar shape of the lookout, the tower of the parish church where she was baptised, her mother and brother alone at the table, the warmth of the hearth. Surely her mother will forgive her, put aside the bitterness of her leaving? But it has been so long and she has had no reply to her letters; she is unsure of her welcome. She knows she must return somehow, even if the journey kills her. She has nowhere else left to go.

The earliest of songs,
light dim on your brow.
Just you and I, my child,
to bear this longest night.

To sing the earliest song,
brave fear for simple joy.
Unmeasured rapture,
love in your eyes, precious innocence.

Their strength you inherit
to conduct your spirit.
These you will never know,
man and boy, your lost ancestry.

It is a mother's wounds
that will not be healed.
Never look upon those fair eyes again
or rest her head again on noble shoulders.

But there are others unforgiving
whose bitter tears we must still endure
Blessed mother, help us now.

Towards sunset, she descends to the river, towards the last bridge at Snape before it becomes too wide and bloated to cross. She finds shelter amongst the ramshackle sheds of the Victorian maltings built by her ancestors, watching through a glassless window as the moon rises. Beyond her in the moonlight she can see the water shining, spreading out greedily over the shallow earth, contained only by low-lying flood plains and untended river walls; she can hear the loud boom of solitary bitterns in the reed beds along its banks. Between her and the sea, the river twists north, then south, then east amongst the Iken flats, where widgeon gather in thousands at low tide, before changing its name to Ore and taking a last sharp turn to the south. After that, it runs parallel to the sea for miles, contained by the natural shingle spits formed by long-shore drift before its last heave towards freedom at Orford. The river is the southern boundary of her early life, the furthest outpost of her childhood knowledge.

Newson Garrett, father of Elizabeth and Millicent Garrett, bought up a corn-merchant's business, with trading vessels and premises at Snape Bridge, and came to live in Aldeburgh in 1840.

She is woken again by a kick inside and then her nursing child's urgent cries; feeds her in the morning dew as she sits on the bank, stroking the child's brow, watching the curlew and redshank wading in the shallow reed beds. The water runs ponderously in its gleaming channel, murky from the mud, now and again disturbed by the popping of a fish grabbing for a fly, or the unhurried stroke of an otter cruising the water.

She eats the last of her food and crosses the bridge into a wet landscape of creeks and sluices separating the river from the heath, her boots again soon clogged with mud, crossing a dyke of sorts before descending into a gulch left by generations of cattle. Deep in the silt she struggles, the river mist low over the salt marsh, before she emerges back into soft pasture, the grass still pricked with meadow saffron, her footsteps leaving a wake of mud in the long stems.

She climbs back up towards the heath and the mud flats give way to a sandier warren of turf, bell heather and gorse, full of inquisitive rabbits. In her exhaustion she is glad for the way the sand lightens her boots and the lichen-covered birch in the plantations turns her hands green. The call of a cheerful skylark rises in the air and she spots a hare chasing through the bright yellow gorse. Each stride brings the steady promise of the waves closer. Her heart lifts a little from the misery of her anxious flight.

The landscape returns in a succession of skins to her shadow. It's as if the heath and woods of stunted oak and birch, the call of the woodlarks in the canopy, are all reaching out to her, drawing her back into their world. Tears of the anticipated reconciliation with her mother begin to stream unbidden from her eyes. The germ of hope grows in her mind. Beyond this last wood lies the heathland around the golf course, the shrieking gulls already filling her heart with anticipation, laying claim once again to her soul, lamenting the foolishness of her absence.

So, as she reaches the final ridge before the outskirts of the town, she pauses for a moment for breath as the coastline is finally revealed to her. She can now sense clearly the distant line of the surf, see the little rows of colour-washed cottages, the 'mean and scrambling houses' huddled against the unrelenting chill of the east wind. The town below is trapped in its own time and geography, bound on one side by the wasteland of heath and marsh, on the other by the unyielding swell of the endless sea, an untidy coastline in constant danger from the forces of storm and erosion. The scarcity of comfort relieved only briefly by a good catch. She had forgotten how much she had longed to escape this – the bitterness of salt, the cold, the damp, the grinding inevitability of their melancholy. How much she had longed for a different life, even though her heart was still here, buried amidst the waves. There could be no joy in returning but she has no choice if her child is to live.

She descends the last slope into the shadows of dusk, passing the massive flint tower of the parish church, hiding as long as possible from the terror of recognition. She avoids the first lights in the windows, passes silently along the familiar streets, past houses of families known to her since infancy, and sees glimpses of their shadowy occupants through the frames lit by the poor glow of candlelight. She can feel the wretched fingers of the sea enter her bones again, tearing at her breast, grasping and deadly. As she reaches the door to her mother's cottage next to the coastguard station, she hesitates and then knocks timidly.

The door is opened at once by neighbours, she sees only dark, dark faces; her clothes and face are in such a state that there is momentary confusion as to who she is. She sees the figure of her eleven-year-old brother through the crowd, standing by an open coffin, his eyes dark and tear-stained. Mourners in black are circled around him. The familiar boom of the chaplain's voice fills the room.

'Martin?' she cries.

A silent scream rents her body as he stares back at her questioning, but wordless and she understands the finality of her mother's death. So there will be no solace, no reconciliation. Her eyes wander from face to face, from eye to eye, seeking answers or a denial, but none will return her glance or speak to her. None will understand.

'Martin?' His bitter reply is choked through tears and accusation. 'Get out, get out – it's you who killed her! Get out!'

In shock she flees this bitter condemnation. Tears flooding now, she runs out into the street, weeping and shrieking. She runs first towards the beach, wanders in agitation and distress between the boats and huts, directionless, knowing not what to do. She hears footsteps in the shingle, neighbours dispatched to find her, and ducks down under a tarpaulin to hide as they pass. Then when she is sure they are gone, she walks as quickly as she can northwards, not stopping to look behind her to see if anybody follows. She half-runs until she is clear of the town and then, exhausted, falters back to a slow walk, her head full of despair. Her steps are tracked by the whispering hiss of the reeds rubbing together in the breeze. In the distance she hears the hoot and rattle of the little train that runs on the branch line up to Leiston. She rests for a while beside a small tea van that is parked by the road. Her baby continues to cry, she feeds her the best that she can, until she begins to simper in her arms. She is so grateful to the kindly old lady who stops and offers her a lift to the holiday village up the coast.

From there, it still takes her a good hour to walk the final mile and a half to her new destination, squeezing through bracken and brambles along a narrow path that flanks the low cliffs above the beach. She enters the walled gardens through the gate by the lantern, the white painted sign 'private grounds' now hanging half off its screws. Eventually her heavy footsteps shake on the gravel path up to the old house. Her hair is soaked, clinging to her face like shrouds of death, eyes red and pale from crying. She is at the point of utter exhaustion, can hardly walk, her heart so close to surrender, the child hanging like lead around her neck. She passes through the shadows flying across the lawns, past the dark statuary, seeking her last remaining hope. Angels and nymphs glower from their lichen-stained pedestals. Past the bronze discus-thrower she knew so well. She sees a few lights in the great house – dim electric lamps in the servant rooms, and a dull chandelier in the library. Vainly she searches for the flickering light in an upper window; the room she knows is his. Timidly she approaches the great wooden door, with its uncompromising bars of iron, framed by a sandstone crest. She pulls on the heavy bell.

In the upper room, Thomas Ogilvie hears the bell but continues to pace the dark oak floor in anguished frustration, his hollow footsteps imitating the beat of the clock. The light of the hearth emphasises the frame of his beech-lined cell. On the radio there is a distant play about the last war, filled with gunfire and gory shouts. He hears the voice of the stranger at the door and wonders who would call at such a late hour and in such weather. He listens to a brief but animated conversation, the soprano notes of a young girl's voice. Then the door closes and there is no further sound. The house phone rings.

'Who was it, Paxton?'

'Nobody, nothing to worry about, sir,' says the servant's calm voice on the end of the line. 'It was just a town girl, lost and incoherent, wanted shelter. I gave her food and sent her over to the gamekeeper's wife. She was in a real state, mind you, ranting on about this and that. Most likely a runaway, if you ask me. Will you want anything more tonight, sir?'

'No, thank you, Paxton – you did the right thing. Goodnight.'

'Goodnight, sir.'

As the servant replaces the receiver, he knows that he has not told the full story. He had recognised the girl, of course and she had even asked for Master Thomas by name, but Paxton had said he was away at college. He had seen the baby in her arms but deliberately not informed his master about any of that. He knows that if he had, his master would have reacted differently; he has a duty to protect him from this. He shakes his head and returns to the kitchen to consult with his wife.

Back in the hushed room, Thomas stares at the half-written letter on his desk. The late visitor has disturbed him. He tries to concentrate again, but the same vision of Amber's face rises each time from the pages, her light skirt flying in the wind, her breath warm on his cheeks. He hears again her short whispered words, strangely perfumed. They are laughing and skipping together in the dunes.

Thomas cannot find the words to write more and so he steps over to the window to look out into the darkness beyond. The gardens are shrouded by leafless branches, like the masts of smacks gathered round a shrubbery of nets and lobster traps. Nothing stirs; the grounds are deserted. He stares over to the lights flickering at the other end of the driveway, imagines the scene in the gamekeeper's cottage. Yes, Paxton had done the right thing – the gamekeeper and his wife were kindly souls. He wonders if he should go over that evening, but he is sure there is nothing that cannot wait until morning.

He returns to the hearth and takes up a poker from the fire, its cold ball heavy in his palm, stirring the last warmth from the embers. A thousand sparks, released into flight, just as quickly vanishing. In frustration, he takes her pleading letter and his own unfinished reply and throws both onto the fire. He wants nothing more to do with her; the memory of his brother's death is just too painful in his thoughts.

And then there was the question of his heart broken by her sudden desertion and Ralph's callous betrayal. He was not prepared; he had never imagined that he would have such feelings for a woman, his spirit splintered into crinkling glass shards, her laughter cavorting within his mind. He parts the curtains to gaze once more onto the chilled scene below; to the line of surf defining the shore. Can he see a figure on the shoreline? Is there something moving amongst the shingle banks? How long can he endure this torture?

My library was dukedom large enough.
Shakespeare, *The Tempest*

He tries to suppress a deeper memory that resurfaces now, that carries both guilt and remorse. Their midnight swims with the other boys, the lights and music from the house, the slight flirting, and the obvious attraction. 'Stand over there between Peter and the recorders.' Hudson organised them all in the background, while he felt the beautiful eyes of Imo, the composer's daughter, burning his face. The king was there with his viola, the famous tenor, the conscientious objector, all of them looking on while the music club rehearsed for its inaugural concert.

'Why did you let him do that to you?' his chiding words to his brother later, as they returned home in their Sunday best.

'*Malo, malo, malo*,' he replied.

Later that night Amber walks down to the shoreline, having left the baby in the care of the gamekeeper's wife and wades resolutely into the black waters. She has so many words in her head, but she is not afraid, each shaped and twisted into a form that holds anger. The night stars shine about her head like ferocious diamonds in the surf; the sea blurred with stillness, cut only by the bluntness of a wave. She sees and breathes all in blindness. The stone terraces shelving away under her feet as she begins to swim. Her body is heavy with the weight of her clothes and boots as she swims out into the vast terror beyond the end of the shelving beach. Her head is soon full of coldness, full of an idea of how she can regain love.

She grasps at the freezing fluid, pulling herself forward on an imaginary ladder until she is far out of reach. Stories wander around her mind lost for purpose. Anger rushes and storms and wanes again as she searches. She fights the sea's lazy drag easily for a while, fights to swim out further, until the late lights of the town form a distant chain on the water. The waves grow higher and her stomach is sick with brine, but she has no fear. She wants this battle; she will fight for it.

As she weakens, the sea seems so light, its surface melting into a cloud before her. It transforms from black to blue to white, all delicate shades of pink and grey. Islands appear and are lifted up like clouds, as if sea palaces rising to meet her. Each of them written in a word in her mind, a piece of verse destroyed, concentrated in the wind, concentrated by the motion of the sea. Her head is full of warmth again, the nausea hot like brandy in her throat. The batik of sea and sky crowded into a whale's skeleton, each rib and bone bent and poised, sinew-like nails spiked into her heart. She cries out for her lost loves.

Slowly, her body slips exhausted into another world, hope revealed in the last moments before her radiance is eclipsed. Her skirt floats over the surface of the sea like the brilliance of sunlight – the colour of ottoman silk and tea and the coolness of day. She stares into its face, its surface like that of a mirror, eyes dancing, apologising for beauty, his arms drawing her to his side. Mother and sister, father and daughter, lover and beloved are all one now. Are all one now at last in that one laugh? Her body soothed by the pungency of oil and milk; a terrible longing in her eyes, a searching of intent. Her brow stroked by the waters, sliding like a sail, irresistible, terrible.

'Amber?' Ralph calls.

They are again silent together in the waves. Amber has left the child she has called Jade behind now – she will make her own fortune. The name of her future written in faint ink on her brow, and Amber's own name is left on the shore, written once more in the sand for a short while before it is reclaimed by the waves.

Come unto these yellow sands, and then take hands.
Shakespeare, *The Tempest*

The next morning breaks in beautiful radiance; Thomas is up early and goes promptly to the gamekeeper's cottage to enquire about the girl, but she has gone. She has left behind her baby and a letter addressed to the child in her scrawled hand. For a time, he is angry with Paxton but then when he understands his new responsibility, he relents.

After a few days, he agrees to provide the gamekeeper and his wife £100 and an annual income for their silence and care of the adopted child. They have their eye on a retirement cottage in Felixstowe. He makes only three conditions to the annuity: never to write to him about the child, never to tell the child about him, his family or the house, and never to allow the child to return to Aldeburgh.

VI – Sunday Morning

Can I see a falling tear,
And not feel my sorrow's share?
Can a father see his child
Weep, nor be with sorrow fill'd?

William Blake, *On Another's Sorrow*

Evening – June 1990
An Art Gallery at Snape Maltings

'Jade, you are so clever, darling – they're brilliant! You must be so pleased.'

'Certainly worth the effort,' Jade replied, unable to contain a sheepish grin. Louise looks around the room across the narrow white pillars and banks of spotlights shining on the mounted photos on the walls. 'I bet you're going to be famous now!'

'Maybe,' she smiles awkwardly.

'Oh, come on, I'm just dying to introduce you to Ben,' her friend says, flashing the rock on her finger and pointing to a fop-haired blond lad, laughing with two other Sloane-types in the corner.

A waiter interrupts them with a tray of sparkling white wine and canapés – they take a glass each and Louise says, 'Ben, darling, this is Jade, our little photographic genius.'

'Well, here's to the next Kurt Hutton.'

Typical Louise-type, thinks Jade, but not at all bad-looking. The crowd is buzzing and she is kept busy with endless introductions, explaining the little stories behind each picture to each group, pitching her ideas on composition here, and there explaining technical details of lenses and filters, a sense of growing pride building within her as she works the room and collects the smiles on people's faces. Suddenly she glimpses a familiar face climb the last step of the metal staircase and enter the room, looking just a little out of place.

'Sal!'

Her friend turns towards her call and rushes over, her

oversized heels clattering on the wooden floorboards, flinging her arms around Jade's neck in an exaggerated embrace.

'Babe, look, I'm so sorry I'm late.' Her rough northern accent seems out of place amongst the local elite, but entirely genuine. She looks around the room and then down at her own clothes. Sal's fashion sense was always a marvel. Her frizzed bleached hair, over-sized earrings, dungarees and torn T-shirt were more Dexy's than the Bangles-inspired rock chick she had probably intended.

'Don't worry – here, have a glass of bubbly.'

Sal gulps it down and wipes her brow then looks around the room once more, this time at the artwork. Louise joins them, holding Ben close to her side. Jade's eyes roll as Sal takes a second glass. She was off already; she leaves them to it while she goes over to the main desk.

'So, how are we doing?' she asks the gallery owner.

'We're doing just great, my dear,' said the be-pearled woman. 'It's a really good atmosphere, and they just love your work. You should be really proud. Look, I've sold two already,' she says pointing to the red dots that had appeared at the corner of two of the beach photographs. They were two of the series Jade had taken with the girl and the seabird and the man snoozing behind her on the beach.

'Oh, brilliant, is the buyer still here?' she asks.

'No, no, he's gone – he didn't stay long. Yes, Thomas Ogilvie,' she says, checking the register. 'He's a bit of a secret collector, lives by himself in a big house up the coast – a bit of a recluse, really. He seemed a bit cross this evening, but a buyer's a buyer!'

'Ogilvie?'

'Actually, Jade, you must know him already. He seemed to know you. He referred to you as the foundling girl?'

Jade felt an uncomfortable chill at the back of her neck. 'I don't think so, but how on earth would he know that I'm a foundling?'

'Oh maybe it's in the exhibition notes.'

'But I'm sure there's nothing in the programme about me being a foundling. Did he say orphan, maybe?'

'Sorry, yes, orphan. I must be confused, forget I ever mentioned it – old age, you know. The good news as I said is that he's a buyer. We like buyers.'

Before Jade can consider this information further, Louise drags her back over to where she was chatting with Sal and the boys.

'Anyway Jade, what about you – who on earth is this, you little minx?' she says, pointing to one of the black and white life shots of Martin that she had formed into a triptych across the wall. Jade looks at them both and smiles a knowing smile.

'Do you really think I'd expose him to you two?' she taps her nose mysteriously. 'He's a bit of a sensitive soul.'

A lot later that evening, back at the hotel, in the crowded snug of the public bar, Martin feels a warm hand slip on to his thigh under the cover of Sally's coat, and a whisper in his ear that makes him blush and feel warm all over, his head already slightly dizzy from the Jamaican rum that she has poured from her flask in the taxi.

Malo: I would rather be,
Malo: In an apple tree,
Malo: Than a naughty boy,
Malo: In adversity.
Latin Grammar

Next morning, Martin is woken from a deep sleep by the insistence of the bright sunlight shining through the hotel window. As he comes to, he has a feeling of momentary panic as he realises that this is not the familiar clutter of his bedsit. Is it a workday, has he overslept? He glances at his watch and then over to the sleeping form curled like a dormouse beside him, half-wrapped in the freshly laundered sheets. He can hear her breathing softly against the pillow held closely to her face, naked brown limbs stretched out across the bed and thick peroxide hair bunched around her shoulders. He feels the sudden guilt of an unfinished transaction with a stranger whose name he cannot quite remember welling in his stomach. He looks down at his own nakedness, and then back to hers, and remembers the incident in the bar the previous evening. So, they had slept together or worse, and in their hurried passion, they had not even thought to draw the curtains. This was a first for him.

Quietly, so as not to disturb her, he slips out of the warmth of the sheets and pulls on his sweater against the cold air. He tiptoes over to the window and looks out at the familiar scene before him from an aspect he had never imagined he would ever see. He recognises the view at once, of course. Beyond the garden of the smart hotel with its scattered deckchairs and potted palms, he can see the row of iron street lamps and his familiar rough childhood beach, littered with straggly weeds of red valerian and mallow, with its collection of clinkered keels and black-tarred huts and beyond them the palest wisp of surf and dirty brown waves.

The room was at the corner of the building and there was a second, smaller window that faced north across holiday villas towards the warren and shingle beyond. One of the fishing boats was returning already, its red keel dragged harshly across the shingle beds by a little yellow tractor. Martin recognises the figures on the shoreline as two of his childhood mates – Jimmy Flynn at the helm. The smell of diesel fumes from the tractor reaches his nose, and transports him back twenty years to the mornings of his youth.

He stares through the window before filling the kettle

that rests with cups and saucers, tea and coffee on the dressing table and switching it on. Tea made, he moves back towards the bed. 'Excuse me, love,' he whispers, trying to remember her name while shaking her gently awake. She murmurs as he touches her and sits up in the bed. The brown cotton of her nightshirt now covered with the tresses of her curled, yellowed hair. She groans and hugs her legs for balance, taking the warm cup from him and putting the rim to her bee-stung lips.

'That's good – you make a very nice cup of tea, young man.' She notes the frown on his face and sees he is unsure of himself. She reaches over to stroke his hair. 'Last night was alright, you know,' she says. 'I certainly had a good time, what about you?'

'Well, I don't make a habit of this,' he replies somewhat curtly.

She glances at her watch on the bedside table and curses. 'It's only seven o'clock! Come on, get back to bed, and take that bloody sweater off!' God, I hope Jade forgives me for this, she thinks.

In the room next door, Jade is aroused from a deep sleep by the sound of the first bells for morning service ringing through the open window. Throughout her childhood, such bells had marked all the movements between human joy and human tragedy. Each Sunday, dragged to the little Methodist chapel off Hamilton road by her adoptive parents, singing and clapping gleefully with her peers to verses of childish repetition; once a month sitting with them in painful stillness, trying to keep awake through the dark formality of the parish Eucharist, occasionally attending a wedding, baptism or a funeral. As a teenager, her lack of zeal had isolated her from those childhood friends as her own acquaintances had expanded in new directions. She had had little to do with religion since her adoptive parents' deaths three years ago, except the occasional anguish of a young mind struggling with worldly preoccupations.

At least – to pray – is left – is left –
Oh Jesus – in the Air –
I know not which Thy Chamber is –
I'm knocking everywhere –
Emily Dickinson, *At least – to pray – is left – is left*

But on this of all mornings, the six tower bells begin to call to her strongly through the haze of youthful memory. Unlike the utilitarian building of her childhood, Aldeburgh church is an absolute, visible for miles – tethering the flat, open land to its vast sky – drawing the eye with strange fascination, just like the sea that drags those bound to it ever closer to its breast.

She is surprised at her own feelings as she debates for once if she should respond to the call; suspend her attempts to deny the existence of anything outside her own closely controlled world, succumb to their seductive sway. What harm to go once?, she thinks. Following the discovery of Thomas Ogilvie's interest in her photographs, there is a germ of an idea in her head and she does want to see the new Piper window.

She lifts the sash further to peer into the coolness of a glorious morning. The bright light and the glitter of the waves on the easterly sea make her wince, her head pounding still from excess consumption at the exhibition opening. It had been a wonderful night and she still glowed from the plaudits that her work had received; like Emily Dickinson, her vanity captivated by 'an incense beyond necessity'. She remembered that in the throng of the gallery she'd lost track of her college friends Sally and Louise, suspecting they had left with the boys before she was done. She might have expected to find them easily enough in one of the town pubs but a brief search ended prematurely in a blank and she opted instead for an early night. After an intense week hanging the exhibition, she needed her sleep.

She looks at her watch and finally commits herself to attend the early service, washes quickly and scours the wardrobe for clothes fit for religious solemnity – her last clean shirt, church white, her best half-decent skirt, not too revealing. She walks along the hotel landing, floorboards creaking, down two flights of stairs, past chintz wallpaper and oversized coastal paintings, to reception, where she smiles and exchanges a quick good morning with the night porter. As she steps out through the elegant porch of the Wentworth Hotel, she notices the air is already warm from the morning sun, poetry awakening in the late summer sky.

> *I do love this town and the music festival. Everyone is concerned in the goings on and there is the sea and yesterday the sun shone.*
> Joyce Grenfell, *Letters from Aldeburgh*

It is early, but she is surprised all the same to see the neighbourly streets still deserted. She passes the White Lion, passes stone-washed workers' cottages distorted by centuries of salty conclave, passes smart weekend villas, their colour-enhanced walls of cornflower blue and rose madder pink boasting stone-washed clothes, past the B&Bs, still quiet in their Sunday indolence. At the crossroads that otherwise lead into town, she turns to the right and climbs the steep path towards the flint-cliffs of the parish church. The bells have already stopped, the bright blue clock on the church tower heeding nigh on 8am. She hurries on with determined strides towards the heavy oak doors guarding the flint redoubt. Beyond the church wall the lush churchyard grass glistens in the dew – dog rose and campanula, an easy fragrance thick in the air, the last red hawthorn blossoms flirting in the trees.

As she enters through the west porch the calm music floods her ears and she pauses, feeling the hushed silence of unfamiliar intrigue, suddenly filled with doubt, no longer sure that she has any traffic with this place. Surely faith and religion are rocks now too far submerged below the changing currents of her life? Infinity and immortality washed but never claimed. If she knows anything, she knows that she does not believe in dusty liturgy, the betrayal of beauty and faith; she lives too much in the present. From time to time, she has thought about it all deeply – through her painful rejection of her adoptive parents' faith to dubious encounters with college Christianity. It would have been easier to conform, to go through the motions, but she could never bear pretence or hypocrisy, for her it has to be real or nothing.

There is a voice beside her. Before she can decide whether to stay, a sideman greets her with a friendly hand and she is caught. He welcomes her and she senses an unspoken question or some doubt at her appearance. She smiles, but volunteers no information, instead following the man obediently to an indicated seat, remaining anonymous, compliant, surveying with her photographer's eye the hushed and greying congregation pasted thinly over dark-stained pews.

The organ growls and she feels its deep vibration rumble through her diaphragm – Bach, she supposes but does not recognise the melody – her eyes panning seamlessly around the church, dazed a little by its interior splendour. Despite her long weeks in the town, she has never once thought to step inside the building. On either side of the main aisle, two arcades of plastered stone columns rise to high vaulted timbers. In the chancels beyond, the great arched windows flow with colour, saints dancing with illuminated richness, rose-red suns shining through ancient glass. She quickly spots the glory of Piper's new glass triptych in the far north window. She had read that it depicts three of Britten's church parables – The Prodigal Son, Curlew River, and the Burning Fiery Furnace – she likes it at once, with its bold colours and strong imagery. Ahead of her, at the entrance to the sanctuary she can just see two wooden angels facing each other and at each end of the rail, two more carved figures facing out towards her in silent prayer. And everywhere, the whitewashed walls are adorned with scrolled tablets bearing the past names of the great and their glory, the most imposing of which has an inscription to *Henrietta Vernon – daughter of Earl of Strafford (Thomas Wentworth), 1786*. She realises how much the congregation is shrunken by the building's majesty and feels like an impostor in this place of richness and colour.

> *Except to Heaven, she is nought, except for Angels – lone.*
> Emily Dickinson, *Except to Heaven, she is nought*

The organist strikes up a dull hymn and the French blue vanguard of crucifer and thurifer advance down the aisle, potent steam wafting through the congregation. Unobserved, sitting quietly, she watches the stately liturgy unfold – the embroidered robes, gilt-adorned altar, and swaying censer. Words she has heard before, a long time ago, echoing caves of distant childhood – words carved from rock, cherished, constant, holding centuries' power. She feels herself falling powerless towards their beguiling arms – the ritual decoration, incense, candles, self-conscious genuflection, all part of that forgotten, uncharted land of primitive symbols, the intensity of religion that has lost its foothold in her own life.

The congregation rises, the sudden movement interrupting the conceit of her thoughts. Expressionless faces surround her, muttering space. She continues to stare absently at the jumble of words in her prayer book, eyes closing; her thoughts already far away.

They sing another more familiar hymn,

I nothing lack if I am his,
And he is mine forever…

This is followed by the collect and difficult liturgy that she follows as best she can – her mind wanders constantly, thoughts of future plans flowing beyond the rich decoration. One of the parishioners reads from the Bible:

'I was ready to be sought out by those who did not ask, to be found by those who did not seek me.'
Isaiah 65

Her reverie is broken once more as the stern crew process past her up the main aisle; the green and gold-clad priest moves forward to join them and recites the gospel text from the shining brass eagle lectern, his voice assured but barely audible, wisdom cased in brittle glass, experienced and calm.

'Now it happened, on a certain day, that He got into a boat with His disciples. And He said to them, "Let us cross over to the other side of the lake." And they launched out. But as they sailed He fell asleep. And a windstorm came down on the lake, and they were filling with water, and were in jeopardy. And they came to Him and awoke Him, saying, "Master, Master, we are perishing!"
Then He arose and rebuked the wind and the raging of the water. And they ceased, and there was a calm. But He said to them, "Where is your faith?"
And they were afraid, and marvelled, saying to one another,

"Who can this be? For He commands even the winds and water, and they obey Him!"'
Luke 8 21–25

When the priest has finished, he leaves the lectern and climbs into the richly carved pulpit. More difficult words follow and they soon leave Jade and the rest of his flock to flounder. She is only stirred from her daydream when the mood seems to change – the old man's voice becomes noticeably more animated, penetrating her consciousness. Jade's eyes rise to the stained-glass image of a wounded figure above the altar. She feels the high vaulted ceiling closing around her as she listens to the priest's words, concentrating on their solemnity.

'Only the wisest amongst us may understand that wisdom is born of fear, solace of faith. We all stand on the deck of that boat in fear of the storm and we are all called to have faith in our redeemer. Think of a time when as a child you hid and wanted to be found, but you weren't found despite all of your plaintiff cries. Well, we have all been found, and we are all blessed if we live in trust, grace will come freely and unsought. Glance for a moment at the fisherman's window at the back of the north chancel and read these words written there: "*Fear not for I am with thee*".'

The priest drops his voice to the barest whisper, letting them dwell on the final words of his homily. When he is done, a silence falls; there is no sound except the uncomfortable shuffling of feet and creaking of pews. The musty air holds the promise of the earth's abundance in its fibre, the pause so long that she wonders if he will continue at all.

Silence is all we dread.
There's Ransom in a Voice –
But Silence is Infinity.
Emily Dickinson, *Silence is all we dread*

At last the music restarts and a hundred fragile hearts beat again in relief to the cheerful cadence of the organ. During the Peace, welcoming hands and friendly smiles are offered and she responds meekly in kind, her knees shaking a little with unexpected conviction. Without thinking, she also rises when ushered to join the others at the communion rail, chokes a little as she swallows the wafer and the sweet wine slips into her throat like an unexpected promise.

From nowhere, the image of her unknown mother is now beside her; she allows herself to fall into her dream shadows again, imagines how it might feel to rise from the rail and hold her mother's hand, dance together slowly in circles of untroubled gladness down the narrow aisles, surrounded by pure arpeggios of sound. She looks up at the veil of satin blue gentian covering her mother's face, the scent of primrose and poppy, sunbeams streaming through the windows. Colours cheaply called flesh – ochre, carmine, and vermilion: insufficient to hold such richness of tone. Her mother stoops to comfort a little bird, confused and afraid, calming it with her voice, holding precious wings between fingers. But the daydream bursts; she reddens and returns to her seat. Anxious now, she abandons her earlier plan to ask the priest whether he can give her an introduction to Mr Ogilvie and readies for a rapid exit, glancing back towards the west door, beginning to rise already from her seat, but something glinting in the candlelight draws her eye, stopping her in her tracks.

On the wall by the door, there is a richly worked bright copper plate; the words clearly visible even from this distance. 'This tablet is erected by their townsmen and women in glad and grateful memory of … who lost their lives in the capsizing of the lifeboat 'Aldeburgh' Dec 7th, 1899. '*Thy way is in the sea, and thy path in the great waters, and thy footsteps are not known.*'

Icicles upon my Soul
Pricked Blue and Cool –
Bird went praising everywhere
Only Me – was still – …
Emily Dickinson, *When I hoped, I recollect*

As she reads the inscription, she is struck hard with compassion, feels a tear rolling in her eye as she sits in the pew, thinking about Martin's family and the loss of his father. Yes, praying quietly, her lips revealing traces of polished quartz as they move to remembered fragments of the Lord's Prayer. She is touched by this brave sorrow; why, when she is so brave, when she has the gift to destroy with a frown, to enrapture with a smile, has this simple memorial moved her immediately to tears? She realises she still feels something for him. Self-consciousness replaces her effortless confidence. Her dark eyes laced with shy shadows, and a landscape reflecting emotion. Still fresh, but tinged with anxiety, breaking innocence, faint lines around her eyes.

Love to the loveless shown, that they might lovely be.
Crossman/Ireland, *My Song is Love Unknown*

Later, once the congregation has disbursed, she enters the vestry to search for the priest, still traces of tears in her eyes. This is the moment she has been nervously awaiting throughout the service. 'Can I help you?' she whispers, as he folds and stores the last of his vestments. The priest appears not to acknowledge her at first, so intent is he on his ablutions, but turns when he has cleaned out the last of the sacraments and smiles kindly. She whispers again, 'I have a favour to ask, I don't know if you can help me?'

Later, when they have talked for a while she receives his blessing and cannot stop herself curtseying before she departs and passes into the churchyard. She kneels for a moment before the fishermen's memorial and places her arms around the stone figures, weeping a little. There is no blemish, no mark of life; no flaw in its gaze.

Once she has composed herself, she returns by the same path to the hotel, and climbs the stairs to room 22, finding under her door a scrawled note from Sally asking her to meet them in the pub next door at lunchtime. But Jade has no time for this; she is in a state of new excitement, with an important errand to complete before she leaves this town. She pens a quick response to her friend to say that she will meet them later for tea and signs it with three kisses. Of course she still has no idea what took place in the next room the night before.

Jade borrows a bike from the hotel porter and sets off north up the coastal road, following the priest's instructions to the letter. The bike ride takes her past the caravan parks on the outskirts of town out through the rough landscape of dunes and reed beds that fall either side of the dyke separating sea from heath land, a summer playground for dragonflies and butterflies. She passes through the deserted streets of the strange holiday village of Thorpeness with its 'Meare' and continues bumping along a narrow unmade path that winds through the dunes, through bracken and heather and brambles, sparse farmland now taking over on the landward side. After another half a mile she sees a sign and a drive leading to the left towards the house that the priest has described to her that morning. As she enters the driveway the house is revealed from behind the hedges: a huge, mock-Tudor edifice built of sandstone, with timber frames and ranks of diamond-barred windows. She carries on along the drive, past an orchard of untended fruit trees, until she reaches an archway and then a gravelled area beyond that, which sweeps into a courtyard in front of the main door. There is an empty plinth in the middle of the courtyard (once bearing a solitary bronze statue of a discus thrower). She has learnt from Father Godfrey that the house now forms the main part of a conference centre.

A great oak door is set into the turreted sandstone entrance to the hall. It is wide open and she enters nervously the once grand entrance hall, with its decorated ceiling roses and great granite fireplace. In a room beyond she can hear cheerful singing and the smell of lunch cooking in the kitchens. A cheery lady emerges and asks if she is looking for someone. Jade responds with the name of the owner. She is directed towards the door of a private wing, where she rings the bell-pull and announces herself briefly to the housekeeper. It appears she is expected – as promised, the priest has called ahead.

A few minutes later she is ushered into the owner's study and the housekeeper leaves her; Jade is in a heightened state of anticipation now. There is no one in the room and she takes advantage of the momentary privacy to feast her eyes on its contents, to look for clues about the man she is finally to meet properly. Finely proportioned, three huge windows face the sea, each framed with oak panels, great shutters that sink neatly into recesses when not in use. Under each window a polished seat in the same wood, beautifully crafted, a high ceiling edged with moulded cornices and a central decorated rose. The walls are painted rose-salmon, finished with beech rails and skirting, framing the golden oak floor. They are adorned with dusty photographs, strange scientific instruments, shelves of butterfly and mineral collecting trays, specimens, taxidermy. Oh, what transport of delight, she thinks – she likes that phrase and feels it fitting for such a room of other-worldliness. A collection of prints catches her eye – a girl with beautiful reddish locks posed in seeming ecstasy, her hands outstretched before her and lips parted, besides a little red bird holding a flower in its beak. She remembers her own tentative communion that morning and the vision of her mother at the rail. 'Rossetti' she reads on the inscription – a faint memory of the tragic story of Lizzie Siddal, Rossetti's muse and Millais' model for 'Ophelia' returning to her mind.

She turns now to the bookcase and runs her hand over the leather spines of a set of Dickens' first editions, feeling their comforting regularity. As a teenager she was always a voracious reader but now she more often chides herself that she should read more. Already she is in love with this room – the Morris fabric, faded settees, the great mantel over the hearth, above which hang a pair of gilded icons, brooding representations of St Peter holding the keys to heaven and an icon of Christus Procrantor. Truly a bachelor's room, it appears the owner has been collecting his relics for decades.

She scans the jumble of papers on the desk in the middle of the room – many are marked in handwriting in the deep black ink that the owner seems to favour, held down on the desk by a collection of great glass paperweights. She picks one up and stares through its honey translucence at the bubbles floating immovably inside. Returning the glass sphere to its paper stack, absentmindedly she picks up a battered copy of *Wisden*, vaguely reading the lists of names and statistics, some marked with personal annotations.

The door opens with a creak and she realises that the long-anticipated interview with the owner is about to begin. She shuts the book quickly, reddening as Mr Thomas Ogilvie enters with a watering can. He coughs and then speaks: 'I hear the town team is always looking for new talent, young lady.'

She smiles at his little joke. 'Tea and sandwich makers, I expect. I'm afraid I've never really understood cricket.'

Mr Ogilvie is a tall man in his mid-forties, slightly bent from stooping too much, and of course she recognises him instantly. She wonders if he recognises her for a second by the way he stares at her as if seeing a ghost, but she is not sure. His clothing is dated, patches on his sleeves, moleskin trousers and a moth-eaten woollen waistcoat. A pair of gold-framed spectacles hangs expectantly from a chain around his neck and she sees immediately the silver ring with its burnt amber stone on his third finger – so she was right in her detective work. He was definitely the man on the beach.

He approaches and shakes her hand. She feels the sweat on his palm as if he is nervous; already she can smell the sweetness of pipe tobacco on his clothing. He motions towards a small silver tray with a decanter and glasses. 'Would you care to join me in a glass of dessert wine, young lady? Château Guiraud – it's one of the best Sauternes, beautiful colour. I'm afraid I'm not much one for sherry.' She nods and he pours each of them a glass.

She settles into one of the threadbare chairs, sipping carefully at the sweet amber liquid, her eyes continuing to devour the exotic titles in the bookcases as he fusses for a few moments about the room, watering the plants that line the french windows and clearing away the cobwebs around the pots. 'You know, this really has been a good year for spinners,' he jokes again, nodding at the open *Wisden*.

His charming manner seems friendly and harmless enough but in her heart, she feels, as she did before, this man is somehow flawed and there is something guarded and falsely formal in his speech. It feels a little like an interview with the headmaster and she is unsure if she is prepared enough for the confession she needs to make. There is a distance about him that she cannot fathom and he has yet to look her fully in the eye. At last he is satisfied with the plant watering and settles down beside her.

'So, young lady, I think you already know that my name is Thomas and you are Jade, I believe?'

'Yes, Mr Ogilvie. It's very kind of you to see me at such

short notice. I hope I haven't disturbed your Sunday morning.'

He ignores the question and continues in his own manner.

'Well, Jade, your name is unusual and might I say suits you very well, truly a very pretty name and I am sure one with a history of its own.' His words are utter charm; he gestures towards two beautifully carved jade figures on the corner of his desk. Jade squirms a little in her seat at the patent flattery.

'They are very beautiful.'

'Yes, presents from a Chinese friend – an antiquarian I have traded with for years. But enough of that: to business, I think. I understand from Father Godfrey that you are doing some family research, and that I might be able to help you. Well, that all sounds very interesting, but if I might say it seems a somewhat surprising pastime for someone of your tender years?'

'Yes, I suppose it is,' she replies. 'But before we get to that, I have a little surprise for you and a confession, if you don't mind?'

She opens her satchel and takes out a package, which she carefully unwraps to reveal two silver framed photographs. Her heart is racing a little now and in her attempt to maintain a cool disposition, she is afraid he will detect her nervousness. She has no idea what reaction to expect from this presentation but turns the photographs towards him in any case so he can see them.

'I have to apologise, I should really have asked your permission before displaying these images. I hope you are not annoyed with me?' When he sees the images, for a second Thomas looks confused and falters, his weary eyes frowning and questioning.

'Apparently, you bought these at my exhibition yesterday?' She pauses for the reaction that does not come. 'I wasn't totally sure at first, but this is you, isn't it?' she proposes carefully, pointing at the seated figure in one of the photographs.

'Well, well, well... I see I am indeed undone, young lady. How clever of you to figure that out. Well, yes, it is indeed me and yes, I was at first annoyed when I found them yesterday. But talking to the gallery owner, she told me about your project and I admit I was intrigued by it. And certainly, looking at you seated with such an endearing smile, I am not sure even an old curmudgeon like me could pretend annoyance with an angel like you. I suppose it is a remarkable coincidence – vanity, I suppose also, so I could not resist buying them when I saw them there. I certainly wasn't expecting the additional delight of a personal delivery from the photographer. But what may I ask has this to do with your family history?' He smiles but his laugh is notably guarded.

'That's very gracious of you, sir. Do you mind me asking who the young girl is? She's very pretty.' Jade ignores his direct question for a second but realises she is probably pushing her luck.

'Oh, just a niece,' he says, half under his breath. Jade sees the lie, knows that his only brother died over twenty years ago. She wonders what he is hiding, and is already creating images of a love child for him in her mind.

Mr Ogilvie gets up and walks over to the bookcase, where he searches for a moment and then takes a book from the shelf, opening it out before placing the gold spectacles on his nose. He walks back and hands it to her, pointing to the book in the photograph and tapping the cover. '*Foxe's Book of Martyrs!*' he says. 'See, the very volume, the binding unmistakable, and indeed, quite a special book in its own right. Given your project, Jade, you might be interested in the inscription.'

She opens the book he has handed to her and reads the inscription written neatly inside the glassine leaf: '*Together with his crown of flowers and the gruesome but improving Foxe's The Book of Martyrs, he is awarded twenty-five pounds in prize money'*. The inscription was signed, Benjamin Britten, *Albert Herring*.

She frowns, puzzled. 'Britten, really? Did you know him?'

'Yes, my dear – our town celebrity. Actually I knew him rather well; in fact, I think he gave me this as a rather unequal swap for my old school Latin primer when I was a young boy.'

He adds, 'It's actually a quote from one of his operas – I'm afraid I was not clever enough at the time to understand his little joke at my expense!' They both laugh, although Jade is not exactly clear what she is laughing about.

Jade looks at him again. He has the expression of a scholarly professor, somewhat remote from the world, gazing down at one of his more tiresome students with a combination of superiority and disdain. She could do without the 'my dear' bit – something of a misanthrope, she thinks – and then draws in her breath purposefully and deepens her voice a little to appear as serious and grown up as possible.

'Look, Mr Ogilvie, I think I should probably come to the point here, but first I have to confess again that I am here a little under false pretences. I do have some family history questions, but not actually about my own family. Still, I hope you don't mind me taking up a little of your time this morning?' she pauses, feeling she has regained the initiative. She notices an expression of relief on his face as she says the words, 'but not actually about my own family'.

'Well, well, that all sounds very formal and more than a little bit mysterious, but let's make it Thomas please, my dear. Please, fire away! It's lovely to have such charming company in the house – it's usually very dreary here.'

She notices from the surface of the liquid in the glass

that his hand is shaking a little and again, he removes himself from her gaze. She had been told in the town that he is virtually a recluse, living with his housekeeper of many years and her daughter in this private wing, rarely seen outside the grounds. He seems quite harmless to her, but as she scans his features and inscrutable expression, she wonders if there is more to him than just a harmless hermit, whether there is indeed some darker side he is hiding – his love child, a guilty secret maybe or even a juicy past she could invent for him, his reserved nature merely a warning to the curious?

'Well, sir – Thomas – the truth is I'm here on behalf of a friend that I'm trying to help with a problem.' She pauses again but his expression is still motionless. 'His name is Martin and he grew up in Aldeburgh in the 1950s, part of a local fisherman's family. I'm trying to help him find his sister, who disappeared just after their mother's death in around 1958. He hasn't seen or heard from her since.' She continued to watch him intently and thought she saw a frown begin to creep across his brow again.

> *Let the ominous thing put out its head, unobtrusively at first, undisturbed by forebodings, and then more insistently, until it holds the stage.*
> M. R. James, foreword to *Ghosts and Marvels*

'Well, that's interesting but I'm not sure how I can help. I've certainly lived here for a long time but I'm afraid I've never had much to do with the townsfolk, stuck out here in this old place. What is it specifically you think I can help you with?'

'Well, I know this is a bit of a long shot, but one of Martin's earliest memories is of two brothers who lived in a big house up the coast from the town. Apparently his sister Amber became friends with them one summer after her father had died and used to go off all the time to visit them on her bike. I was wondering if you might be one of those two brothers and if so, whether you remember her and more importantly, whatever happened to her.' It was her longest speech so far, and she could see that she had disturbed the equilibrium of his composure with her questions.

Thomas pales for a second and she notices that his hands begin to shake even more. She wonders whether he might have some sort of nervous disease. As she had observed last year on the beach, he is still handsome, slightly greying, with strong, kindly features. She thinks again of her previous daydream that he might be her father, and thinks that would be rather nice, with a lovely house like this. His hair is a little too long, in need of a trim, like his eyebrows and his clothes lost somewhere in the 1960s, but she could soon sort him out. He turns away from her gaze again and pauses for a long while, as if searching his memory and unsure of what to say to this determined young woman. Of course, from the name and her eyes, he is by now in no doubt as to her true identity and feels a dreadful wrench of emotions between the need to maintain a distance and to open his arms to hug her to his chest.

'Well, Jade, I admit you have taken me back a little. Gosh, that's a very long time ago and to be honest, something I had almost forgotten about. But now that you remind me, I think I do remember that family – they suffered a whole series of tragedies, didn't they? The father drowned, if I recall?' He was barely able to keep a straight face as he uttered those words, so close to the uncomfortable truth they hid.

'Yes, that's right, absolutely. Martin's father was drowned in 1953 in an accident at sea and it badly affected his sister's balance of mind. She became more and more detached from the family and eventually she ran away from home before reappearing almost out of the blue on the evening of their mother's wake, a year later. There was a row and she ran off into the night – Martin never saw her again. Do you remember her? Her name, as I said, was Amber.'

He swallows hard and then stammers, his voice rising distinctly in pitch. It was years since anyone had spoken that name to him. He had heard that the gamekeeper and his wife were dead now, the remittances had been returned by the bank, but he dared not go further to find out what had happened to their charge. All those years maintaining a lie, and now the girl's daughter stood before him in the very house he had made them promise never to allow her to enter.

'Yes, yes, actually I do, but it's really very complicated and... and to tell the truth, a little painful. She was an occasional visitor to us on her wanderings along the coast. You may not know this, but I lost my brother about that time, also in a freak accident. He fell from the Martello Tower and broke his neck. Yes, I do remember her, but I'm afraid I really can't help you at all with where she is today. I have not thought about her for years, and I'm afraid I have no idea if she's even still alive.'

His manner was evasive and his voice cracked a little as he tried to be forceful and final with the last sentence. She could tell he was hiding something; the photographer in her could see the beads of sweat beginning to form, his eyebrows drawn up towards the middle of his forehead and the tensing of his skin. She smelled blood and decided to press home her advantage.

'Oh dear, I'm very sorry. I certainly didn't intend to stir up bad memories for you. Look, I know it's a terrible imposition, but any background you can provide would be fantastic. I haven't got any clue at the moment where to look, and even the smallest thing might be helpful.'

He looks unsure how to respond as if he is trying to make up his mind what to do.

'Jade, I would like to help you and your friend, really,

but it's such a long time ago – a very long time. In some ways they might be events better left forgotten, really. I'm not sure…' He rises from his seat and begins to walk falteringly towards the door.

Jade feels her hold over the conversation slipping away.

'Oh! Look, I'm sorry – I really had no idea this would be so upsetting for you. I certainly don't want to open old wounds, but is there anything you can tell me? Please, anything at all?'

He hesitates again and paces up and down the room for a few minutes, then looks at his watch before turning back towards her.

'Look, I'm very sorry, young lady. I have to join my guests now for lunch and really, it was lovely to meet you. Let me give it some thought and see if there is anything I can recall. Leave your name with Dorothy and have a pleasant ride back to town. In fact, if you'd like, you're more than welcome to wander round the gardens – there's a lovely walk down to the beach. She used to enjoy the garden.' He disappears hurriedly.

'Don't worry, dear. Really, he was pleased to see you again,' says the housekeeper as she shows Jade to the front door.

Again?

June 1953

The late afternoon sea mist had dispersed to reveal a calm evening, peaceful but portentous. Thomas and Ralph had returned earlier from the festival in their uncle's car. The house was full of guests up to stay for the festival and a round of golf, so the boys had disappeared off to the beach to escape the grown-ups. They had wondered south towards the 'Ness' that formed a headland just north of the holiday village founded by their ancestor. Although the late afternoon mist had gone, its briny aftertaste was still bitter in their throats and they could smell in the air the deep concentration of the approaching storm.

The sun had nearly set but a half-light hung in the air, the first stars just visible in the north. They were out on the shoreline, lying on their backs in the shingle banks, when suddenly they heard the quite distinct sound of another human voice shrieking and then a crack like a lightning strike.

Ralph started up first and pointed towards the shoreline. Thomas turned to where his hand indicated movement in the surf. They watched for a while in silence, straining their eyes against the dimming light, alarmed but excited by the sound of that passion, by that cry. They could just make out a figure moving slowly through the breakers, their breath gathered around them in moist clouds in the clammy night.

The shape came steadily closer, stepping with difficulty through the water. Thomas's heart was already beating like bellows against his chest. He could see now that the figure was a young girl, her dress tacked loosely around her, some sort of cloth bag tied to her waist, floating in the water behind her. Her face was silvered and ashen, as if aged by the starlight, and she was clearly distressed, tears falling uselessly into the shimmer that lay on the surface of the sea.

Eventually, she emerged fully from the water, walking towards them. In that light, her appearance was ghostly, distracted, not acknowledging in any way their presence. Neither of them spoke and they hardly dared even to draw breath. When she arrived at the top of the dune, she stopped and turned back to look at the sea, expressionless, adjusting her hair endlessly, wordlessly. Thomas noticed how thin she was, more bones than flesh, sodden clothes clinging to her wet body defining an elfin shape. It was impossible to tell from her face if she was awake or just in a dream.

'Well, give her your coat, Tom – she must be freezing,' his brother said.

Thomas stood up and approached, offering her his jacket at arm's length. She started when she saw him at first, but then reached out her arm and took it without a word or a smile, wrapping it around her shoulders as if she had just received an expensive mink from the doorman at the Ritz. She gazed into his eyes for what seemed to be the longest time until he had to look away, her stare was so intense. Then she turned back towards the sea, her hair fluttering as it found the strength of the wind. For a second, he caught the sweetest smell in the air, like rose incense, and his heart was suddenly full of unexpected feelings. Protection, love, pity, who knows, but they were feelings he had not felt so strongly before. He sensed the force of Ralph's hand on his shoulder, pulling him back down to the sand. His fingers held to his lips.

'It's that girl from the village, the one who tore my shirt.'

The girl started to sing, gently at first, then increasing in intensity. The words seemingly sung in her own singular language, lilting and rising like the sound of the sea; caressing, consoling, seducing one moment; pencil-sharp and shrill against the agony of the night the next. Her voice was both irresistible and chilling. The brothers looked at each other but were transfixed, powerless to interrupt. And then without further notice or signal, she just as abruptly moved back towards the waves, reaching into the tide until the breakers covered both her body and form.

'She'll drown!' cried Ralph.

'My jacket,' Thomas called to her under his breath, but somehow he knew he would not see it again. They both ran into the waves, searching through the breakers, but she was gone without a trace.

The storm was approaching rapidly now and the clouds began to move quickly across the moonless sky, stars uncovered by the fleeting shadows as they fled, each seeming to whisper the name of each point of light from the beginning. They searched a while longer for clues in the fragile darkness, but there was only one: her name, written in the sand by the movement of her feet.

'And her name was?'

In 1940, just after the Battle of Britain began, Thomas and Ralph had been evacuated from London and sent to live in Bly House, near Aldeburgh with their uncle and aunt. Bly House, or at least its predecessor, had been a part of the Ogilvie family's story for generations. It was once a much grander place, a vast thatched palace surrounded by hundreds of acres of spacious grounds and parkland. That original building burned to the ground in the early 1920s after a fire started in the kitchens during a grand society party. The fire took quickly and the thatch meant it spread before any of the local fire engines could get there. It was almost completely destroyed. However, the family were determined to replace it and a new house was built a year later in the Tudor pastiche that still stands today, though at less than half the original scale. This time they were wise enough to roof it with tiles to avoid a repeat of any thermal accidents.

After he is sure that Jade has gone, Thomas walks agitatedly back into the study of Bly House. In the late calm of that Sunday morning in 1990 he looks at the old photographs on the wall above the piano. The rooms of the original building had been stuffed full of old paintings and memorabilia – prosperous ancestors with money made from timber trading. It had been a fabulous place – sparkling with parties, gramophones roaring, cigar-smoke on the balconies, glamorous girls dancing in their cocktail dresses – but by the time Thomas and his brother had arrived in 1940, those glory days were long gone and the place already somewhat forlorn and battened down for war.

Barely a month after they arrived, both their parents had been killed in separate incidents on the same dreadful night.

It was late 1940, the most intense part of the Blitz. London was bombed by the Luftwaffe for 57 consecutive nights and their father was working for a secret government project in the city when a bomb destroyed the building. Their mother was killed later the same night, searching for him as the fires raged through the streets. It was fortunate that the boys had been evacuated to Suffolk, but they were both under five at the time and there were long family arguments and endless meetings with solicitors about what to do with them. Later that year, Bly House was commandeered by the Army. The boys themselves continued on in one wing with their uncle and aunt, their new guardians, for the duration of the war.

After the troops departed, the main part of Bly House was left in a mess and there were further long discussions on what to do with it. Eventually it was sold to a private boarding school and most of the parkland sold off. However, the family were able to continue living there in the wing that had been taken on by their uncle. With a school now on their doorstep, it was natural that they were also sent to study there. It turned out to be a strange place, with a largely experimental curriculum. The students were able to study almost what they liked and some subjects, like maths, were not even taught unless they (or more usually, their parents) wanted them to be. In the holidays between terms, what remained of the grounds was virtually theirs alone to roam to their hearts' content. They had private tutors come and go but most of their time was spent under the vague protection of their elderly relatives and the more effective eyes of the housekeeper and his wife.

Thomas remembered how it was always cold back then – the house had an innovative heating system that broke down on regular occasions. Eventually it was decided it was just too expensive to fix, so they had to make do with the heat from the range, electric fires in the bedrooms and the smoky open fires in the main rooms. Even at the height of summer, he remembered the chill that seemed to hold the place in its grasp. There was frost on the windows in winter and always a pervasive smell of damp. Ten years ago, Thomas had relented and installed proper central heating – he wasn't going to continue to live in a cold old morgue, despite the extravagance.

So, his early memories were of these iron winds, salt in the air and the raw cries of gulls mixed with the incessant beating of the surf. But of course, the advantage of being on the coast was that there were also long periods of quieter evenings in summer, when the air was warm and still and the place regained some of its old twenties magic. On these evenings, Thomas and his brother would lie out on the terraces, with the radio playing in the house, watching the swifts swooping amongst the eaves and listening to the distant thud of the waves against the shingle. During the holidays, with all the other students gone, there was not much to do. They had to make their own amusement, often wandering the beach all day, searching amongst the driftwood and cast off fish netting, inventing landscapes and adventures. In their daydreams, they would fight invaders on these Saxon shores, build dams and entrenchments; stride like giants across the ancient causeways.

> *Thence all evil broods were born, ogres and devils and evil sprites – the giants also, who long time fought with God, for which he gave them their reward.*
> Anonymous, *Beowulf*

Thomas gets up from his desk and walks to the window. The house is perched no more than 200 yards from the sea and looks down over abandoned gardens and a wide terrace that descends through a series of steps and further terraces towards the shoreline. He can see Jade as she walks purposefully through the grass towards the gazebo at the southern corner of the garden.

After her interview with Thomas, Jade emerged from the house into the bright noon sunlight. She decided, as he had suggested, to clear her mind with a walk between the yew trees and roses, rather than cycle straight back into town. There was much to think about, she knew there was something he was not telling her in that interview, but for the life of her she could not figure out what he should have to hide. She followed a path that led away from the house and sun terrace towards the far end of the walled garden. Here, she climbed the rickety wooden steps onto the upper storey of copper-domed gazebo and entered a room glazed on all sides like a lighthouse. There are two seats with floral cushions and a small metal table with a cloth. She sits to take in the wonderful panorama of the coast laid out before her. Against the sea-facing panes a telescope is trained towards the headland to the south.

She thinks there is something fine about that stretch of shore with its mild elevation and sandstone cliffs. The startling seascape, the three narrow bands of sand and sea and sky, solid and fluid and airy cloud; the sea a moving sink of power that washes in against implacable opposition, restless, rippling, disturbed; and then the sand so calm and unmoved. She watches a flock of avocets bustling along the shoreline, searching the debris for food – the third amongst the legendary Suffolk trinity of marsh harrier and bittern; a flurry of white on a wave crossing the sandbank, catching the sun's power in a flash, the air slipping pleasantly past, turning the pages of a book left by one of the conference centre guests on the table.

Jade can see white spikes of sailcloth breaking the horizon and a gull, lone and expectant, standing looking over her above the beach, cresting before it sinks to the water's edge. She wonders where the boat is heading, heeling into the wind, and the decks almost awash with the waves.

VII – The Depths of the Sea

There hath he lain for ages and will lie,
Battening upon huge sea worms in his sleep,
Until the latter fire shall heat the deep;
Then once by man and angels to be seen,
In roaring he shall rise and on the surface die.

Lord Alfred Tennyson, *The Kraken*

Late afternoon – June 1957
The beach north of Aldeburgh

The third time Thomas had seen Amber was several years later– it must have been around 1957. She was lying on the beach below the gazebo, reclining like a nymph in the narrow strip of sand where the waves lapped, oblivious to the world. He had watched while her legs crossed and uncrossed in the air as she turned the pages of some paperback romance. Her bike lay in the sand by her side.

A chance encounter, but it was enough. He was about eighteen or nineteen and must have watched her secretly for an hour from there, admiring the way her white socks contrasted with the healthy tan of her shins. He remembered her plain cloth dress, drawn in at the waist with its loosely knotted belt, stained with salt from the sea. Her hair fell untidily about her shoulders – every so often as she turned a page, she had to brush it out of her eyes. He liked the way she did that. Her hair shining with a thousand colours that changed in the light from amber to gold to red, as if made of some precious thread spun from copper and bronze. The longer he looked on at those silken skeins, the deeper the colour became, the more he wanted to hold its fullness to his face.

The girl was a couple of years younger than him and the freshness of her features still those of a child, as if freshly polished by the action of the waves. Her lips formed two cups of carmine pink that could not have been painted more perfectly. He remembered the pair of rope sandals that he had found abandoned on the beach a week earlier and wondered now whether they were hers. Tiring of his lookout perch, and eager to find some excuse to talk to her, he retrieved them from the loggia where he had placed them, thinking they belonged to one of their guests, and walked down the path towards the shoreline.

He was still unsure whether he should approach her and for a while sat on the edge of the shingle, crouching amongst banks of sea kale, studying her further as a pair of Silver-studded Blues fluttered aimlessly around the pages of her book. One of the pair, as if caught by the wind, flew off and the other, now companionless, settled onto the gentle crest of her back, its wings opening and closing like delicate bellows. Something caught her attention and she raised her head, and then as if she had suddenly felt the intensity of his gaze, turned to face him.

'It's rude to stare,' she shouted across to him, an uncompromising sternness to her voice, and those deep green eyes flashing like emeralds. He coughed and blushed, but her mock severity was broken by a smile. Behind them the summer heather was at its gaudy best, the hillocks of sap-green rolled on to more distant olive mountains of yellow gorse. A lone colony of yellow poppies swayed in the wind, cups of pollen reaching out to the sun, the heady scent of salt in the air.

'Sorry,' he stammered, 'I didn't mean to disturb you.'

She allowed the faint smile to broaden but kept her eyes fixed on the book and continued to read. The marram grass, coarse and spiked, pricked his arms uncomfortably. Drifts of chilled sea mist rolled in banks from the sea, past the sad-speckled paths, yellow and purple with heartsease and gossiping ferns, into the scorched heathland beyond.

He tried to regain her attention. 'You looked so intent there, I was afraid of surprising you. I wondered if these might be yours.' He held out the rope sandals that he hoped she had abandoned.

She laughed a private sort of laugh, and then said distantly, 'I wondered where they'd got to.'

Rolling on to her side to face him, she closed the book, consciously stretching to allow him to glimpse the flesh between her blouse and skirt, and then looked away towards the still horizon, absent-mindedly drawing circles in the sand. Her hands were thin – bony, but delicate and strong as coral. He continued to watch her wordlessly, the fitful sun beginning to throw shadows across her legs.

'You know, gentlemen really oughtn't to stare at girls,' she said, without looking up. 'Especially when they're training to be priests and all.'

He was surprised by this intimate knowledge that she possessed.

'OK, do you mind if I sit down beside you then?' he asked.

'Can I really trust you?' she teased, patting out a flat spot in the multi-coloured sand. 'It's a bit damp here, though.' She laid her bag on the sand for him to sit on.

He settled onto the prepared seat, watching the light fall on her face, the auburn tresses blowing in the wind, throwing a handful of pebbles, one by one, towards a large stone at the very edge of the wave-line.

'I remember seeing you here before a few years ago – you took my jacket and you never even told us your name.'

'Didn't I?' she replied, almost as an afterthought. 'You know, I think I did.'

'Well?' He noticed how her legs glistened, guessed she'd been swimming earlier. That was why the sand was damp.

She thought for a while. 'Well, OK then, if you don't remember – it's Calypso! CALYPSO!' she shouted. 'That's me!'

The butterfly still fluttered around the bow of her skirt-belt. She held out her hand, and allowed it to settle on to the back of her wrist.

They both laughed, and she brushed the hair from the side of her face winsomely, to reveal a pale blush of rose at the crowns of her cheeks. 'Come on then, don't be shy,' she said, and she leaned over and kissed him, just lightly, like a child might kiss her father. He blushed.

Once, once only, once on the crest of his burning cheek, was that enough?

Of course she had come back to visit them many times over that fleeting summer, but how many more times since in those long years had he returned to that place to find only memories of that fleeting kiss amidst the burning sands? You have to understand that it was once and once only, but enough to ensnare him for a lifetime. If he had his time again he would have fought harder with Ralph for the prize that he stole from him, a betrayal that would result in tragedy.

Her eyes sparkled like sunlight on the crashing waves. Her body like the complexities of a nautilus shell, surfaces and compartments of glazed delight. Crazy days, sunlight spilled at a time when senses were truly colour, a time cradled and lived again and again.

Is anyone ever certain of the future? Can anyone ever really know what lies beyond the azure fields of evening? There comes a point in your life when the future is not everything, when you no longer believe that you can be or will do anything. History and time begin to encroach, experience begins to exert its dead weight, and the future becomes a calculation, an analysis of remaining possibilities, with none of the charmed freedom of limitless probability. There comes a point when the die is cast; it creeps up on you and then you can no longer change with freedom. You have responsibilities, ties, expectations.

Reflection, soul-searching, a catharsis, all releases of sorts, for a time, while they last, but you cannot live your life that way. You cannot continue on the brink, on the edge of the river, waiting for the signal. And sometimes as you wait, the calculation is just too difficult, too close to the heart; sometimes you just have to jump. After all, catharsis is pointless, if it has no effect. Sometimes you just have to jump.

'It's just a piece of foolishness.' He hears his brother's verdict again, and now it is too late, and there is nothing left. 'It's me she fancies.'

If he had the choice again, would he have acted differently? Faced with the same choices, would he have chosen the same course? Regrets littered like faithless companions, like the grit of sand in her hair, like the murmur of the waves, burning with Amber.

Two weeks after that kiss Thomas sits, precise and controlled, within the generous shade of an apple tree. His arms rest on the surface of a small writing table, round and substantial, covered with a coloured cloth. From time to time Thomas lifts his head to watch a pale blue butterfly that has alighted on the cotton-painted surface, frozen in perfect miniature, each wing glistening with its complex crystalline structure. Around his legs the warm breath of the July breeze flows and shifts like a jealous cat. His mind is alive and fresh, exhilarated by the unexpected conquest, expanding into the glory of the garden.

He considers the sounds of the day, attempting to capture their form with a well-turned phrase. *The far-off longing of the gulls, the persistent rapture of a cricket's content, the faintest roll of the surf, delicate, almost intangible in its slow caress.*

His occupation is peaceful, each minute of time stretched and enjoyed, tasted and reversed and tasted again. His pen draws neat shapes of incredible patience on the writing pad, each word considered and gentle and bold transferred to paper with deliberate strength. The deep black ink marches in regimented dark furrows across the white paper so that the forms belong and become complete.

His brother Ralph lies in the sun before him, a cream and white deity of shining linen, wrapped by the dark green slumber of the lawn. Ralph is sleeping gently, the straw of his hat tracing a delicate trellis of shadows across his sun-reddened face, an unread book held loosely in his hand.

Into this undisturbed framework strides the very antithesis of their order, her temper expanding like a storm across their bored civilisation; engulfing and enrapturing with its urgent conquest.

Thomas was writing but as soon as he saw her climbing the last steps from the beach, he lay down his pen on the half-filled page. He watched as the shape moved towards them like a cloud rushing through the sky.

She walked quickly, her unshod feet gliding across the stone terrace towards the garden's flat plain. He could see that this time her mood was completely different. In fact she seemed to be in some distress, her dress torn and ragged. She had the urgent look of one who sought help. He could see blotches of red around her eyes, her face dusty and marked as if she had been struggling with something in the sand. She stopped when she saw him, startled as if shaken out of a trance, seeming to realise her location for the first time. She looked round in desperation as if searching for a familiar landmark or path and turned to leave.

'What's happened, are you in trouble?' he asked.

She hesitated and stared at him, as if knowing but not knowing his voice, the voice of a forgotten friend, struggling to remember. Ralph's breaths were heavy behind them, the oppressive sweetness of honeysuckle grasping his throat, causing him to cough and snore in his sleep.

'I meant no harm,' she said quietly, as much to herself as to Thomas.

She stood with one hand on the balustrade, maybe twenty yards away. He could see she had been running, her lungs rising and falling still as she caught her breath.

The dress that now hung torn and ragged around her limbs was similar to that she had worn all those years previously. A single piece of cloth, a slit for her neck and arms, draped and tucked around her body. The material secured with a belt shaped like threaded daisies. However, as he approached her, he noticed that the cloth was not really plain, but bore a very faint pattern of interwoven flowers and leaves that were picked out and glistened with silver thread in the fullness of the sun's light. She had indeed been crying, the stark intensity of her green eyes heightened by the red circles that surrounded them. Her hair fell in long wild tresses about her shoulders, burning the pallor of her skin. Had he ever imagined then that such beauty could sustain so much tragedy?

She sits down heavily on the wall, seemingly tired, rolling her face in the long locks of hair to remove the dust. Thomas walks to sit with her and puts his arm out, but she seems to shy away from his touch.

'You'd best not come near me.'

'Why?' he asks, concern modulating his tone.

'They say as I'm dangerous.'

He looks at her face, into those deep green eyes, but this time it is she who drops her gaze first. She is clearly distressed; she looks as if she has not slept all night. He scans her body but cannot see any outward sign that she has come to any harm. She starts to speak hesitantly.

'I seen him again,' she says, biting her lip as she kicks her ankles together.

'Who?'

'My pa, I seen him in the waves, calling.'

'In the waves?'

'Of course,' she says resolutely.

I hear those voices that will not be drowned.
Benjamin Britten, *Peter Grimes*

How could he deny her these claims, her belief seemed so total? Of course, the stories of her moody wanderings had reached even their fortress world, the tragedy of her father's death – apparently her mind had been affected, the townspeople thought she was going mad. However, she seemed totally harmless there in the brightness and protection of the garden, a vision of natural beauty.

'That's fine,' he says gently and lays his hand upon her brow. She is burning hot. He wonders if he should take her inside, ask the housekeeper, Dorothy to feed her. 'Can I get you something to drink?' he asks.

She nods and follows him cautiously through the roses and ivory shrubs to a seating area by the house in front of the conservatory. He brings out a pitcher of lemonade and two glasses and she drinks slowly, her lips cracked from the sun. This patio is cooler than the open garden and she shivers a little from the change in temperature.

'I'd offer you a jacket but last time I never got it back!' he jokes, referring to that evening several years previously. Indeed he had never seen that jacket again.

'Still playing the gentleman,' are her only words.

Above the house, a skylark sings, bursting in sudden flights of iridescence sound through the powder-blue sky. The air smells cool, a gentle fragrance from the garden mint. After she has drunk the lemonade, they walk back out into the full sun and she rubs the skin peeling on her shoulders. A first smile appears in the delicate light. She recovers some confidence of beauty, the first understanding of this already playing again with his mind.

'Shall we wake your brother?' she asks with an obvious interest that hits him like an arrow to the heart.

When she returns a week later, he is again seated at the table in the garden, this time sorting specimens for his mineral collection. She is wearing a makeshift crown of the sea pea and yellow-horned poppies that grow along the shore.

'These are so beautiful,' she says, lifting the stones to the sky so that their rough shapes eclipse the sunlight from her face. In its place, spirals and prisms of rich crystal shadows, blues and ultramarine and intense scarlet reds fill every pore and crease of her cheeks with coloured light. She twists them in her palm, admiring the changing patterns of light as the facets turn.

'The purple one is amethyst, the red garnet.'

'You must be very clever to know all their names.'

She replaces the specimens in their cartons and takes out a piece of polished honey-coloured glass. She stares through the translucent resin, embedded with pockets of air.

'It makes the world seem like a dream, like a painting,' she mutters, a reflected sunbeam passing across her face.

'The Persians called it Ambar, the Greeks Elektron – the tears of Phaeton's mourning sisters, washed up by the sea.'

'Well, I don't know about that, but I do have a present for you.' She replaces the polished stone and draws a rough pebble of uncut amber stone the size of a hen's egg from her own pockets.

'I'd been saving this, but I think you might like it.'

In his study earlier, as he had talked to Jade, Thomas had lifted the same egg-shaped stone again from his desk drawer and turned it in his palm, marvelling at its lightness. He had known from the moment he gazed at her on the beach that he would love this girl, this sea spirit, known that he would treasure the stories of her personal mythology, her tales of journeys to the depths of the sea; fall with her into the boundless depths of her imagination. But it had all gone wrong, so terribly wrong. He sits back now, alone again in the study chair and closes his eyes, the sky turning the colour of her name, and he watches her dance across his thoughts once more.

Of course that was not the last time they saw her. It was just the beginning of their troubles. In that, life imitates art.

There was another time when she had almost knocked the box of precious stones from his hand, coming out suddenly from behind the mulberry, grabbing his shoulders first, and then passing her hands over his eyes. Her insistent enthusiasm felt hot on the back of his neck. He longed to turn round and hold her body to his, but false propriety stopped him again.

'Guess who?'

'Who else?'

Somewhere she had found a wide-brimmed hat with flowers in the band that expressed her state of womanly transition better than any words he could command. In the few weeks that she had visited them, she had unleashed a flood of creativity in him that had transformed his previously awkward stanzas into verse of intense line and strength – screaming passion from the page. He felt alive in her presence; she swept through their dusty afternoons like a spirit.

She stood for a moment in silence, measuring the value of the stones, fixing every shape with the movement of her eye, straining the quality of every colour with her unmerciful gaze. Ralph came over to join them. Undeterred by false modesty, he passed his arms around her waist and kissed the top of her hair. She turned her head to give him a peck on the cheek. Thomas uttered a silent scream. *No!*

'Still playing with those coloured rocks, Tom?'

Thomas was mortified but Ralph seemed indifferent to all this of course, insensitive to his pain. For him this was idle flirtation, for Thomas it was all but life and death.

Over the next weeks, she visited so often that it was almost as if she was living a secret life amongst them, concealed from the world, protected from discovery by the grandeur of the house, the feudal distinction of its inhabitants. It appeared that she had no other friends.

'Come on, Tom – let's go swimming,' his brother said.

His brother was the archetypal sportsman, stronger, more handsome, and unworried by life or art. His golden features might have been hewn from crags of brawn and sinew, shining before them like an icon of good breeding. Of course, he also excelled in everything: tennis, cricket and football, whatever. For him girls were a chore to be endured from time to time, but this one was different. She held her own; she was Ralph's kind of girl. He was beginning to take quite a fancy to her, and Thomas could see with despair that the feeling was returned.

The swimming pool lay behind an old yew hedge, watched over by six weather-worn dryads, their comic expressions frozen alternately in outrage or contemplation as if despairing the indignity of such a watery chore.

Jade now walks across the lawns to where the swimming pool lies. She walks back into the small, dark loggia below the gazebo and shivers at the cool relief from the torpor of the afternoon sun.

'This is where bathers used to change,' says a voice. Jade jumps, she had not noticed the figures in the gloom. It is the housekeeper and her daughter. The younger woman is speaking, her voice strangely familiar. They are sitting in rocking chairs in the shade, blending into the shadows of the sandstone walls, half covered with a peeling stucco of sea-shells and flint. 'This was once our miniature sea-palace, guarded by two great fishes that used to spew water into the pool. I'm afraid they are no longer working,' she says. Jade closes her eyes and imagines the water falling from the fishes' mouths into the pool.

After the three of them had satisfied themselves in the cool water, they lay by the entrance to the loggia, letting the sun dry their bodies, talking lazily in the airless shadows, disturbed only by the cooing of doves from the dovecote.

Thomas began to read aloud from his book: 'Beauty is not the same as perfection; it requires a lack of balance, a fault in the symmetry to create life. True art captures that beauty.'

'What perfect rot!' declared Ralph.

'I don't understand, what does it mean?' Amber asks.

'It means that to create a thing of beauty has value in its own right, it isn't about money or wealth or power.'

'And you believe that? More fool you!' said Ralph, shaking his head.

Jade looks into the shadowy loggia. The woman and her daughter have gone, leaving only a book and sunglasses in the chair.

Amber's visits were capricious twists of vanilla in the long laziness of that summer. Her friendship was given freely without thought, bestowed on them without a plan. Gradually she transferred to them the whole magical kingdom of her imagination – the beasts and the sea-creatures, the stories of seafarers and far-off ports. She made the sea-palace by the pool her own palace, decorating it with shells and sea holly and salvage from the beach. They could have spent a hundred years like this, as she weaved between them. She was a fairy-spinner, beguiling with innocence, so that gradually their freedom began to unwind into her heart.

One day, tired of lazing around the pool, Ralph suggested that they meet her at the Martello Tower, a good four miles to the south. They started before the sun was high. It was a long walk through uncertain paths and heathland to Thorpeness; from there, they could get a horse-drawn carriage the rest of the way into town. The cliffs were covered with a soft, springy turf that provided habitat for wild orchids and stonechats and delicate blue butterflies. As they moved away from and then back towards the sea, the land ran off into the hinterland of bracken interspersed with bright islands of heather and the first bilberries. The air was thick with summer.

They found one of the horse-drawn carts that operated throughout the tourist season between the holiday village and the main town of Aldeburgh. It made slow progress, but eventually they reached the high street and continued on foot down the main causeway towards the strange military structure at its end. The tower was in fact a fortress built above the shingle, a complex form of slanting sides, ledges and narrow windows built to deflect ordnance from invaders who had never arrived. A million bricks arranged in strange quatrefoil design. Above the old bricks was a more recent superstructure built as a penthouse studio by a local artist.

She was waiting for them when they arrived.

'My home ground this time!'

'I'm too hot!' said Ralph, throwing off his shirt and shorts, and plunging straight into the sea. A hundred yards from the shore was a raft used for mooring pleasure boats, its anchor chained to a buoy. Amber shrieked with laughter and jumped in after him, her strong back arching like a porpoise through the waves towards the raft. Her smock flowed through the water, like a scarf around her legs. Thomas followed slowly, more deliberately. He was also a strong swimmer, but moved with precision and form, not with the carefree athleticism of his brother. She reached the raft before either of them and pulled herself up onto the sun-bleached logs, ahead of his brother's grasp, so that her legs ran through his hands like a fish.

'Ha, Calypso, I want to eat you alive!' he said, and his jaw closed around the wet folds of her dress. She squirmed and writhed, flushed and giggling in the grip of the bronzed sea-monster. Thomas's stomach churned with nausea as he watched them.

'Ars gratia artis – art for art's sake,' Thomas repeated for them like a mantra as they climbed the last steps to the entrance to the tower. They were twenty feet above the shingle now and the flat expanse of blue on one side and the marshy estuary on the other seemed like two giant quilts spread over the land. Only the narrow line of shingle broke the two blankets of cover.

'Tom is going to join the church, you know,' Ralph winked. 'To be a fisher of men.' His brother's words struck like a betrayal. He looked into her face, expecting disapproval.

'Well, I'd rather marry a fisherman than a priest,' she said enigmatically.

Laughs and screams from the loggia, unhappiness in my breast. Love led him like a martyr to his stake of flames.

The following week they were back again.

Amber beckoned to Ralph, keeping maybe fifty yards ahead of him, skipping lightly over the stones. Every so often she looked back, taunting, giggling, allowing him to catch up a little before setting off again, the cloth of her skirts flapping in the sea breeze.

'Catch as catch can,' she laughed.

They were almost at the tower. She stopped, resting her back against the massive brickwork, looking up at the sky, no sign of breathlessness. Ralph stopped too, twenty yards short, bent over with his hands on his knees, chest heaving, gulping in the salty oxygen, looking up at her reddened cheeks, the splash of sea thrift in her eyes, the strands of unkempt hair billowing wildly in the gusting wind. Out of breath, he was unable to speak.

'I'm going to get you, Calypso!' he panted.

'What are you waiting for?' she laughed, pushing herself off the wall into the force of the wind. He staggered the last twenty yards, attempted to catch her in his arms, but again she ducked her shoulder and ran off, laughing uncontrollably.

'Much too slow!' she teased.

'Hast thou, spirit, perform'd to point the tempest that I bade thee?'
'To every article.'
Shakespeare, *The Tempest*

Thomas could hear the echo of feet crossing the small bridge over the moat, bare feet on sandy steps. His brother had set off again, following the hidden stone stairway that spirals through the walls of the tower. He saw him emerge onto the platform, where the four rusty canons guarded the cardinal points. Amber had vanished, hiding somewhere, calling from time to time to egg them on. Ralph seemed to be searching ever more frantically and signalled down to Thomas to look, but neither of them could see her. Ralph searched everywhere, over the parapet, over the sheer sides of the fortifications, then stopped and appeared to be staring into the sea, sheltering his eyes from the sun. Thomas wondered if Ralph could see her diving through the struggling circle of water that broke around the breakwater beneath him. The waves were pounding at the beach, the lace of white air racing like breathless armies to the surface.

Then it was as if some sort of rash heat seized his brother's blood. He was usually so calm and considered and avoided undue exertion. If you were to debate with him the merit of an opening batsman or a particular horse he might, perhaps, allow the thrill of competition to rule logic for a second, but not for long, and then only in the theatre of a game. He was the best example Thomas knew of the balance of beauty, but maybe Nature loses interest in perfection. In any case, there was no rail to hold him back then and later they found that the coping stones were loose.

He hesitated for a moment on the brink and then dived as he fell. It was crazy, but too late for thought, too late for reason. There was not a word of hers hanging in the air to guide him.

Dive together.
Follow her down.

His body was captured to Thomas's terror in mid-air, suddenly transformed; inert no more, reacting with rashness that was untested. A man conveyed by powers unknown. No turning back, he had made his choice. Reason and compromise lay with his shoes and jacket on the dusty walls above.

The light of the surface of the water came to meet Ralph, reaching out to receive his body. As his shoulders penetrated the icy brine, he felt its fingers tearing at his throat and chest. There was no sensation in his limbs save that of rushing thunder. The clarity of glass in his mind, his breath held precious in his lungs, like a pearl diver against uncertain danger.

Sea-rippled legs kick.

It was as if her eyes had drawn him to this danger – eyes of jade, causing him to forget reason for long enough that everything was now risk, nothing stability.

Loose cotton shift floating freely.

Middle-air was no place for the faint-hearted, no part of his history. He was now chasing the girl who cried for her lost father in the waves.

Shoulders robed in silken filaments.

Surely there was something worthier than ambition here, something pure and precious. Trust me, her eyes said, for I know life.

Ungirdled skin, shining in surging sunlit shafts.

Down he fell, deeper into the pool. So deep that his eyes found no light, trusting in touch for recognition, scarves of green and silver tugging at his body, the exquisite thrill of nausea filling his cheeks.

Deeper down.
Shimmering shadows.
Aquamarine, turquoise, cobalt.
She finds his shape, beckons to kiss.

Thomas stood below on the beach, beneath the brick edifice; gazing on in horror at the dark form of his brother falling like a great seabird might dive from the tower above into the maelstrom of reefs and currents. He shouted silently while he was still in mid-air, knowing the fatal danger. Even if he found the deepest part of the pools left by the surging tide, the currents could still hold his body captive; seek to draw him through the undertow, back into the ready jaws of the rocks below.

Breathe again.
Breathe through her.
Further,
deeper,
down to the bottom.
She smiles – eyes glistening.
Stroked silken hair.

Kissed lips, coral-soft.
Again,
and again.
Breathe.
Again,
and again.
Floating, weightless bodies.
Rolling, swaying in the current.
Kiss again.

Why had Ralph pursued her, this girl who glowed into that fatal dive? He must have known that Thomas was already in agony with love. Was it just another stupid game for him, a dare that had gone too far, or had her siren attraction really driven him to such madness? Had Ralph seen in her the longing for the deep, her limbs strong, her song and the face that lights darkness, singing still on the morning after a storm, in the first blushes of dawn as the sand clawed her feet? Had he seen in her the form that wandered that first night in the waves, listening for her father's call?

Deep down.
Surging currents.
Writhing.
Flowing.
Schools of red and orange and yellow.
Deeper still.
Gasping for breath.
Ears bursting.
Pain.
Swallow.
Starbursts of light.
Can't breathe.
Must get up.
Fight to escape.

Clutching arms.
Gasping.
Can't breathe.
Up.
Must get up.
Ears exploding.

Yes, but she was beautiful. They named her after the stones that were washed onto the shore.

Up to the light.
Surface swirls of white and
Foam-flecked waters.
Glint of the sun.

She had eyes of jade, hair like amber.

Salt-water,
Nausea.
Unconsciousness.

Dread throbbed through the veins of the rescuers. Accounts grew wilder in the town. No one paid attention to the sight of Amber waiting beyond the crowd with helpless tears, except for the gulls diving in the evening air. Although he saw her there, Thomas in grief could not bring to himself the courage to walk over to comfort her.

It was a dull airless evening. Eastward was the gray majesty of the sea, hushed in breathless calm; the horizon line invisibly melting into the monotonous misty sky; the idle ships shadowy and still on the idle water. Southward, the high ridge of the sea dike and the grim massive circle of a Martello tower, reared high on its mound of grass, closed the view darkly on all that lay beyond. Westward, a lurid streak

of sunset glowed red in the dreary heaven, blackened the fringing trees on the far border of the great inland marsh, and turned its gleaming water-pools to pools of blood.
Wilkie Collins, *No Name*

The memorial service was held in the Moot Hall, a rectangular upper room reached by an external staircase, with two small windows facing the sea. The dark oak furnishing, two ranks of desks with leather button seats and twisted medieval beams gave it a formal gravitas. On the south wall was a great chimneybreast, at its centre a steel disc, a hideous sea monster, blackened with soot, staring from its dark recess.

Father Godfrey spoke slowly, deliberately, keeping all in his gaze.

'What are we to make of Ralph's death? What are we to make of this waste of the life of one so young?'

And what was in my own heart? It was me who loved her, me who should have died.

After the service, Thomas wandered the length of the beach, but she was nowhere to be seen. He had searched the narrow streets of the town, her footsteps not to be heard. She had slipped away in the night, into the blackness.

VIII – The Water Nymphs

Then hurry home at dawn,
Proud of what you've done,
Smile to think
I slept alone!

Benjamin Britten, *Albert Herring*

SUNSET – NEW YEAR'S EVE, 1980
BOWSCALE FELL, CUMBRIA

Martin and Sally lower their rain hoods to breathe more freely the liberty of the astringent air. Breathless but exhilarated, balanced on a narrow outcrop as they look down over the route of their ascent, they fill their stale lungs with the unpolluted air. They have been walking all morning and the day's early drizzle has just begun to thin to a fine mist, the buffeting wind the only disturbance threatening the hills' deep slumber.

'Look!' she cries, pointing to the slopes steeply dropping away beneath their feet, towards a ribbon of silver that defines the valley floor. 'Now you can really see the waterfall.' The peat and flowerless heather of the higher slopes meet in watery confusion.

Directly below them a plantation of spruce and birch crowds the calmer banks of the beck, sheltering the green pasture around a lonely farm. On the far side, the hills rise in random patchwork to meet the rolling mist. In silence they sit together on an outcrop of rock, absorbing the waves of colour, watching the hill at the far side of the valley. Martin turns to look at the place where the slopes twist into a saddle, half-veiled by the cloud base and sighs.

'Dreaming about another woman?' she asks, only half-joking, breaking the self-indulgence of his thoughts with a well-timed dig in the ribs.

Martin looks at her, smiles grimly, and then looks back at the hills. He'd been with Sally for six months now, his longest ever relationship. After that first night in the hotel room, she had grown on him like a drug. Her body and the freedom of her affection still excited him, but the initial thrill of all that passion had already begun to turn commonplace. It wasn't that he was bored of her, or didn't fancy her anymore, she wasn't clingy or even particularly demanding, and he just missed his own solitude. Commitment was proving to be a trial.

'Come on, Martin, cheer up! You can't go on torturing yourself. Just say what's on your mind. Say something, anything.'

He knew he was behaving badly. He continued the thoughts from an earlier conversation as they had climbed through the open fell. 'I still feel guilty about Jade,' he said.

She takes his rough hand, and places it against her mouth with genuine affection. She looks again into his face, sees the ghost there still, the bitter scars, and waits for a moment for him to say something more, but he does not react.

'You really can't keep on torturing yourself like this. Look, I've been thinking, I've got some vacation owing – I think we should both get away for a while. Will you come away with me?'

'Where to?' he asks.

'I don't know, anywhere, Europe, maybe?'

'I don't know. I've just started this cabinet-making course and I don't want to give up now.'

She sighs, her breath enhancing the creeping mist. It is beginning to rain, so they turn to descend the path. The stones are slippery, but they scramble through the heather at a jog. Halfway down, he falls, and she shouts back to him but her voice is lost in the wind. 'I'll wait for you, Martin,' she says.

They return to the small cottage that belongs to her parents, in the quiet working Cumbrian village where she grew up. It is now quite dark. She goes inside to prepare their food, leaving him to sort out the boots. Their meal will be simple fare – she is not a great cook but she can certainly warm up something her mother has left in the fridge for them. He enters and she glances at him, pacing around the sitting room. He just needs cheering up, she thinks, and opens a bottle of wine and switches on the radio. 'Come on, let's have some music,' she says.

At her request, he builds a fire in the grate and then continues to pace around, picking up this and that, staring at the walls. 'Martin, just sit down and relax, will you.' She points to a copy of Wainwright on the kitchen table. 'Read that and work out where we can go tomorrow.' He takes up the volume from the table and settles down in a comfortable armchair to study the guidebook.

She serves up and calls him back to the table. The rich juices of the stew and freshly baked bread warm them up. They have finished the bottle of wine before they know it.

'There's a ceilidh in the village hall later, do you fancy that? It's always good fun.'

He shrugs. 'Would you trust me at a party in this mood?'

'You're right, maybe not, but I'm sure we can find something to do here then.' She winks.

She pours them both a glass of single malt and then puts another log on the fire. She stokes the grate so it flares and then sits down on the arm of his chair and places her arms affectionately around his shoulders and folds her knees across his legs. 'What am I going to do with you, lover boy?' she says, stroking the back of this head.

This time, he responds in kind, and kisses her warmly as he begins to unbutton her shirt, nestling his head in her arms.

'Hey, what about you?' she says and fumbles with his belt, before pulling him down on top of her onto the floor.

Later, covered only by a blanket they lie together, her head resting on his chest. He feels her weight warm and glowing all over his damaged body. Her hands absently stroke the hairs on the nape of his neck. 'You're tired,' she says. 'Close your eyes.'

His eyes quickly grow heavy and in two or three more moments he is far away, and soon a new dream begins to float across his sleeping horizon.

'Life hurts less when you dream in colour,' she whispers.

A new horizon.
Distant heat-haze.
Purple, snow-capped mountains.
A vast and dusty plain.
Bodies surround him.
Limbs, blood, metal, leather.
A field covered with dead.
Torn and deserted banners.
Shrouds for the fallen, sullied with dust and blood.
Everywhere corpses.
Blackened with smoke.
Piled high, like discarded stone.
Dressed for death.
Dry, desert winds blow.
Blasted, battered faces.
Carrying the stink of decay.
Black clouds of flies, swarm.
Everywhere dust.
'For what are we but dust?'
Thirty or forty prisoners tied by a cord,
marching in sad time.
Naked.
Dragging weary feet.
Downcast eyes.
Horrible wounds.
Another group, two hundred or more, a single guard.

'They grieve the Cross?'
Which cross?

In the distance, rumbling.
Growing in intensity.
Ever louder.
Squeaking wheels.
Heavy machinery.
The air split with shrill whistles.
The impact,
when it comes,
deafening.
And the ground,
to his left,
simultaneously,
explodes,
and implodes,
into the deepest crater.

Summer 1983 – a newly opened section of the M25

The powerful car gathers speed as it progresses up the new highway, heading northeast out of London.

'Impressive, isn't it?' Louise says. Martin has never driven a car like this, pushes again on the throttle and feels the beast respond immediately.

'Well, thank you so much for escorting me – I just hope it wasn't too boring for you,' she says.

'No, it was great, really,' he lies. *The Turn of the Screw* was not exactly his choice for an evening out, but the perks of driving her father's fast car into town and back made up for it.

He pushed the throttle further to the floor. They are cruising at 80 mph now, 85, 90, the speed warning flicking on and off.

'Next turning!'

He applies the brakes and they slow down rather too quickly while he slips the car off the motorway onto a sliproad for the A12. They turn and soon the vehicle is picking up pace again, pulling gs like a jet fighter. Fifteen minutes later they get to her parents' house. His battered old mini stands less proudly in the driveway.

As they pull up, she asks, 'Would you like to come in for a coffee?'

This is the fateful question, capable of both innocence and ambiguity. 'I don't know, I really ought to be getting back – I've got a heap of work to do,' he says half politely, unsure if he is supposed to accept or decline.

'Come on,' she says. 'It's Sunday and Sunday evenings are just so boring. Keep me company, there's no one else at home.'

She opens the front door and they pass through an opulent entrance hall into her own private sitting room at the back of the house. She lights the fire, turns on her hi-fi and pours them both a brandy.

'So, where's Ben?' he asks.

'He's travelling as usual, some corporate deal. That's why I'm staying with my parents – he'll be away now most of the time until Christmas.' She clinks her glass against his and kneels down on the floor by the side of the leather chair he has slumped into.

Martin looks around the sitting room. It certainly reflects her home county tastes – floral curtains, music books everywhere, sports team photos and gymkhana rosettes on the walls. Outside the windows he can see a spot-lit terrace, with statues and Greek urns and a gleaming pool beyond.

'Would you like to swim?' she asks. 'It's still warm outside and we heat the water.' She slides the bolt and opens the french windows, letting the warm breeze fill the room with perfume from the bougainvillea.

'Are you sure there's no one else around?' he asks. She shakes her head.

'OK, why not?'

'Right, well I'll go and get you a towel.'

He strips off quickly before she returns. The water proves not quite so warm as advertised – must be the habit of the estate agent's pitch in her – but he manages a few rapid lengths of backstroke before starting to feel the cold. His shoulders and back muscles are tense but he feels them begin to loosen as he strokes more vigorously up and down the pool. He sees Louise come out of the house, carrying towels and a silver tray with a bottle and two glasses. She is dressed now in a silk kimono, jewellery adorning her fingers, and freshly powdered cheeks offsetting her smartly bobbed hair. Who else would dress up for the swimming pool at night?

She isn't exactly beautiful, her eyes a little too wide and keen and her mouth somewhat boyish, but she is always good fun and impeccably mannered, with long, elegant legs and an athlete's body. He indicates to her that he is ready to get out of the water and she turns her eyes away for a second and holds out a towel for him while he climbs the steps. He accepts the towel and wraps it rapidly around his waist to avoid any misunderstanding.

Soon they sit either end of a garden bench, sipping their wine.

'Ben loves swimming here too,' she tells him. 'He says it's the best thing to cure jet lag.'

'So, would he approve of a naked man swimming at night in your father's pool, then?'

She shrugs. 'Well, neither of them are here to object, are they?' she chuckles, lifting her feet up to rest them in his lap. 'So, what is this secret project then, Martin? It does sound rather exciting,' she continues, rapidly changing the potentially dangerous subject. She sees his face light up. Gone is the brooding melancholy, his voice at once more animated.

'Well, the commissions are really coming in thick and fast now, so I'm planning to set myself up in my own workshop, but I haven't found anywhere suitable yet. I'd like to get out of the city into the countryside – somewhere I can use local materials, be in control of what I do.'

'Art for art's sake?'

'More like money for God's sake!'

She studies his face and snuggles her feet a little more deeply into his lap and then her eyes light up. 'Do you know, I think I might have just the place for you. It's a bit run down and needs quite a lot of work, but the location is fantastic and there's loads of space.'

'Really?' he asks doubtfully.

'Yes, it's not that far from here. Why don't you stay over and I could show it you tomorrow before you go back, if you want? We've got plenty of spare rooms.' She chinks her glass against his and pulls her feet into the folds inside the towel covering his legs, so that he can feel her toes wiggling against his thighs.

'That is if Sally wouldn't mind?' she winks.

'She's not here to object, either,' he smiles.

Something more bitter than death.

There was another time that followed, between Christmas and New Year. They were all four of them in a trendy wine bar, near the Barbican. They'd been to a play together, something angry and Northern. Sally had an early flight the next morning up to Manchester and Ben, now Louise's husband, had offered to drive her back to her flat in Chiswick, leaving Louise and Martin alone in the bar. They had had too much to drink and the flirting and touching started again. Under the table at first, then hands, then lips in the crowded darkness. The re-arousal of their earlier swimming pool encounter was broken only by the unexpected return of their partners, trying to find the car keys.

Her love caught you like a trap.

IX – Moonlight Crossing

'Know ye, that we, the aforesaid Abbot and Convent, with our assent and consent, and with consulted minds, for good and reasonable causes, our minds and conscience especially moving us, of our certain knowledge and mere motion, willingly and freely have given, granted and confirmed, and by these presents do give, grant render, deliver and confirm to our most illustrious and invincible prince and lord, Henry VIII, by the grace of God, King of England and France, Lord of Ireland, and Defender of the Faith, and on earth the supreme head of the English Church, all our lordship, monastery or abbey of Coggeshall, and all the circuit and precinct of the same monastery, also all and every manors, lordships and messuages, gardens, curtilages, tofts, lands and tenements, meadows, feedings, pastures, woods, rents, revenues, services, mills, passages, knights' fees, wards, marriages, reliefs, escheats, bondsmen, villains with their followers, commons, liberties, franchises, jurisdictions, profits of courts, hundreds, view of frankpledge, fairs, markets, parks, warrens, pools, waters, fisheries, ways, waste places, advowsons. And we do, of our certain knowledge, and with free and willing minds, renounce the same by these presents, and grant this renunciation by these writings. And we, the aforesaid Abbot or Commendator and Convent, and our successors, will warrant against all men forever by these presents to

our said lord the King, his heirs and assigns, the aforesaid monastery, and all and every manors, lordships, messuages, gardens, curtilages, tofts, meadows, feedings, pastures, woods, underwoods, lands, tenements, and all and every other premises, with all their members and appurtenances. In witness whereof, we, the aforesaid Abbot of Coggeshall and Convent to this our present deed here jointly put our seals. Given the 5th day of the month of Feb., in the 29th year of the reign of our aforesaid lord the King that now is.'

Bryan Dale, *The Annals of Coggeshall*

Evening Moonlight – May 1990
The River Blackwater, Coggeshall

Martin sits on the wall that separates water from earth, spreading his fingers against the cool stones to ease the cramp in his hands. He is tired, and his palms rough and sore from the constant scraping of metal against skin. Beneath his hunched body, the river floats calmly amongst the reflected ripples of evening, creeping slowly, almost apologetically, slipping between reefs of leaves and debris, its surface lower than usual after a month of drought. The young fish have congregated in the shadow of the bridge. Every so often he hears the splash of water as a river bass surfaces for a mayfly, watches the shadows roll out in circles, dancing their quiet *passacaglia* through the turbid whirlpools, their easy motion mocking the tension in his limbs.

His heavy eyes are closed, fixing for a moment the scene, as if framing the landscape in his mind. He feels the stillness as an illusion, knows that soon the light will finally depart, as on any other night, and take with it the fading colours of day and the blurring clarity of line; knows the river will continue, moving under its moonlit surface through shadows of steady conviction seeking the certainty of its own briny goal.

As night draws in, he shivers in the colder air, and rises to return to the house, to regain its protection. Here for a time he has lived, untroubled. He has achieved certain stability and calm in this house that lies in the cradle of the river, between the willows and the cornfields, fixed within the frame of wood that has become his world and workshop. With industry he is able to protect himself from the ghosts that still bear heavily on his soul.

He crosses the terrace, paved with herringbone brick of uncertain antiquity. He notices how the thick London clay given up by the river flares, red and rich, in the last rays of the sun.

The house is ancient, organic. It has grown and changed; weathered and cracked over two thousand seasons. It has kept its own counsel, guarding the marks and scars of witness. A building that has stood for half a millennium, that has seen the full cycle of human experience, that has earned its own calm. Here too he has found peace for a time, in his own fragile construction.

He recognises as his own footsteps the echoes that reverberate throughout the complex chambers of its shell, that ring in sympathy with the distractions of a mind searching for a journey's longed-for end. These floorboards and beams are shores and shingle and clinker to him now, teasing imagination, and such confusion, like his own. Who shaped it so? What mind could conceive a structure so crooked and haphazard?

The ancient frame, twisted by each transient tenant, stretched to each new generation, broken and branded by the lives of others. He feels the pain of each reflected in his own shadow, in his own sadness.

When he knew for sure that Sally had finally gone, he had lain down in the park, felt the clouds press down upon his chest, his whole body stiff with grief, immobile, unable to breathe; eyelids reddened by the colourless sun.

The dew had moistened his shirt and he had clutched the grass, fearing to fall from its horizontal ledge. He had gripped so tightly that the earth pared his fingernails and tiny rivulets of blood stained the turf. He had stayed there for an hour, two hours, an afternoon, while all around no one noticed, and all the time the sun reddened his eyelids and the fragile skin burned around his nose. Such was the pressure of the clouds that had borne upon him that day.

Why had he been so stupid with Louise?

He enters the house now through the back door, the river door, closing the bolts carefully. There are no intruders here, but old habits are hard to lose. He does not welcome casual visitors, maintains his distance from the traffic of village life. The kitchen holds the chill of the evening air, the glow from the lead-black range too weak to reach beyond the hearth. He opens the heavy iron door and adds a log to the simmering fire. The soot that once found no escape clings still, like a metallic frost, to the uppermost reaches of the chimney.

He strips to the waist to wash his upper body at the stone sink, beginning with his strong shoulders and running the soap over the firm sinews of his forearms. The cold water shocks his body, running off his skin in waves of dust and plaster. Satisfied by its greyness, he soaks his hair and runs a comb through the matted strands, releasing each hardened knot of his inky scalp. He turns the tap to full, bracing against the chill, until the last grains of plaster have disappeared into the drain; closes his eyes and wraps his face in the fuzzy warmth of a towel.

Every day now for six years he has laboured in his workshop by the side of the house, rising early, breaking only for the briefest of meals. Most evenings while others might slumber in front of the television, he has restarted his efforts to work on the house. There was much to do; decades of dereliction and neglect to unravel. With the energy that is left in him he has restored this sick old body. Painstakingly applied splints to its sprained timbers; set and braced its tired joints; anointed bruised walls with the balm of plaster and wash. At some point in the past there had been a fire in the attic that had done much damage, but he had made good the purlins and rafters. His contract will be made good only when this ancient structure has been purged of all the iniquities of neglect.

Did the house choose him, or did he choose the house? He is no longer sure, so entwined have their lives become. In the wilder fancies of his mind, he imagines he may have worked here forever, reaching the point where love and loathing cannot be separated, until true obsession takes over. They now share a mutual sentence.

Louise had taken him to see the place and it had intrigued him, but he was not sure about the distance of almost 50 miles from his London client base. He had put in a cheeky offer, which after a while was accepted, and then there was the interminable work of lawyers. The second time he visited, just before he had to hand over most of his savings, he was again filled with doubt, its lines picked out in the faltering gloom of a wet December night. A brooding sentinel concealed from the road by a short gravel path, so badly rutted it caused the old black station cab to shudder in its shocks. He was so discouraged that he sat stunned in the back seat, listening to the rain on the roof, to the ticking of the clock, unsure whether to ask the driver to turn round and leave.

'This is it, you staying or what?' the cabbie asked impatiently; keen to return to the station for his next fare. He paid, then braced and forced the cab door against the heavy gale.

In the dark and rain it seemed like a completely different place to that which he had viewed with Louise months earlier. The exterior of the house shifted grimly in the damp undergrowth, walls dripping loosely with a confusion of creeping vines and flaking plasterwork. There were shattered panes, gaping holes that held no light, the roof so devastated by neglect that it hung ominously to the west. His feet slipped on the moss-iced doorstep as he inserted the key into the worn aperture of the lock, feeling around until it met resistance and engaged. The door sighed; he hesitated to push too hard. He shone his torch around the hall, up the stairs, over walls and floors scattered with the careless debris of abandoned occupation, ceilings scarred with rot. He had realised at once, of course, that it was perfect, irresistible. He was glad to hand over his savings; it was a new start, now there was nothing left but to make this project work.

Six years later and still each evening he wanders from room to room, inspecting his progress with pride, reminding himself of the extent of his artisan achievement. He has renewed the structure, where necessary. Beams reshaped faithfully from stumps of seasoned oak to replace the ravages of water and beetle. He strokes the limbs of new wood, smoothed by his own certain hands, feels their delicate and uneven contours, veins of sugar and honey traced into the grain. Works of naive art, skills almost forgotten in an age of concrete, strong and still. Native oak of the type that thrives in the deep local clay, left to dry naturally, hardened with age until it had become stronger than steel; left to sag and warp in the frame. He tests the sturdiness of each new joint; he blows gently at the webs that hang from his handiwork, testing his breath against the strength of their threads. The smell of new wood, the structure now complete, and like the web's creator, grown, untwisted, renewed.

After the boatyard closed, he had been eager to learn new skills. Encouraged by Sally, he had used his redundancy to spend a year at Rycotewood College, and then studied alongside master craftsmen in a furniture workshop up a nondescript alley in Spitalfields. He was good; he rapidly gained distinctions for his work, designed commissions, survived the summer riots and saw the beginnings of sustainable income before deciding to strike out in late 1983 with his own workshop, here on the Essex/Suffolk border.

As he became more competent, he had veered away from the commonplace and specialised in beautiful and perfectly made tables and cabinets, retaining his earlier affinity with the material the designs were made from.

English oak, perhaps the hardest and most majestic of the oaks, traditionally quarter sawn; ash, in tightly packed figure-bands; cherry, close grained, silky and warmer in tone; native elm, sycamore and walnut. His designs were organic and unfussy, using solid wood and sensual flowing lines, carving and shaping deep into the wood, either with pairing chisels or cutting with his band saw. The water and nature of his childhood were his inspiration. He was especially skilled at steam-bending oak, which he sourced from local woodland, developing the ancient techniques he had learnt in the boat sheds, used for centuries to make fishing boats, and combining these innovatively with his own functional designs. He created simple flowing pieces; visually light, but strong and ergonomic. Yes, he had transitioned from journeyman to artist himself: a perfectionist, a creator of beauty, fishing for the moon.

And as he worked in parallel on the house itself, he had also developed an admiration for his ancient predecessors and their handiwork. The cutting of the joints the most difficult job – each frame unique in the details of its joinery, attempting to recreate a lost art without a pattern to work from. He has had help, of course, but now that the heavy tasks are over, he prefers to continue alone. This day on the framing, the next on studwork; moving through the house at his own pace, glad of solitude and time. He repaired the fragments of wattle, mixing mortar from horsehair and lime, re-pointed the flaking brickwork. The roof no longer leaks, the rotten casements fixed, the buckled floorboards repaired… yes, the worst is behind him.

And as he works, he lets the stories this house can tell unravel in his skin, like so many letters crammed into a spinster's drawer, unread and forgotten, released by the curiosity of youth. Despite a lifetime of manual labour the intensity of the task has taken its toll on his body. Some nights he is so exhausted that instead of undressing, he simply sits in his chair by the window, watching the river in the moonlight, awaiting the solace of sleep before the sun's rising, before the first pale tints of dawn begin to embrace the casement above the bed. He feels too the tension in the walls, the insistent creaking of the timbers, the silent voices of a score of generations; the scorching of a hundred summers. Sighs carried by the wind over the contorted geometry of its rooftops.

He works alone so that sometimes, he finds it hard to distinguish clearly between the days of the week, so distant seems the crowded rush of the boatyard, or the time pressure of the Spitalfields workshops that once filled his life. His furniture commissions now fetch such prices that he can choose his own work, set his own pace. So the tasks that fill his days are indistinct and carefully chosen.

The passing of time marks the seasons as they march through the valley. He notices subtle changes in the level of the river, a lengthening of the shadows on the moss-laden terrace, the rushes, the sagging willows; small signs. He feels that he should write down these thoughts for posterity but struggles to reconstruct them amidst the night images, already confused and blurred. He will remember again, when the time is right.

Remember to love when you sing in colour.

The Rood House lies by an ancient river crossing mentioned in early Saxon writings. A ford lies parallel to the bridge that spans the river, two constants in this man-made geography. At the end of the cloth trade the town had sunk into a period of atrophy, only recently regaining its former vitality. The river is dark and secret, flowing ever eastwards, disappearing into endless fields towards its seaward grave, the ancient bridge now shrouded in modern concrete supports to hold the traffic. The house too had decayed, alone in its grounds by the river, abandoned and forgotten; condemned to rot, until he had reached out to save it before it was too late.

Once there was a structure to the building, a whole idea. He had had to reassemble the original layout, resolve the puzzle, and discard the later modifications. At the time the house was built, wood was plentiful and used in preference to brick. He has not had this luxury, scavenging lesser timbers and reclaiming beams from salvage yards. The house is an insane jumble of prefabricated frames, joined precariously by wooden dowels. Each timber originally prepared and planed at the carpenter's yard, each joint numbered and disassembled prior to transportation, each frame reconstructed onsite, and lifted from the ground with ropes and pulleys and chains. It was a sixteenth-century flat-pack house, the tie-beams and braces still preventing the frames from collapsing.

In 1699 the widow Common was tried three times for witchcraft, each time by 'swimming' in the river by the ford.

Since he has lived in the village he has also taken the time to learn its history. He is familiar with the tales and village myths of past tragedies, accidental drowning, hangings, earthquakes, ley lines, martyrdom. The Portobello pub down the road is named after Edward Vernon's victory when he raided the Spanish port, with six ships defeating a 300-strong garrison. The full force of English history concentrated in just a few acres. Three years ago, after the great storm, the gentle stream had risen into raging, muddy flood, its banks overrun by water running off the fields, leaving anguished householders to lament in the howling of the east wind. In the last century, many had left the village, to find a shore remote enough that they could build anew, uncluttered by the shallow layer of humanity that strangles the earth; bereft of their wits.

Knocking down one of two windmills as there would not be enough wind for both of them.
Traditional – *Coggeshall 'jobs'*

They suffered the dream of desertion. He too had considered this option during his earlier despair after the boatyard closed – that was until he had met Sally and Louise and started his own stuttering process of renovation and renewal.

Just before dawn is the most difficult time, before sunrise, when the trees still are heavy patches of grey in the sky. He stares from the open window at the frailty of the sky, watching the earthy waters slip sullenly along their artificial channel, past the willows, past the three-arched bridge of hand-fired brick, past the lichen-stained walls built to contain and direct the waters away from their ancient course. Colours still unknown, lines blurred, the sigh of giants confounding remembered eyes.

He holds Sally's head in his eyes as the tears run down his cheeks, her silken hair shining in the moonlight. But just as the darkness seems too great to bear, day arrives, and peace of sorts returns to his soul. The river returns to him serene, his tired eyes contemplating its steady flow. He takes out a history of the village from his bedside door and continues to make notes against the wilder chapters.

'He was a man of polished erudition, as well as of temperance.'
Edward Lewes Cutts, *Ralph of Coggeshall*

Red dawn, shepherd's warning, the house is still again in the morning air. The shipwright, he still thinks of himself so, sleeps restlessly in the uncertain heat. The serenity of the previous day has descended into night-time terror, his sleeping mind crowded with events and shadows of faces that will not let him go. His dreams recur, leaving him to sweat deep in a forgotten world. Dreams of childhood and earlier sorrow thrash together in relentless torment, always starting thus.

Of course there is a beach, the sea lapping at the shore, shingle illuminated by the languid shafts of the moon. There is the vastness of the ocean rolling up the sky in turquoise pleats, washing salt into every wound and sorrow. The evening tide like a dark blue gown cast over a courtesan's bed. The shore is hidden in emerald fog, washed by yellow foam. Two children playing, crouched on pebbles of granite and quartz, clothed in rough cotton. He follows his sister through the margins of their sea-world, searching for shells and amber along the shoreline.

Sometimes in these dreams their mother joins them, kneels, contented, peaceful, bathed in pools of silver light, and behind them always the beating of the sea. He hears the waves on the shingle, the woman singing quietly to her children. It is a hard but peaceful dream world, undisturbed and fragrant in the waiting light. They are waiting for their father who would never return; trying to forget their pain.

And then a night without darkness gives way to the still notes of dawn. A dawn filled with floating pleats of rose-tinted chiffon, phosphor waves radiant with the day's fresh glow; the soft roar of the tide breathing the breathless sighs of the wind. He is no longer alone on the shore; there is a young girl, frozen in impasto oils of brilliant intensity–citron yellow, coral reds, blush pinks, extravagant flashes of silver and gold. She bears bold flux-lines of colour, the graceful movements of a dancer. In his dreams, he rises to put his arms around her shadow, nestling his head in the fold of her neck, kissing the sleep-tangled curls. Together they shatter the crusted shingle, the waves flowing backwards and forwards, forcefully and rhythmically. Together they dance in the shingle. But the joy never lasts; she is an impossible illusion, an illusion that is spoiled once again.

So soon he is alone again and falling, floating freely above the earth, small and distant and detailed, while the wind rushes past in accelerating expediency. There is a brief silence, and then the pull, and the tug. Although he is floating, he is no longer truly free. And in the blue envelope he watches as the stars shrink and counts the gulls in flight, and sees the world as it is: small and distant and detailed. And the sun that has burned his back, and an angel or two that passes overhead, and then the pull again and he is down again in the dunes, feels the clouds pressing down upon his chest. His whole body is stiff with grief – immobile, unable to breathe, eyelids reddened by the colourless sun. Her body floats still in the water before him where the sea kale grows, its frosted flowers turned in away from the sea, a child's plaintiff cry in the distance.

A boy searching for driftwood,
Finds a stone left by the waves,
translucent as dawn.

Often he wakes in tears to the fierce reality of daybreak.

As morning arrives the fresh air that hugs the river blows coolly through the house. Unrefreshed by sleep, he breakfasts in the half-light. His body feels worn out, not from physical exertion but from the sickness in his heart. A strange calm pervades outside, as if to accentuate his weariness, the birds already at full voice in the patient shade of the willows. Another day lived in the tyranny of his past; another day to spend somehow, to consider his own.

In the heavy branches the call of a wood pigeon massages the night's tension from his limbs. He sees nobody, he counts on nobody; he has learned to live apart from the world. He knows he must break the spell, but has no energy left with which to fight. Often he is frozen for hours in this lethargy, watching the dragonflies hovering over the reed beds, his mind drifting with the river away from man towards a forgotten sea.

He realises that he has made two great mistakes; the first when his youthful rejection contributed to Amber's despair; the second his rejection of simple unconditional love from Sally. He has not forgiven himself. He calls to mind days they spent an age ago, when the sun shone on their faces; replays each moment from beginning to end. He remembers their smiles, their smells, their voices; the softness of their bodies. He recalls the powerful interplays of circumstance that stalked and eluded them; the arguments, the sadness, repeated and reflected in this darkness. Truthfully, was there ever a time when he did love? Emotion was beyond him. He remembers the days when even the patterns of mist frowned as they walked the shoreline, the strands of their lives woven thickly.

He knows he is searching for Amber still and the search will destroy him. Sally was to be his salvation, and he has spoiled even that last chance of happiness.

Here are sounds and smells that have been heard for a thousand years. The rustling of heavy cloth, the dull clink of metal, careful pouring of precious liquids, whispered liturgy, the sudden explosion of a match into its sulphurous glow. Words repeated under his breath; rapidly, accurately, rich but worn, the heavy incense of tallow, psalms sung in silence, without audience, without accompaniment. This is a lonely task to bring each night to its end and each day to a new beginning. This is a time for quiet prayer, for selfish devotion.

If you study a picture long enough, close enough, you will eventually see the clouds move. You will see the riches of rich hours waning. Confounded by love, Martin was once full of such impatience and youthful ambition. He had sent the blue sky into brooding dark clouds, called together savage elements, transformed the sunlight into shadows, the trees into dark sentinels, the rooftops into sharp angles of rain. Great expectations descended into rumours of nothing. Through this intense dedication, he had lost his muse, he could not hold to the demands of her commitment. He had traded the promise of utmost fidelity for casual sensation seeking and she had moved on.

X – Sam Crow

I walked around a room,
and saw such fireworks on display,
that the air had burst on fire.
So bright shone the sun that day,
with shades and colours yet unnamed,
that snow melted in the wind.

And if light,
really could be so bright,
can we withstand,
the frailty of such a hand?

And if sea and sky and grass,
are all in all reflections,
that become wheat that flows,
and quilted grass bejewelled,
how patterned is this mind that sows?

For are they lilies now or ice
that float within that crimson lake,
and who defies those poppy clouds,
that rampage the endless skies of summer?

Within these envelopes
of coloured air,
do I dare,
to stare,
at love,
at air on fire?

Sunday Morning – August 1990
Coggeshall

It is Sunday, the one day he takes for rest. At the edge of the allotments he climbs a small stile into a walled garden of overgrown vines and nettles, his footsteps startling a family of rabbits. There has been a vineyard in this place for generations, now sadly left to seed. He clears a path with his stick. Maybe this should be his next project.

The path climbs through the gentle candelabra of horse chestnuts as he passes step by step through the terraces leading to the top of a small ridge. From here he can see the river in its full glory, a shining confusion of ever decreasing coils, winding through the red roofs of the small town, through the dappled mirage of landscape, towards a distant imagined sea.

The cricket willows sway like feathers in the wind. They beat in delicate silver-green against the more demanding colours of the early corn, the smell of chlorophyll overpowering, heaven-blue as night behind the gossiping clouds. The air thrilled with the intensity of light.

He rests for a while on an old oak stump; the late spring heat burning his head. He runs his hands through his hair, feeling the warmth of the sun on his fingertips; closes his eyes against the brightness of the fields, the wood pigeons soothing, cooing in the trees.

Well, are you satisfied? he asks himself, surveying the view with his palm over his brows, as carefully as a landowner might count every field in his manifest. There is a sudden flash of light from the river as the reflection of the sun is caught in its flow. He wipes his brow with a handkerchief before replacing the battered cap that is his trademark companion. His linen flannels give him an air of glory, reflecting the gleaming air like a gladiator, his jacket every so often rippling impulsively as it is caught by the wind from the valley. He is struck by how healthy he feels away from the workshop, the pallid tiredness of winter completely banished from his skin; his arms and legs tanned from frequent excursions.

He walks east along the drover's path, flanked on one side by hawthorn hedges and the other by a wide field of green corn, crosses the main road and then descends the hill by the path that leads down past the asparagus fields towards the Abbey Farm. As he approaches, he can make out drier patches in the grassland that mark the long disappeared walls of Stephen and Matilda's Savigniac abbey; the shape of the one of the cloisters, the cow byre that was once part of the refectory.

> *If thou should never see my face again, pray for my Soul. More things are wrought by prayer than this World dreams of.*
> Lord Alfred Tennyson, *Morte d'Arthur*

Here and there, amongst the walls of the farm lie finely carved fragments of masonry.

> *This wall, rust stained and covered with moss, has seen one kingdom after another, stood in the storm, steep and tall, then tumbled.*
> Anglo-Saxon, *The Ruin*

He crosses the river by the old cart bridge, a morass of mud in winter, but now quite dry after the recent drought, pocked with the hoof marks of cattle and horseshoes. At this point the river has slowed and its surface is covered in a thick skin of bright green algae. The meadow that surrounds it is waist-high in cow parsley and borage. There is a flash of turquoise, a kingfisher; he looks to where the bird has flown. No more than a momentary blaze across his vision. There is a lonely drone of a single-engine light aircraft in the deep blue sky.

It's about time we had some rain, he thinks.

He crosses the bridge and walks over into the field, filled with buttercups and dandelion clocks towards a solitary oak. A few cows give half-hearted inspection before resuming their nonchalant grazing. He sits down under the broad shade of the tree, watching the sun sparkling in the river.

> *What would it be like to swim through a watercolour? To dive into its surface, and feel the blues and yellows soaking through your skin, making ripples as your arms stroke the wash. Or to sing in colour, they say music is chromatic, but actually to sing in colour? Like a girl on the shore lit by a silver moon, but bathed in the coloured light diffracted by the prism of her hair. Once he saw the moon and there was a great silver halo around it and on the beach lay precious jewels of every colour and hue; but for the most precious of all?*

A small white butterfly flutters around his head, settles on his back, opening and closing its wings in the sun. The wind rustles in the upper branches of the trees like a far-off sea. He smiles and wonders why.

Do I regret the discovery of life; a time so short, so bright it has illuminated my being? And if I had to, would I choose the same again, choose between love and the grand achievements of my primitive craftsmanship?

> *150 years earlier a highwayman called Crow and his gang robbed travellers and householders along the road that led*

away south from the village. When they tried to arrest him, the accounts say he escaped, and ran into these fields. He was eventually caught at Tilbury trying to board a steamer and died in ignominy in Chelmsford jail.

Her body was light as air, and I have never wished to hold another.

Often alone, every first light of dawn, I have lamented my sorrows.
Anglo-Saxon, *The Wanderer*

He catches his own smile. It is just a story, of course.

London – 1990

Under the fluid metal of a steel blue sky, the thin body of a young woman strokes silently through the dawn waves. The pool is empty. Fifty or so lengths completed, she climbs the steps, showers off in the cool morning air and heads for the luxuriance of the tepidarium. The air inside is warm and humid, infused with the merest hint of eucalyptus; she relaxes for a while stretched out on the hot tiles, breathing deeply, droplets of water forming timidly on her skin. Ten minutes more then she showers again, before diving back into the cool energy of the outside pool. She lets her dive continue until the rush of water has indulged her senses and then allows herself to float slowly upwards, opening her eyes only as the light on the surface approaches.

A second splash, and ten, fifteen, maybe twenty feet away, under the water she sees the body of another girl twisting in the arcs of the spotlights. Her limbs ripple from the surface reflections, air bubbles teasing the firm muscles and tattoos of her back. Jade blinks and the half fish is already past her; her long flowing hair breaks the surface and she gasps for air.

The siren is transformed back to human form as her old friend Sally swims up alongside her. 'Sally, oh my God!'

After Martin had split with Sally over the incident with Louise, there had been only limited contact between them over the years as their careers and lives developed in different directions. On the back of her photo exhibition, Jade had rapidly been offered other work and had soon forgiven her former flatmates. Their friendship was more important to her than quarrels over a man who had never responded to her in any meaningful way as a woman. In fact not only had she forgotten about Martin, she had also completely abandoned her family history 'project', especially after that frustrating interview with Thomas Ogilvie. She had moved to Brussels, drifted to Paris on fashion shoots, danced and sung in her spare time, worked briefly as a model herself, fallen in love, received more than one marriage proposal, each rejected of course; won a small international photographic competition. But freelance was what she really enjoyed – a few illustrated articles for trade magazines, a glossy interested in taking her work. She was good, really good; all she needed was the right subject and she could weave the photos and a story around them. She had worked her way right up to lead the photographic team.

Meeting Sally again now made her think again about those times a decade ago. She wondered if her phase of growing fondness for Martin had penetrated his cold despair, whether it might have been different. There was never anything physical; he was always careful to keep his distance, even though she would have been happy at the time for something deeper to develop. But nothing happened and in retrospect when Sally hooked up with him, she was fine with that. There was no argument, no ugly scene – the choice had been his. So she had left them to their own journey. They seemed to be getting on fine for a while and it seemed the cloud was beginning to lift from his gloom. But then there was that unfortunate incident with Louise in the Barbican bar, after which he had virtually disappeared from all their lives – in fact apart from sending him Christmas cards, to which he never replied, she had all but forgotten his name until the need arose recently. His workshop would be a great location, a transformational life story for an article in the series she was thinking of pitching.

'I'd like to start with some shots here in London before we move on to your workshop,' Jade tells Martin over the phone. That suits him. It would be good to get away for a day or two; he had some things to get done in London.

'I assume you'll let me keep my clothes on this time?'

He agrees to her request for an article, probably too readily; he justifies this as a return act of friendship. At least working shots will mean he can continue without too much disturbance and it will be good to have some company. He no longer needs the money or exposure – he is way beyond five pounds for a few modelling sessions now – but he owes her for getting him started. A few introductions set him on the right path.

Gino's buzzes to the thick techno beat from the speakers, treasury dealers, Calvin Klein and oysters. Louise has joined them and the three girls are high, even before they burst through the door.

'Heck, you should have seen my boss's face, Jadie!'

'Sal, you've got a nerve!'

As they head for the bar dark-haired Mediterranean-skinned bartenders move with poise, collecting orders, serving food, flirting with the female clients. The owner, silver mane swept into a ponytail, rushes between kitchen and bar.

They pull themselves up onto high barstools, carefully smoothing their designer skirts, adjusting ostentatious seams.

A waiter pushes past them with a full tray of glasses. Sally winks and catches his right buttock with her fingers.

'Sal, he's only a kid,' Louise frowns. The poor boy flees.

'Fair game. Anyway, how is Ben the banker?' Sally counters.

Louise makes a face then glances down at the bump around her midriff. 'Well, he finally came up with the goods.' They shriek with laughter.

Lunch over and with Jade and Sally more than a little tipsy now, they leave Louise to continue her baby shopping and take a cab to the Barbican flat, where Sally is now living. Jade has been scouting locations for the shoot and needs a modernist background for a profile.

'No problem,' said Sally. 'Use my pad.'

Before they enter, Jade looks up from Silk Street to the tower above, its crown jagged as if a giant has broken the top off an even higher tower. They find the lift, ascend to the nineteenth floor and enter a triangular space. Three doors lead off the atrium and Sally puts her key in the lock of one of them. They enter an interior hall opposite a small dining room, with bedrooms off to the right. Beyond the dining room is a larger living area facing northeast at the apex of the tower, opening out onto a narrow balcony. Off to one side there is a tiny galley kitchen, the walls overflowing with a mixture of contemporary artwork. Jade inspects the small space, setting up potential interesting angles in her mind, while Sally coaxes the expensive coffee maker into action. The room will be more difficult to shoot than Jade had expected; a room with so many aspects, so many faces; every wall a twisted plane, every facade a miracle of eroded pigment. She knows the northeast aspect will make the light a problem, the shadows moulding ever-shifting shapes as the sun pivots on its axis around the evening glow, but she is happy enough. She has the story and shots for her article in her mind, the words already beginning to tumble into place, like a jigsaw she has cut and now needs to rearrange into her own coded sequence.

'Sal, it's perfect! I think I'll need it for a couple of evenings next week.'

Martin arrives early at the address she has given him – Cromwell Tower. He knocks on the door and she lets him in, wading through the assembled collection of his most treasured pieces mixed in with all her photographer's paraphernalia. The tangle on the living-room floor causes him to have second thoughts. In his mind the thought of his beautiful furniture appearing incidentally in some bland women's magazine – squeezed in between PMT and this month's diet – is not attractive. Pride of authorship, of course but isn't that the point? she says. Surely there's no such thing as bad publicity? He notices the bedroom doors shut off to the right of the entrance and swatches of material and drawings laid out over the dining-room table.

'Is the flat occupied?' he questions.

'Yes, but they're away. No problem, we won't be disturbed,' she says. He is oblivious to her tiny lie.

As she shoots the pieces they have selected, Martin wanders on to the balcony. The evening sun is setting, the light scorching the last views over Hackney towards the Lea and Stratford. He watches through the open door as she works. She certainly knows what she is doing, he thinks. Petite and lithe like a dancer, she moves quickly and efficiently around the room. She looks little more than a schoolgirl, with her short boyish bob and slightly upturned nose, but he can see the fiery intensity in her focus. Jade catches his stare and emerges to take a few shots of him in profile against the skyline; then inside again with the furniture before indicating she is done.

'Before we go, there is just one other thing. Someone I want you to meet,' she says somewhat apologetically. He looks at her and shrugs.

She walks over to the first bedroom door, stepping over

the lighting boxes and pushes it open, speaking conspiratorially to someone inside. A cat appears from the open bedroom door, quickly followed by the silhouette of a taller woman dressed in a silk kimono-like wrap, blonde as Marilyn, a towel wrapped around her hair.

Martin's face drops in genuine surprise. 'Sally?'

'Come on up, I'll tell your fortune!' She laughs.

Jade coughs. 'Well, I'll see you back here same time tomorrow, Martin,' she says hurriedly and leaves before he can object.

Down in the willow garden
Where me and my love did meet
As we sat a-courtin'
My love fell off to sleep
Traditional, *Down in the Willow Garden*

'What on earth are you doing here?' he asks. By now, the ambient light has fallen to a level where he could not exactly make out the expression on her face. 'Don't tell me this is your flat?'

She beckons for him to sit down on the sofa that runs alongside the eastern window. 'Sorry to surprise you, but it's not as bad as it seems. Jade was looking for a flat to use and this seemed perfect. Do you want a beer or something?'

They sit in half-shadows, their words calm and pregnant – a lightning résumé of work and careers, small talk to avoid the central issue. He summons up the words to express the silence.

'I know I was wrong to run out on you over Louise, you must really hate me.'

She laughs. 'You mean if I hadn't stormed off to Europe and given it a chance? Don't worry, you weren't solely to blame.'

He raises his eyebrows and is silent for a while and then speaks very quietly and very gently.

'You know, you've changed – you're so confident and sophisticated and you look a million dollars in that dress. I just can't get over the transformation. But please tell me that at heart you're still the beautiful Cumbrian lass I fell in love with. I'm an idiot, aren't I?'

She moves closer and holds his hands then lifts her eyes to his. 'Just kiss me, idiot.'

He reaches over to her and gently passes his hand through her hair, brushing her cheek as they kiss.

'Martin, I think I really could love you again, you know,' she sighs.

Jade arrived at the Rood House in a smart chauffeur-driven car the following week. As Martin helped her with her luggage, he realised that she appeared to have packed for a month. The changes she made over the coming days were subtle but meticulously planned. The crockery not in its usual place, the furniture rearranged; his old walking boots scraped clean and stacked away neatly. The first thing Martin had the nerve to challenge was the tiny antique vase with its innocent sprig of field flowers.

'What on earth is this?'

'I found it in one of the junk shops – five pounds, and a bargain.'

She was a law unto herself and it took him a while before he realised she was moving in with him.

Today Jade sits at the kitchen table, astride a stripped-beech stool, leaning on its back. She holds a steaming mug to her lips with both hands; she has been jogging, little droplets of sweat have begun to form at the tips of the fine hairs above her cheeks.

'Jade, where's the frying pan gone?'

She points to a shelf on the wall over the range. Her cheeks flush, her eyes flashing innocence, flattering the powder blue of the jogging suit. Five gleaming copper pans glint pink in the morning haze, replacing his single familiar skillet. She rises to her feet, the chair scraping on the earthenware floor. 'Sorry, got to dash – the main crew will be here at nine.'

What could he say?

'How long will this take then?'

'A few days, maybe a week should do it.'

'Five-to-seven! Hell, I forgot to set the bloody alarm!'

Jade throws her duvet aside, pivots her legs to the floor, and has to sit still for a minute to let her head steady after the sudden rush of blood. No dressing gown. She pulls an Icelandic jumper over her shoulders and staggers towards the door, stumbling on discarded shoes. Her shoulder meets the bathroom door a little harder than she'd intended. It flies open with a bang. There is a splash, and then a shout in the steam.

It is a second before she realises what has happened. 'God, I'm sorry!' She closes the door quickly. Further splashes from within.

'I'm really sorry,' she giggles through the door, 'but I'm running late.' He emerges, still dripping, a towel wrapped around his waist. She notices again the strong musculature of his torso, buff like a film star.

'I didn't mean…'

'I'll dry off in my room.'

She laughs and so does he, for once seeing the funny side.

'I'm really sorry,' Jade says again in the kitchen later. 'It was so stupid of me.' She stands transformed, dressed in one of the suits she has brought with her from her last Paris shoot. One hand holds a piece of toast, the other tea.

'Forget it – I think you've seen it all before!'

She points to her eyes, 'No lenses.' They laugh again. 'I've got to dash – I'll be back this afternoon to set up.'

'Really?' he asks, uninformed of her plan, but in reality he has given up all resistance.

Sunday morning, a week later, and she is woken rudely by the sun's fresh rays puncturing the darkened gloom, a distant hangover agitated by the doves stirring noisily on the pan tiled roof. In the warm cocoon of her bed she stretches playfully, tensing the muscles in her back against the hard mattress. She feels vigour return to the length of her legs. Despite feigning indifference, she secretly savours the expectancy of these colour beginnings: the white hedgerows newly fitted with frosted hawthorn, the cow parsley already flapping high as a man's waist, early blossom covering the paths like confetti forgotten by the sexton's broom.

In the garden below, nettles clamber over the river walls to stroke the placid surface, trapping a litter of reeds and leaves. A proud willow shakes ringlets of jade and emerald in the breeze. She hears the sleepy murmur of wood pigeons. A sapphire-bodied dragonfly, floating on gossamer, ascends gracefully towards the open window. These are days that belong to a different time; it is all freshness after the darkness of an endless city winter. Free of the cynicism of her adoptive world, she is feeling renewed.

She rises and glances at her face in the mirror, a youthful lustre creeping slowly from her eyes. She notices the freshness in her cheeks, the absence of darkness beneath her eyes; is pleased by what she sees. For the last week she has jogged out from the village each morning, venturing further each day. She extends her circuits into the fields and spinneys that shelve gradually away from the river, filling her lungs with the coloured air. She feels her whole body melting into summer, with a rhythm and warmth that teases her womanhood. Spring is nearly over and everywhere the air is on fire. All she needs now is a young gallant to round off her nearly perfect life.

The church bells peal for the early service. She rises quickly, without stopping to eat, and pulls on her trainers and jogging suit. But this time she is not going to church. She runs past the worshippers slipping through the lych-gate, smiling inwardly as she runs into a churchyard full of untended iron-fenced monuments, pyramids and fallen headstones. The doubtful whispers of the horse chestnuts return her greeting. Fitness now is her private religion, fashioned on the run while others quench their thirst in more sedentary pursuits. Outside, the air is still tinged with the sharp scent of night. The path from the churchyard passes through holly and yew bushes through a stile, into a field of grass filled with regiments of dandelion clocks. She stretches against the wooden rails and then leaps the gate; glad to inhale again the intoxicating vapours. Her trainers bounce lightly off the tufted soil. Beyond the cornfield, fields of rapeseed spread before her in a lemon-curd haze, quickly coating her leggings with angel dust as she wades through the tall green stalks. She feels the oxygen coursing through her body, feels powerful and young, her heart lifting its pace to a new tempo.

To the north, the village is bounded by thick coppiced woodland. She enters, keeping up a steady pace through the bracken and tree roots, her eyes adjusting gradually to the shadows of the encroaching canopy, full still of the bright images of the sun shining on the fields. She reaches a point where there is a choice of paths, and chooses the rightmost, jogging carefully along a lane green with new growth, listening to the birdsong as she runs, smelling the fresh incense of late bluebells and lilies as she sings along to her Walkman.

Do you dare,
to stare,
at love.

It seems there is no other sound in the plantation apart from her music and her feet bounding through the leaves, the birdsong hushed by the deepening gloom at its centre. She rests for a while amongst the exposed roots of an ancient beech, switches off her music and takes in the enchanted silence, the moisture forming on her cheeks as the hot blood brushes the air, the ground still thick with dew. She is in a clearing, where a stream has been blocked to form a dark pool. The damp air tinged with the feint resinous smell of sap mixed with wood smoke from the forester's clearance of fallen trees. She stares for fifteen minutes or more, transfixed by the magic carpet stretching for a quarter of an acre or more, drowning the undergrowth of the open glade in a sapphire sea of bluebells and wood anemone surf.

Alone, remote, unhurried, perched on a fallen trunk, floating in leaf-coloured light. She opens her backpack and takes from it an old biscuit tin, which she places carefully on the log. Gingerly she lifts the lid of the tin and takes from it Martin's family scrapbook, which she has 'borrowed', her interest in his past once again reignited by their renewed friendship; turning the pages slowly, looking at the pictures carefully. She has been through this all before, but now she is searching for more clues, anything that could help her. She remembers that last interview with Ogilvie, how he had seemed so defensive about Amber. After deciding there is nothing more to learn from the photographs, she reads the scraps of letters again, taking each one in turn from their stained envelopes. There is not much here either: short letters and postcards written by Amber to her mother, a few place names. She re-reads the letter that mentions a man called Crow and the woman Sarah with whom Amber was apparently travelling for a while. Nothing more in that, either. Sighing, she refolds the letter and tucks it back into the plain brown wrapper. She looks at the dull lilac stamp on the front. It is a picture of the Queen and a Welsh dragon – 'British Empire and Commonwealth Games,' she reads. And then suddenly she notices the postmark: Coggeshall, Essex. She frowns as she processes this new information.

By the time she reaches the house, Martin is already up and about. She takes the scrapbook from the backpack again and points out the postmark. 'Look at this!' she says breathlessly.

'For heaven's sake, Jade, where on earth did you get that tin?'

'Never mind, Mr Angry, just look at the postmark more closely.'

He reads the words.

'Coggeshall, wow! Now that's a strange coincidence...'

Braintree for the pure,
Bocking for the poor;
Coggeshall for the jeering town,
And Kelvedon for the whore.

'Martin, this Crow character and Sarah, are you sure you can't remember anything about them, anything at all?'

He shakes his head. 'I don't know. I don't think I ever heard my mother use those names – there's nothing apart from this letter in the scrapbook?'

She pauses for a second. 'It's too weird though isn't it, now that you live in Coggeshall?'

There is a moment of silence during which she thinks she sees him wince as if in pain. She looks into his eyes; they seem more tired than normal, lacking all brightness, as if he has reached a point of defeat.

'Jade, I know you're trying to help, but even if this Crow

guy or Sarah does still exist and even if they knew Amber, I'm not sure I really want to find her anymore. I'm settled now, doing OK. If you don't mind, I want to give it another go with Sally.'

She has no answer prepared for this.

'Of course,' she says, 'nothing would make me happier – you're made for each other.'

So her plan had worked at least in that way. But all the time she is also searching for a clue in his voice or expression, but there is nothing, no hint of recognition. She realises that her questions about Crow and Amber have upset him; maybe she has made a mistake bringing the subject up. There is no sound now in the room apart from the steady beating of a clock on the sideboard.

Suddenly he rises awkwardly and walks to the bookcase, taking a slim volume from the uppermost shelf, very deliberately turning the dog-eared pages.

She sits in anticipation, the rhythmic pulsing of the long-case clock and Martin's breathing the only sounds. He breaks the silence.

'It's strange, you know, but I did come across somebody with that name when I was doing some research on the house. Hold on… if I can just find it…' He begins to read from the book:

> *'Concerning the image of the Crucifix in the highway by Coggeshall, I will, on the suggestion of B record the following facts.'*

He stops reading and pauses to look at her before restarting,

> *'The house at the corner of the bridge on the left which stands a little back from the road is called the Rood House in the title deeds; very likely it took its name from the erection in the small space before it of a Rood to mark the entrance to*

the Abbey demesnes, cast down and removed shortly after the Abbey's dissolution.'

He pauses to recover his breath, gently turning the thinned paper with the tips of his fingers.

'In the year of our Lord 1537 the idol named the Roode of Coggeshall, whereunto was much and great resort of people; for at that time there was a great rumour blown abroad amongst the ignorant sort, that the power of the idol was so great that no man had power to shut the church door where he stood, and therefore they let the church door, both night and day, continually stand open. Wherefore these men (whose conscience were sore blasphemed to see the honour and power of the almighty living God so to be blasphemed by such an idol) were moved by the Spirit of God to travel out in a wondrous goodly night, both hard frost and fair moonlight. They forced the church door open, and took the idol from his shrine, and carried him a quarter of a mile from the place where he stood, without any resistance of the same idol. Whereupon they struck fire with a flint stone and set him on fire, who burned so brim that he lighted them homeward one good mile of ten.'

'OK...' she begins in confusion. 'But I didn't ask for a history lesson. What's this got to do with Crow?'

'Wait a second, if you really want to find the truth,' he adds, looking at her sharply and begins to read again.

'There were three of them hung in chains, all but the ringleader escaped.' He pauses and adds, 'One Samuel Crowe, disappeared into oblivion – probably sent off to the colonies. Even stranger coincidence, don't you think? It says there's a fuller transcript in the County Museum.'

'This is weirder and weirder.' She closes her eyes, understanding that he is indeed teasing her somehow.

Whether out of cruelty or affection, the effect is the same: she is still at a dead end.

'Come on, let's get out of here, and let me show you what I'm going to do with the vineyard,' he says, more positively than she has heard him speak all week.

They walk without conversation, passing through a wooden gate onto the path that runs along the river to the West, all manner of questions forming in her mind. The sunlight plays tricks with her eyes in a little shadow theatre on the ground. She determines that she will keep her patience, try again and try and catch him off-guard. Perhaps she should not have warned him, allowed him to prepare. Out in the fields a lonely skylark sings its intricate psalm. Martin stops and signals that they should pause. They sit and silence rushes in. Jade rips petals from a flower head in petulant frustration, while Martin closes his eyes in guarded sleep. Nothing stirs amongst the willows apart from the engaging call of a cuckoo.

The trees are moved breathlessly by the wind. He opens his eyes again; he is obviously still upset by their earlier discussion. She opens her satchel and takes out a drawing block.

'Do you mind?'

How to begin? This was always the problem, when faced with that accusing block of white emptiness. The gift of composition, what should she leave in, and what to leave out? She knows the golden rules – thirds, tones, perspective. She knows to start with the lighter colours. 'Paint what you see, paint what you feel,' but there is no agony like that which governs the first stroke, and no ecstasy like the completion.

I'm a poet. I like telling stories and jokes between poems.
Luke Wright, Coggeshall poet

She feels this is a test. A test of her ability to capture something in his face that she will afterwards be able to interpret, that will take her further, although presently she has no idea what to expect. Swiftly, she moistens the paper, taping it to a board, applying a light wash to postpone the moment of decision. Her hands rise to form a square between thumbs and forefingers until she finds the view. She starts to mix scrapings of pigment. Soon the rhythm is in her fingers, and the washes flow like hazel tears.

As she begins to sketch, massive perpendiculars fill the white space, linearity stencilled confidently against a hazy blue sky, framed by ancient shadows, frothing red campion that floats amongst the thistles. The figures dance while each wash dries. Time is measured only by the changes in tone and the conduct of the weather. When she is finished, she rises, looks out across to the field of blowing wheat, the dark copse of oaks beyond. She is pleased with her little sketch and shows him. He nods his approval and the spell is broken.

'Look, Martin, I'm not trying to dig up painful memories. I just thought I might help, that's all.'

He breathes in, his eyes still closed, the old cap casting a dark shadow over his brow. 'Please trust me. I just don't know. Maybe she is still out there somewhere, but I just don't know and unless you have a magic wand, there's no way to find her, is there?'

'You know I think there might be a way.' She speaks carefully, conscious of his mood. 'But I need more than a few postcards.'

She points to a small stone monument to a drowned child set down by the river. 'It's important to believe passionately in something; something will not rest in me until I help you find your whole story.'

Amber was so much like you, he thinks, though you could never know all the secrets of her life. He looks into her eyes and sees the pleading there.

'OK, OK. I'm happy for you to carry on, just don't bug me about it!'

The words fall like rain on the dusty silence. She searches the cipher of his face, but can see no clue. There is no more she can say today. He glances at his watch.

'Look, we really must get back. Perhaps you could try the County Library or something? Maybe they will have something on this Crow. Do you want me to take you over there tomorrow?'

'No need, but it would be fantastic if you could lend me your bike.'

He couldn't help but smile at her determination.

Next morning Jade is up again early and running into the woods. In her new favourite place in the world, she strips down to her costume and wades into the water. Two or three strokes of crawl, and she reaches the far end of the dark shadowed woodland pool. Her limbs tingle from the icy water. She takes another dive; a plunge back under the surface and reaches the far end in five or six further strokes. She repeats this for another twenty or so lengths of the short space. The air is heavy – difficult to breathe, a thunderstorm threatening. She dives back into the water. *Who needs a gym when you've got your own natural swimming pool?* She lets her dive continue until the rush of water cools her and she begins to float back towards the surface.

Rising from the water, she dries herself quickly under the dappled shade of a willow. It is only 8am but already the day has begun to heat up. In the distance she hears the promise of skylarks, the gentle blueness of morning surrounding her like a veil. She begins to retrace her path, but halts at the stile to look over the churchyard. Amongst the manicured masonry she notices the white face of a marble angel figured in stone and imagines its frozen face smiles at her. She sits, breathes deeply, watches the swallows turn and tilt; can imagine no existence so peaceful, so free of responsibility and demands.

The Norton roars as she speeds through deserted lanes, hedgerows rushing by. The wind tugs at her neck as she accelerates into the bends, the brightness of the sun repeated in the alien chrome. She is dressed in dark leather, riding at hellcat velocity, crashing through the pretty silence. She feels the thrill of speed in her blood, the adrenaline in her veins, her arms shaking with the vibration of the machine. It is hard for her to avoid smiling, a laugh broadening under her helmet at the freedom of the moment. She pushes the bike further, her body electric tense on the frame, finds a straight where she can push the little red needle closer to eternity, the exhilaration making her head light.

When she enters the County Library building, her body is still buzzing, heavy boots sending earthquakes through the sound-sucked corridor. Inside, the red carpeting is worn and stained like an old-fashioned club. There is a quaint disorder: books stacked too carelessly for research, shelves stuffed with paperbacks and discarded textbooks crammed under the high roof of the former gymnasium. Over-zealous white paint yellows on the radiators complementing the legacy of floor wax and sweaty shoes.

In the centre of the room, an old man turns the pages of a newspaper, studying the classifieds with a magnifying glass as if reading clues to some ancient text. Two ageless women chatter by the romance section, their hair and figures ravaged by motherhood, their squabbling two-year-olds pulling each other's hair. One child looks at her and pulls a face. Jade pulls one back, while his mother is not looking, and the child bursts into tears, hiding under his mother's skirts.

She approaches a man her own age standing behind the desk. He looks up at her and smiles, eyes wide and eager, ridiculous girl's eyelashes and unkempt curly locks that could do with a trim. 'How can I help?'

'Where would I find local history for Coggeshall, please?' she asks.

He points towards a bookcase under the window, squeezed between the rungs of old climbing bars. He rises and walks over with her, her heavy boots squeaking on the floor. The section on the village is small. She quickly scans the titles, rejecting most, settling only for a couple of histories and some box files of cuttings.

'Unfortunately, most of the good stuff is in the Public Records Office,' the young man explains. He helps her carry the box files to a table and smiles again. 'I'll leave you to it, but please ask if you need any help.' She notices a sweet sign of eagerness in his voice.

After fifteen minutes, he is beside her again, offering help she feels she really does not need. His presence irritates her a little – she wants to crawl in under the shelves, make herself a hole beneath the books in which to read in warmth and privacy. She can feel his clumsy eyes, taunts him a little with a careful twist of her fingers through her hair, knowing exactly how this reveals the delicate flesh around her neck. The confines of the space are such that an easy conversation could be arranged if not for the enforced silence and feigned lack of interest. She watches him as he watches her, allows herself to be a little flattered by his blatant interest – maybe he is not that bad-looking after all, she thinks.

'Find anything?' She wonders whether to tease him further, indicates wordlessly the need for a box on the upper shelf. He climbs the steps and she touches him with the slightest unnecessary physical contact as he descends, watches the skin around his neck redden. She smiles inwardly at her own ability to create such reactions in men.

'Thank you, you're really too kind.'

'It's a pleasure.'

She turns to him, and then stares for a second in disbelief at his librarian's name badge.

'I'm sorry, but your name's Sam Crow?'

He nods and she lets out a nervous laugh, but he has not finished, 'Yes, me and my father and his father before me!' He pauses doubtfully, spotting the surprise in her expression. 'Well, it's not that funny a name is it?'

'No… No,' she shakes her head a little as if to clear it. 'It's just a… a coincidence, that's all.' He does not understand her comment and is in any case intent on securing another liaison.

'Look, I wasn't going to ask before, but didn't I see you painting in Coggeshall yesterday?'

She is left reeling a little by these twin revelations. His taut frame is picked out against the shadows as he waits for her reply. She notices the narrowness of his hips under the tightly buckled denims, more like a boy than a man. She is unsure whether she likes or loathes this young brave.

'Were you spying on me?' she asks boldly. He blushes.

'Of course not, I assumed that was your boyfriend with you?'

She feels wrong-footed by this young man, unsure of where the conversation will take them. An unexpected thought crosses her mind.

'Not exactly, just a friend, but anyway what were you doing hiding by the riverbank on a Sunday afternoon, if I might ask?'

He blushes again, cheeks burning like the redness of the sun at dawn. She notices the rather too red layer around his mouth, the darkness about his eyes. She can tell there is something more he wants to say. He is handsome enough, she decides – brawny, no doubt with a string of admirers of his own. She wonders which girl he had met by the river in this Sunday afternoon liaison; if they had continued their own commerce in the bushes at the same time as spying on her.

'Seeing as you like my name, can I buy you a drink later?' he chances, cheekily.

Later becomes silver and darkness creeps into the night. Jade and Sam have been walking along the river path and she has brought him to the old barn with the blue diesel pump in the fields beyond the river. She hitches her skirt up around her knees as she climbs the wooden ladder into the loft, shakes out her hair and Sam follows her lead, sinking gratefully onto the blanket she has laid across the hay. He has brought cheap wine. With the minimum of fuss she proceeds with her plan. The crickets rasp in the background, while quietly and efficiently she extracts the arousal she needs from him. She leaves him exhausted within the blanket, his body tingling with her warmth. He is now a figure shrugged and thoughtful, maybe a little older, as if in a dream.

'Mr Crow,' she whispers, in triumph. 'Now maybe we're on to something.'

'What moves you that you should leave your child unchristened so long?'
'We be bound to do nothing contrary to the word of God.'
'Why: Baptism is commanded by the word of God.'
'His institution therein I do not deny.'
'What do you then deny?'
'I deny all things invented by man.'
'What things are there, that are devised by man, with which you are so offended?'
'Your oil, cream, salt, spittle, candle and conjuring of water.'
'Will you deny that with which all the whole world and your father were contented?'
'What my father and the whole world hath done, I have found nothing to do with, but what God has commanded me to do, to that I stand.'

'A faggot will make you do it.'
'No, no, a fig for your faggot. What God thinks should be done, more will I not do.'
'What can be a better reminder, when you are out riding, than to see the Cross?'
'If the Cross were such a profit to us, why didn't Christ's disciples take it up and set it on a pole, and carry it in procession with Salve festa dies?'
'It was taken up.'
'I know it to be true, and do not believe the contrary.'
'Are you the same man as before?'
'I am no changeling.'

Interrogation of Thomas Hawkes, gentleman of Coggeshall by Bishop Bonner from Foxe's *Book of Martyrs* (abridged).

XI – Calypso's Return

Splendid in my rage, I go,
shaking out my burning hair,
spreading terror to and fro,
searching, searching, everywhere.

A. D. Hope, *A Reply to Blake*

Morning – September 1990
The Rood House, Coggeshall

There are mornings like these when her mind will not allow her the respite of sleep. She is tingling still from her evening exertions. Rising quietly from the mid-summer heat, she pulls on her joggers. Outside there is only the half dawn of grey mist, drifting like phantom messages over the reed-encrusted solidity of the river. She leaves the house and passes quickly through the green clouds of nettles and comfrey into the marshy area beneath the willows. The trees stand in perfect alignment, their rich silver foliage swaying royally in the gentle breeze. Soon her clothes are covered in dew from the undergrowth and she feels sweat rise to her brow with the determination of her strides.

She is beyond the village grounds into deeper countryside, only the fizzing of the river disturbing her thoughts. She sees a water vole slip from its riverbank home into the water, creating long V-shaped furrows in its wake. The gentle clatter of the pumps from below the sluice shakes the ground beneath her feet. She comes to an old iron bridge, feels her way carefully across, recalls the framed yellowing photograph in the window of one of the village shops: Sam Nunn, the blacksmith's bridge, forged in some distant time, once famous now forgotten.

As she moves through the air she feels its coldness around her neck, freezing the nightmare images from her mind. Such darkness cannot survive the truth of morning light. She remembers an illustration in a book – an American pioneer, spearing fish from a canoe, distinct and primitive, unspoilt by the academic artistry of later schools. She feels connected to such simple images, like her own handiwork, devoid of pretension, honest but profound. Above the sluice she returns to the deep pool, now her own secret place where she can be quiet and think alone in the privacy of nature.

She is aware that there is another reason for her coming here this day. The pursuit of solitude requires more than privacy, it requires also a cleansing of her spirit. She feels a compulsion to immerse himself in the luxuriance of its dark waters – cover her head until the blackness tugs at her lungs and she is forced to break the surface once again to renew her life. She is a good swimmer. Remembering her strong body gleaming in its candid reflection, cutting through the water like a sturdy knife. Too quick and lithe, her strokes animalistic, like an injured seal. She seeks immersion in these quieter dark waters, a private cleansing, and a second baptism.

It feels to her as if Martin's life is still trapped in the confusion of childhood. His body is strong and mature, but his mind still as fragile as an adolescent. He does not allow himself to acknowledge doubt openly but the doubts that betray his eyes never leave him. With this new revelation about the Crow family, she is determined now to continue with the search. Partly because he is the only one left, and she is the only one left to search, but even if ultimately there is nothing to be found, she is hooked on the mission. And she must at least keep her mind honed for the possibility of achieving some sort of redemption for him. And of course now with Mr Crow there is a new complication, a sweet reason for pursuing the story to its next phase. He had made her feel good about herself with a passion she had not felt in a very long time.

When she was growing up, others had blamed her teenage introspection on the absence of her parents, but they were wrong: the tragedy of loss, of not knowing, only enhanced their heroism in her eyes. She would have continued to grow in good humour and in the free exploration of any teenage girl. The darkness came of the gradual loss of faith, a source of light that had slowly slipped away beyond her grasp. They had not explained this to her, of course but she knew enough from idle gossip and her own discoveries to piece together her version of the story. And without any counter she had no reason to doubt her own version of her mother's memory. And then those that she could never forgive, who she believed were hiding the truth from her, were no more.

Sometimes she wonders what her life story is all about. What the confusion between characters really achieves. She knows there is meaning somewhere, something quiet and fine, like the extension of a note beyond its natural resolution. There are people she knows, she has met, who have no difficulty with such uncertainty. Not the distraction of unknowing, eating like a canker at the mind's edge, ever present and corrosive. She can play the scenes of delicious childhood over and over in her mind, but of course the endings never change. Always the jewel-like quality of memory is tarnished by cruel separation.

Now if she builds she also destroys, nothing carved so perfectly that it cannot also be broken by her terrible hands. The figure of her mother standing beside her in her dreams is cold and lifeless from the burning of her blistered hand across its surface. She cannot stand to let beauty or poetry sit undisturbed in her mind, always it must be dragged off from its golden temple into the troughs of stubborn jealousy. There is nothing left of glory, nothing of joy, as if its very presence hurts her, piercing in its ordinariness. It is an irony that love corrupts so.

True, there are sounds that generate this helplessness; that can arrest her lungs, cause her to breathe shortly. The gulls are one, the sea another. These will stop all other sounds to demand her attention – until she finds some evidence of her mother there.

Returning to her room to shower and change, Jade is excited and impatient. Later she will walk with her newfound lover, leave the village along the path that leads out from the corner of the churchyard. Together they will walk across an area of tidy allotments, crowded with flowers and vegetables. She has many more questions to ask him.

'There should be a good crop,' he will say, tapping a marrow with his stick. 'Let's see how much of this we see for Harvest Festival.' She knows they will dance around the truth, but she has a plan and unlike him, she will have more than one thing on her mind.

The link to Crow she had found while looking at Martin's documents now opened up by the chance meeting in the library had reawakened in her some reflection about her own family. To have not known your mother seems to her a fate, against all the basic justice of the world. She had never suffered for her orphan status, her adoptive parents had made that easy for her, and people were generally kind or disinterested, but this lack of knowing was for her an incompleteness that grew and grew as she became more aware of her own loss. She always knew she was searching, too; she held a hope in her breast that there was some terrible mistake and the finality of her mother's absence would someday be broken, like a dream that if you slept long enough would be overcome.

Her search for Martin's sister therefore was not a thing done out of pity, more a substitute – the need to find for herself the answer to a question that still lay hidden, that could be uncovered if she was dedicated to the cause. It was like a challenge or a quest, with vicarious history the objective.

There was of course the chance that what she would never find was what she was really looking for or even that she would, and would not like what she would eventually find. That was always the danger, that some discovered fact would break the cherished mystery of her mother's goodness. But she doubted it: she knew both too much and too little for that. You do not need to know how to believe, but at the same time she could not leave the truth unsought.

In this space unique,
these lines assume their form,
performed and played
to walls of aging brick.
birds circle, carp wheel,
and on their hidden trapeze,
glide down to a watery stage.

For this is my song, Calypso caprice,
composed and performed now,
for the loving of you.

Above this blue-brushed scene,
the clouds float and wisp,
dragged by linen-rags,
across the wide, cornflower sky.
Green lily-pads, rushes of gold,
swimming in silence,
hushed in their shadowy stalls.
Silver plane, cheeks flushed with rouge,
drawn by silken chords, to western shores.
And the willows become swaying palms,
sheltered islands in the warm, tropical breeze.

And in the fading light,
I remember perfume,
orange and oleander,
and scented night.

Did you want to seduce me?
What are you scared of, what are you running away from?

Jade and Sam walk to the top of the hill with their picnic basket. The elevation of the path along the droving road that crests the ridge is sufficient to afford a view across the golden cornfields framing the river. They descend back down towards the river itself. It is late August and as hot as any day of summer, the larks breezing in the cloudless sky, flies swarming the hedgerows. The earth is cracked and dusty under their feet. He throws his rucksack to the ground and lies in the long grass, mopping his brow, watching the sun play on the fishponds by the river.

Her glare, his smiles, he can guess what her next words will be. 'Your shirt,' she requests confidently. He does as he is told and raises his arms. She pulls it over his head and notices the way his muscles dance on his bare back. 'OK, now your shorts.'

'OK, so now you've got me naked, what next?'

'Well, are you going to swim?'

'After you!'

'Well, turn round then.'

He turns round as she has requested. She kneels and pulls the dress over her shoulders; already the sun is warm on her skin.

He sits on the bank soaking up the warmth, watching her while she walks towards the cool shadows of the river. In a dream he hears her shout, and then there is a splash and the sound of laughter. After a minute he jumps in beside her and they slide and squirm through the dark waters, shrieking and giggling. When they emerge, they remain unclothed, drying in the sun by the riverbank. She runs her hands over the muscles of his chest.

'Draw me,' he says.

'What?'

'You know pencil and pen. Draw!' He pushes the instruments from her bag towards her.

She looks at him, his face motionless, frowning and waiting irritably for an answer. She takes up the pen, lays the pad on her knees. His body is abrupt and poised, waiting for her to begin.

When she has finished, she calls him and it is as if he is dragged back from a dream.

'Not bad, you'll make an artist yet!'

They are nearly dry already in the warm sun and the breeze.

It is still dry, although ominous dark clouds gather in the sky. They watch a car in the distance. It is Martin; he has the hood of the old Herald down, leaning his arm over the door belt, feeling the cold air trickling through his hands, like water slipping through the fingers of a boy. He drives slowly through the narrow lanes, crawling through newly-harvested cornfields, winding past low hedges entwined with ripening blackberries and the tufted remains of wild clematis, past colour-washed farmhouses with their dark-tarred barns, and little bridges of hand-fired red brick. The dark greens and olives of the oaks in the higher fields remind him of islands stranded in a bleached-golden sea, and in the lower fields, lines of silver-grey mark the river's course.

'It's getting late, I think we'd better get back,' says Jade, and she takes Sam by the hand and helps him to his feet.

'They say if you close your eyes, you can mistake the wind in the corn for the roar of the sea,' he says.

As Thomas removes his jacket to lie on the beach below the lookout tower at Bly House, his mind goes back over thirty years. In his daydream Amber laughs, her eyebrows flying again in the way that he loved. 'What now?' he asks.

'You remind me of that story – you know the wind and the sun.'

She was right: after the entire struggle, he could still be at home with her on this balmy shore.

He was certain that he had seen her once as she wandered, defiant, rampaging the blue-grey storm that blew at her skirts. She was walking along the shoreline, separating a man from his love, a child from her dream. All the achievements of the world, judged by men, perhaps never understood, except that sometimes you must love, once at least, bring newness to life, and then…

All she has left of her mother are her eyes.

That same evening, Jade and Sam take an evening boat ride in a skiff along the river. A lone candle floats in a glass dish on the centreboard, the thick night air cut only by the rasping of crickets. He drops the oars into the gloom that supports the river's dream-like surface, hardly able to make out the contours of her face.

'Well?'

'It's a story about love, really.'

They drift on, she moves in the boat and it rocks dangerously. Silence while the moon threatens to emerge from its cloudy obscurity; for a moment he thinks he can see her laugh.

'Sam, do you know much about your dad?'

'Not really – I'm named after him but he was a bad 'un. He left us to fend for ourselves, that's about all.'

'And what about your mother?'

'Her name was Sarah; she died about ten years ago. She was a kind woman, but after he deserted her she had a heavy heart and our life was hard. I was an only child.'

Sam Crow and Sarah, that's too much, she thinks. She can hardly speak now from excitement.

'Look, I have a photo I'd like to show you.'

She pulls the photo out of her locket and passes it to

him. He gazes in shock at the photo, in recognition of the shadow and takes another sip of wine to warm his stomach.

'Sam, say something. Sam?'

'It's my mother and father and that child is me. I used to have a very similar photo. Where on earth did you get this from and who is that other woman?'

'Sam, it's my mother.' Tears flood her cheeks. 'Please tell me you've still got that other photograph,' she says, weeping

Once too Sam had jumped, floated free above the earth, small and distant and detailed, while the wind rushed past in accelerating expediency. It had been brief, and then the pull, and the tug, and he was floating, but no longer truly free. And in the blue envelope, he had floated and watched the stars shrink, and counted the birds in flight, and saw the world as it is: small and distant and detailed. And the sun had burned his back, and an angel or two had come to pass the day and then there was the pull and he was floating.

There is a small space between the sky and the earth where a man can fall without tempting harm, and in that space before the grip of gravity asserts, before the flimsy canopy opens to its puppet strings, you may find a peace. In that space you are free to fall, through nothing, unharmed, burnt only by the sun; and the earth below is small, distant, detailed. And surely there is a way to find that space, and to fall for a time unleashed from the cares of the world, listening to the angel's idle chatter, gliding with the birds, carefree before the pull, and the tug and the flimsy canopy asserts. During that time, that brief space, the earth is small and distant and detailed. But it never lasts.

'Did you know you were seducing me?'

Back in the Rood House, she can hear the chapel bell over the fields, far off on the other side of the river. Three o'clock in the morning. She reads for a while, contracts the hours remaining until the first rays of dawn. The wind batters the panes of the window. Can she hear voices outside on the terrace? Her ears strain to discern the sounds fighting with the window, maybe just an owl shrieking. The voices float now around the timbers of the room. She hears a creak, then a noise on the stairs. Are those footsteps outside her door? Is this now a ghost story?

The next morning, Martin is at her bedside with a cup of tea as she wakes. Immediately she blurts out what she has discovered. Martin shakes his head.

'Well, I found something yesterday while you were out with lover-boy as well.' He shows her a small cloth bundle. 'I was replacing the creaking floorboards in your room, this was wedged between two of the struts.'

She looks at his face for a clue and seeing nothing, turns back to unwrap the little bundle. Within it she finds a small brown envelope containing a collection of newspaper clippings: 'Dockers on Strike', 'Armed Police Board Trawler in Aldeburgh Sea Drama', 'Tragic Death in Fall from Martello Tower'. Wrapped with them is a colour printed engraving torn from a book. She recognises the image. 'The depths of the sea,' she reads and turns it over. On the reverse, written in heavy blank ink is a poem with a simple dedication: 'For Amber'.

'My God, Martin, I know that handwriting.'

XII – Storm

The Crown Court, March 1849

It having been arranged that the trial of the various members of this desperate gang should commence this morning, an intense interest was excited in the neighbourhood of the Court, where hundreds crowded, anxious to hear the details of the cases. As soon as the doors of the Court were thrown open the galleries were filled almost to suffocation by respectably dressed females. The Grand Jury returned 18 true bills against the parties, and the first case was; The Burglary at Mr Ham's.

The indictment charged Samuel Crow, William Ellis, and William Tansley with a burglary, attended with great violence, in the house of Martin Finch, at Bradleigh, near Coggeshall; and Wm. French and John Crow as accessories. Mr. RYLAND opened the case at great length.

Highway Robbery with Violence

Samuel Crow was charged with robbing Mr D and Martin Filer with receiving part of the stolen property. Mr RYLAND for the prosecution, Mr T. CHAMBERS for the prisoners.

William Wade proved that in October 1847, he went with Crow and Tansley into the Bramchurch road, and after waiting for some time Mr D. and his daughters came up on horseback; Wade first took hold of the horses, and Crow took them from the horses, and after laying them upon the ground he searched D's pocket and took the contents of his purse.

The prosecutor, a member of the Society of Friends, gave corroborative

evidence, speaking
positively to the
identity of the
prisoner Crow, and
said that Crow
stopped his breath
while he was upon
the ground. The
blood flowed from
his nose and mouth,
and after taking his
fingers from his face
he stroked it down
the cheek of Crow.
As for his youngest
daughter, she would
never be the same
girl again.

On the way Crow
put a shirt over his
clothes and a white
cap over his face,
with holes in it for
his eyes and mouth.
Tansley, Ellis and
myself blackened
our faces with some
stuff Crow had
with him. Crow
began to unfasten
the door with a
plough coulter, and
Crow said, 'We
want money!' Finch
said, 'I have not got
any' and the
housekeeper went
into her sleeping-
room, followed by
Crow, who had a
pistol in his hand.

I told them not to
hurt the old man,
and after hanging
him over the heart
for a short while,
they let him down.
Crow said he
would put her on
the fire, her gown
caught fire and I put
out the blaze when
Crow said, 'Don't
do that, you fool,'
and he and Ellis left
the house with a
load of ham and
port, and then I left
with a load.

Evening Rush Hour – September 1990
Liverpool Street Station

It was lightning that cracked the tree.

Sally heard the whistle go just as she passed the ticket barrier. Damn, she was just too late onto the platform to catch the express to Colchester! It had been pouring with rain and she was already soaked. She had been drinking vodka and lime in the station bar when too late she noticed the time. As she ran, she remembered with guilt all those Sunday night sprints along empty platforms, echoing wooden bridges, bags heavy with food and laundry, late, as always, for the last train. Never mind, it was only 6pm and the guard told her there was a stopping train in ten or fifteen minutes.

The station stood in its brightness and light – neat red and blue benches, parked between the newly sand-blasted pillars. Liverpool Street Station was different now, no more the smoke-hugged cavern of earlier years. The old arches, once inhabited by seedy pubs, were cluttered with hall-domed wine-bars. The concourse was full of flickering monitors and chrome-tube barriers that corralled the homebound flock. It was a worthy monument to a brave new land, although she noticed the paint already peeling round the edges.

She was excited, if a little nervous, to be seeing Martin again but if there was one thing that she hated, it was a train journey at rush hour. The ugly spawning of a thousand steamy raincoats, sharp-spiked umbrellas poking you in the head, newspapers raised defensively on every side, standing counsel to the soul-sucked faces. She had thought about taking a hire car, but the train held the hint of romance for a lover's journey like this.

A platform number appears against the next train. She walks to the carriages, the first to board, settles in a non-smoking window seat. The carriage fills quickly, until every space, save that opposite her outstretched legs, is taken. Maybe she should have paid for first class, but that went against her northern roots. At the last moment before the train departs, a boy slides towards this last seat with visible relief. Politely, she retracts her legs, gives him more room; smiles distantly.

As the train leaves the station and rounds the first bend she catches a glimpse of the terraces behind Spitalfields, where Martin had taken his first apprenticeship. She remembers the lazy Sunday afternoons spent with him in his seedy digs or drinking together with their friends in Portobello Lane pubs. That was nearly ten years ago now; it was a sacred time.

Maryland, Stratford. She glances across the carriage at the young boy. She is a collector of faces. He is quite pale, and bony-chinned – boyishly pretty, impish. He is dressed in art student black – jeans, felt hat, silver earrings, bracelets, rings. She remembers the student party she had once attended in Stratford, getting too drunk, ending up sleeping beside a boy like him who had stroked her hair and the curvature of her back tenderly into the early hours. A boy whose name she could not even remember the morning after, but whose touch she could still imagine on her skin.

Romford, Shenfield. The boy opposite has taken paper and pen from his bag and draws freely, with a light, flowing stroke. Quick, choreographed lines, swept with a rollerball. She had shared a flat in Shenfield once, as close to London as she could afford at the time, when she was starting out.

Those were days of more parties, more boys; more lost souls.

Ingatestone. She must be near Louise's parents' house now she thinks, looking out onto the dark countryside, straining to see the house lights on the hillside. In the window's reflection, she can see the young artist's work without staring too directly. She realises with delight that his drawings are costumes, instant paper wardrobes – a blouse, a simple skirt, a jacket. She tries to picture how she would look in them. Not really her style, more art-student chic. He draws non-stop, seemingly without thought or effort. Maybe she has found a little genius at work, a fashion prodigy, a new discovery, and is intrigued. There is text too – funny, gawky, childish letters, strung into drunken lines. Descriptions, instructions, colour notes (not all teenage fashion is black then, she thinks), all written in thick black ink.

Chelmsford. 'Chelmingrad,' they had called it. She had worked here for a while too, on the local newspaper. Not the greatest of jobs but it had been a good grounding and the nightclubs provided plenty of fodder for their light amusement. The brief journey was bringing back all sorts of memories; it was funny how something so mundane as a railway line could evoke such long-forgotten moments. It was as if she could get off at any one of these stops and step back in time into real conversations with lost friends and lovers.

The train lurches and the young boy is forced to give up his drawing for a moment and puts the pad down on his knees to look out the window. She attempts to read the inverted text but the vibration and the unreliable glow from the lights defeat her. She is fascinated by this creative demonstration. Until this moment, his hand has hardly stopped. Another page filled and yet another. Getting more sophisticated now, this is more in her line of fashion. An elegant cocktail dress, gloves, silk vest, lingerie, all crammed into his A4 spiral pad. The train slows for her station; she looks at his face and his ponytail and passes him a card before she leaves. 'The fashion writer?' he questions, his eyes lighting up before she gets off with a wave and then blows him a kiss.

The night is jet black; sheets of rain lash her face as she runs across the car park to the waiting cars. She recognises Martin's, unchanged in ten years, and struggles to open the door against the wind. Once inside she slams it quickly to shut out the elements. The interior is peaceful, a haven of old leather and wood. Her perfume fills the small space instantly. There is a moment of silence that neither seems able to break and she wonders whether this was really such a good idea. This was not something that you could row back from easily, with a pleasant smile and a polite good night.

'Sorry, I'm late!' She reaches over to him and there is an awkward brief kiss.

'It's mighty good to see you again,' he says a little nervously, savouring again the once familiar scent of her favourite perfume. 'I've got supper ready back at the house.'

'Well, I'm starving. I hope you've had a better day than me.'

'Go on?' he laughs.

His hands turn the key nervously in the ignition, desire and anticipation make him feel both anxious and warmer already.

The river near Coggeshall, the moon emerges briefly, its disc reflected in the water – the ground glistening with the heavy rain. Three figures stand on the riverbank shrouded by the rising mist. Two carry spades, the third a strange object on a pole and a torch. They leave the river, creep towards a building: Crow's Barn. Tools poised faces stern and determined. One of them holds back, the others walk on. There is a sound, like an owl screeching – a signal. The others climb the fence. They run across the field towards the shadow of a tree. There is a second screech, and then the third rejoins them. 'Do you really know how to work this thing?' The rain sleets down mercilessly.

'Yes, of course,' replies the second. 'Just keep the torch still.' He scans the ground with the pole as it emits at first a strange electronic beep and then a gathering rush of sounds in a staccato crescendo.

'Here, dig here.' The three work with spades and after a few minutes there is the sound of metal on metal.

'I've got something.' They work furiously with hands to release the object from the cloying soil.

'What is it, coins?'

'No, it's just an old plough coulter. Damn!'

Martin drives slower than usual because of the rain – the car's ancient headlights struggle to illuminate the road against the rolling mist. Up ahead there are lights swinging in the road, barring their path. While he has been waiting at the station, a telegraph pole has fallen in the storm and blocked the main road. A policeman in oilskins suggests they turn back.

Martin reverses the car with a horrible mechanical whine, turns and sets off back past the station, takes the main road north and then after half a mile turns left down a less familiar lane. They are crowded in by high banks and dark hedgerows either side. The note of the engine rising as the road begins to steepen, pistons turning over like the expectant click of a roller coaster as it climbs towards the first drop.

'We'd better watch out for highwaymen – this is where they used to lie in wait, you know.'

'Stand and deliver!' she laughs. 'But I already have my own Dick Turpin.'

The old Herald reaches the summit, and then begins to gather speed on the downhill stretch. He shifts down a gear, uncertain of the road ahead. Still the car accelerates. He touches the brake pedal gently, and then more forcibly. The needle of the speedometer flickers upwards: thirty-five – forty – forty-five.

'Martin, please slow down a bit.'

He crunches the selector into second, the gears complaining as the engine roars. He pumps the brakes but they are wet and failing.

'Too fast!' she gasps.

He holds the wheel even more tightly with both hands – his knuckles white against the rim, the engine screaming. Here is the bend, sharp left past the old mill. His grip tightens again, tugging the wooden rim clockwise. There is another light ahead and they see two figures in the road this time, their faces lit up clearly for a second by the headlamps. Almost too late, he swerves to avoid them.

'Christ, what the hell...?'

There is a third figure standing straight in front of them; Martin turns the wheel sharply and the car heads into the hedgerow; they brace for the impact. But the car bursts right through the hedge, down across a cattle gulch and straight into the river.

Maybe if he had not been so tired, he would have seen the man ahead. Maybe if he had not been so tired, he would have been able to hold the bend. Maybe if he had not been so tired, he would have been able to avoid the hedge. Maybe everything would have been different.

The old car that is his only world now lies shattered at the bottom of the embankment, half-submerged in the rushing waters, balanced precariously on the shoulder of the riverbank; headlamps extinguished, wheels turning slowly, frame sliding ever deeper into the river's clammy grasp. Inside the steel shell, he feels a silence that suspends time, hears his remaining lifespan measured by the ticking of the seconds on the dashboard clock, the outcome unresolved, contingent on dark confidences. Outside he hears gloomy fingers tearing at the bent metal, water clawing around the doors, steam issuing urgently from the radiator. The river and his life flow without mercy. His body, reflecting his native landscape, fathered and fatherless; heart long-hardened, head long ago lost to hope. In this shattered cage all are one; the child, the boy, the man, all searching the landscape through frosted glass, struggling determinedly for life, searching.

It is only seconds after they have come to rest but he feels already a first watery breath around his neck; his feet wet, the chassis of the car creaking ominously in its cradle as the swollen river rages by. Time and tide are against him again, just like from the beginning.

The beautiful woman that lies beside him is also weakening, her dreams washing away as the water rises, her lifeblood ebbing just as quickly. A moment ago he heard her scream, but now there is no sound. He has sensed the futility of their struggle, feels they are losing, wonders whether he has reached the point where he has to die, wonders whether they both have to die, trapped together in this metal cage.

On the bank he sees a water vole panicking in the flood. He wonders how he can feel so calm, so unaware of pain, in this darkness, in this car, on the brink of disaster, listening to the voice of the river singing through the gloom, listening to Sally's fading breath. He feels pain in his legs, cannot move them, and wonders whether he has the strength to try to move, to push his shoulder against the crushing weight of the river against the door once more. He wonders if he cares enough to live, in the darkness, in the gloom, in this fluid ambiguity.

He wishes to see her face. Hear some word of comfort, some promise of encouragement, some breath of life from her lips, some confirmation that he is not to be left alone. He shouts again for help, unable to move his body in any useful way to escape.

The ticking of the clock distracts his mind. He feels for fragments, strains of meaning in the silence. Gathers moments of their shared experience into memory; calls her name, unsure whether she can hear him. She does not answer, maybe she cannot answer. Without her he must make the choice, decide their fate. He must storm against life. Confidence betrays him. Is there no other way to escape?

He peers again through the mud-scraped glass into the mocking shadows, into despair, into night still far from dawn, the world blind to the peace that might emerge from its fine overlays of colour. This cruel separation they have both suffered, damned by tragedy, the darkest shadows stifling every hope. They have shared stories of the sea, of the moors, stories of storms, stories that will not give them peace.

A minute or two has passed and already the water is up to the belt line of the car. The feeble glow of the moon penetrates the cabin. When the car had first come to rest, he had stared through the window at its sallow disc, disbelieving, still numb from pain, thinking of a thousand things apart from salvation. He had seen her face in its light, cold as silk, unmoved in its supernatural reality, the inside of the car illuminated briefly by the carelessness of a fleeing storm cloud. Her body is stretched out on the seat beside him, like a dress discarded carelessly after a party, features barely recognisable, and limbs already slipping from a faded world. It was no great leap of imagination to see her arms wrapped in the folds of the river, flowing helplessly through darkened fields, her spirit moving ever more quickly towards the final resolution of the sea.

He strokes her forehead, watched by the pitying willows, her hair thin like a silver fish writhing breathlessly in the flood. His mind tormented by the demon: he must choose.

Choose whether he also would float in that river, drift with her in the moonlight, connected only by the fluid landscape to those lifeless limbs.

The water has reached his chest now, filling the car as if sucked in by the futile action of his lungs. There must be a solution, a way out. Drown in a river? That would be some little irony. He fingers the chain with the little cross that hangs about his neck. Looks at her face again, wonders if these are to be his final thoughts, their final moments? He remembers the cold terror, the cries of desperation, and the bitterness of loss.

She murmurs in her seat, the water lapping around her neck, as if she has been disturbed in a dream. He wants to sleep, exhausted, in her arms, fragile in her embrace; dig deeper together into the night. What would he give now to have time to talk, to reconcile? If only he had more time… but there is none, not even seconds. He has left everything too late; he has depended too long on an empty journey, a fruitless search.

Of course there was bitterness. Over the last six years, without her balancing presence he had descended once more into solitude. It was as if his life had been lived through a hundred bodies, all searching, pilotless, for a dream, a chimera of promised dawn. He closes his eyes, and his mind becomes the darkened landscape that threatens to engulf them, the lifeless body on the shore, this fierce woman's anguish. All hope of renewal washed away on the tide.

Are they to die together? Is there to be any escape from this conclusion?

In the moonlight, her eyes flicker and he reaches out to her mouth, feels the feeblest breeze from her lungs. He collects in his palm the last vestiges of a soul that could love him, truthfully and faithfully, despite his coldness, despite his rejection, despite his anger. Without hope he throws his shoulder against the door, oblivious to pain, but it is wedged solidly by the force of mud and water, and does not yield. If he could just get some help. He calls again, time moves with inexorable slowness; he sounds the horn again. Is there anybody out there to hear?

He had been taken aback by the ferocity of his guilt, reeled for a while in its intensity. He was unable to hold her, unable to let go; unable to return the completeness of her emotion, to return the fullness of her love. Her forgiveness had left him defenceless. Like two lovers counting ripples on the shoreline. Like a man raising his shoulders above the storm to see again the blue sky, to see far-off days, full of frantic joy. And then, more recently, he had walked with her again, proud, softened, for the entire world like a giant with a boat above his head. The sea grass had swayed in the breeze, ripples on the shoreline. He was comforted by the peace of the sea, all the accusations and confessions blown away by the wind.

He brushes her cheek with the back of his hand. Her body is chilled; soon he will know that warmth no more. He looks at her face, and sees her likeness pale in its shadows.

I drew a sabre through her
It was a bloody knife
I threw her in the river
Which was a dreadful sign?
Traditional, *Down in the Willow Garden*

He calls her name urgently, shakes her motionless body, his words met by silence as he cries out to her in the darkness. During these last moments while he struggles, a man drowning in glistening sadness, he realises his life has been nothing. More than anything, he wants her to know, for all that it hurts, that he loves her and knows that she loves him.

He remembers how the sun burnt in the waves the morning after the storm that claimed his father's life. He remembers the wailing of the women, his sister's frantic song, her sudden departure, his mother's funeral, their bitter final parting. Everywhere, water on fire.

'I love you!'

There, he has said it. It is such an irony that in the coldness of this river, he finally releases the heat that was always there, bottled in by his pride. And now that he looks back, he sees that there were moments when this truth, that has remained concealed in his breast, could have been shared, awoken by rage. Did anything good ever happen that he didn't destroy? He regrets the loss of time. It was so very long ago, before the shadows had pierced their lives, that they danced together, under the stars. He feels it all now – rage, anger, guilt, striking out at the truth that has lain unspoken, crushing his body. Tears are shining on his cheeks.

He thinks her more beautiful than ever in this cold light, her face pale in the gloom, cheeks once bright now merely ripples in the waters. His hands across her face again, brushing her cold lips one last time. He strokes the dyed blonde hair that he loves. Her own words recur to him, spoken before she left him in despair: 'Life hurts less when you sing in colour.'

The car shudders in its slippery bed. He looks at the windscreen, at the creeping fingers, sees the silver threads breaking its completeness, and sees there is a way to escape, a way he can still get out. The smell of fuel is strong now, but if he breaks this cage the water will follow, and she will be free to float. Only he, in this car, in the darkness of the river, watching her dying, can decide. Stay or leave, sink or swim. And there is so little time to say goodbye. There is so little time.

'Will you ever forgive me?'

A mighty pyre.
Faggots piled,
around the stake.
Chains.
Soldiers pulling,
crowds pushing.
Rich on his steed.
Be calm now,
and know the grace of God.
The bell tolls.
The fire's set,
smoke's rising,
faggots cackle.
Martha screams.
'O my dear wife, how I love thee.'
Flames, heat, scorching now.
Terrible pain –.
Be calm.
Know the grace of God.
'Jesus receive my spirit into your tender, loving arms.'
Terrible heat.
My lungs burning.
My father's eyes,
he cannot look,
'O Father, I have found freedom.'
Must give a sign.
Reach out to heaven.
O clap for joy,
Heaven's open,
with all its angels.
O clap for joy.
Once,
twice,
three times.

The crowds gasp,
the horses cry,
the wind rushes.
O joyous flame.
Now, it is finished.

XIII – Passacaglia

In ceaseless motion comes and goes the tide
Flowing it fills the channel broad and wide
Then back to sea with strong majestic sweep
It rolls in ebb yet terrible and deep.

Benjamin Britten, *Peter Grimes*

SATURDAY EVENING – LATE SEPTEMBER 1990
ALDEBURGH BEACH

'I thought you might like to see this.' Thomas passed Amber the open book. She pulled aside the glassine paper that protected the plate and stared at the deep colours.

'The Depths of the Sea,' she read aloud.

Her face reflected already the possessive danger of the mermaid's eyes, clinging to her handsome prize, dragging him down, ever deeper, towards his submarine death.

Under the fluid metal of a steel-blue sky, the body of a young woman strokes powerfully through freezing waves, her legs extended, the winter ice chilling her skin, her arms reaching for resolution in the morning air. As she glides through the lazy current, she disturbs the balance of the channel, releasing a surge of rings, strong and certain. The greens and greys of the water's surface thick like sugar around her waist.

A stone's throw from the water, a man huddled against the cold sits in the lee of the fisherman's huts, nursing the flame of a calor gas stove in the fickle wind. The faintest wisp of steam emanates from a small stained kettle resting on the stove. The beach lies bleached and barren before him, an outsized desert of pebbles and seaside jetsam, undulated by the force of winter storms into ridges between deep furrows.

Jade leaves the waves and collects her shoes and towel from the water's edge, the athletic bearing of her body assured against the bright outline of the sky. Her hair is blown by the wind so that the expression on her face is lost to his eyes. She seems small and young against the vastness of the ocean.

'That was good,' she says, pulling the towel through her hair.

'You're mad, it must have been freezing.'

She pulls on jeans and sweater over her wet bathing suit and nuzzles up under the protection of his arm for warmth.

'But you're lovely and warm, Sam. Warm enough for me.'

Silently he pours the boiling liquid into two cups and passes her the foaming soup. She drinks without waiting for it to cool so that he thinks her mouth must burn. Her face and neck shine with the reflected sun.

'Thanks for coming, Sam. I really appreciate the support; especially after all you went through Friday night. How are Martin and Sally doing?'

'Recovering slowly but they'll be fine. They were lucky that we saw it happen – if they'd hit a tree that would have been it. He is really besotted with her, isn't he?'

'Yes, she's exactly what he needs.'

'Do you mind? I can tell you had a thing for him.'

'No, you're my hero now.' She hugs him tight and nuzzles her head into his chest.

'What else could I do?'

'I'm so in love with you.'

He sips his soup thoughtfully now that it has cooled.

'So, tell me more about this picture you found.'

'Here, look.' She unravels a folded sheet from her bag. 'To think it was lying there in Martin's attic all those years. No doubt about the handwriting.'

Sam inspects the picture and the inscription 'To Amber' and on the reverse, 'To my sea spirit'.

'It's a strange sentiment for a picture of a man in the death grip of a mermaid! Burne-Jones, isn't it?'

'Yes, but I think he knew what he was doing.'

'So what did this Mr Ogilvie have to say about it?'

'He made some lame excuse about her admiring the picture in a book of his. He's still hiding something. I'm sure he knows what became of Amber – it's something to do with his brother's death. I can't work it out.'

'Maybe it's as simple as he just doesn't like curious women?' he said, teasing her. They roll over in the sand and she kisses him hotly.

'To Amber,' Thomas remembers writing still on the back of the illustration in his dream.

'Let's swim again tomorrow,' Amber says.

Girl.
Sand.
Hot, sharp grains.
Warm breeze.
Smile.
Moon-jade eyes – like burning coals.
Defiant, kiss-daring smile.
Half-waistcoat of hemp and ribbon-appliquéd stones.
Lapis lazuli, emerald, rose garnet.
Waves of desire.
Gift-proffered shell.
Fragile, smooth, twisted spirals.
Held in her palm.
Listen!
Hear the sea!
The sounds of the deep,
the sounds of Calypso.

Sam pulls back the hair from Jade's cheeks and kisses her in return, full on the lips.

'So, do you think you've really found her?'

'Maybe,' she says, shaking her head, 'but I haven't got to

the bottom of it yet. The coroner's report said Thomas's brother Ralph fell and broke his neck. He couldn't have dived in, that tower was always twenty yards from the sea. The lady from the Trust once told me that they had had to replace the coping stones when they became dangerous. Maybe he just fell, maybe he was chasing Amber, maybe Thomas pushed him… I suspect we'll never know.'

'You are becoming quite the detective, Sherlock.'

'And then there's you and your silly name.'

'Crow?'

'Not just Crow: Sam Crow, from a long line of miscreants and highwaymen. How did you just drop into my life?'

She takes out the locket from the bag and opens it so she can remove the picture. 'Sam, Sarah and me at Felixstowe,' she reads.

'All ghosts now?'

'Who knows, but if this is really your mother and father as you say, and the woman is my mother, then did they know what became of her?'

He pauses and reddens.

'Oh, sorry, there's something else.' He fumbles in his pocket. 'The hotel receptionist at the Wentworth was anxious I give you this.'

Spidery black writing covers the plain white envelope, 'Jade' the only inscription.

'Sam, you idiot, that's his writing!'

She slits the envelope breathlessly. Inside the first envelope is a small brown package; faded writing, a lilac 3d stamp, the letter unfranked and unposted. She unfolds the package. Inside is a note, a love note; a letter unread in a quarter of a century, a letter from a mother to her daughter. She shakes her head, her hands trembling. 'Oh my God, Sam, I can't read it. Please can you read it, please?'

'Dear Jade…' he starts.

And before he reaches the second sentence unchecked tears run down Jade's face.

'...my darling, Jade, I don't know where you'll be or how old you'll be when you read this. Please don't think badly of me or believe that I had a hard life. I loved a man – Ralph, your father. I lost him in a terrible accident. I loved another – Peter, your grandfather – lost to the wrath of the sea. My mother, Ellen, the most wonderful mother a girl ever had – we share her green eyes – is dead now too. And Martin, my dearest baby brother, I've hurt him so. If you have not already done so, please find him. He was the kindest brother that any sister could ever have. Jade, don't think badly of me. Believe in yourself, don't give up like me. I've left you with a friend who I hope will care for you better than I ever could. Love your life and pray for me always. I love you so. I will always watch over you. God bless you, my little darling.'

At the northern end of the same beach a middle-aged man wades in confusion into the black waters. He has so many words in his mind, each word shaped and twisted into a form that holds completion. The night stars shining about his head like diamonds in the surf. The sea blurred with stillness, cut only by the blueness of a wave. He sees and breathes all in the blindness of his guilt.

The shingle terraces shelve away under his feet and he begins to swim. His body is heavy with the weight of clothes and boots, as he proceeds out into the vast terror beyond the end of the breakwater, his head full of coldness and despair.

He grasps at the fluid, pulling himself forward on an imaginary ladder until he is far out of reach. Stories wander around his mind, lost for purpose. Joy rushes and storms and wanes again as he searches.

He will fight the sea's lazy drag for a while, fight to swim out further, until the late lights of the town form a distant chain on the water. The waves grow higher and his stomach is sick with brine, but he has no regrets: he wants this battle, he will fight for it.

As he weakens, the sky becomes light so that the surface of the sea melts into a cloud before him. It melts from black to blue to white, through delicate shades of pink and grey. Islands appear and are lifted up like clouds, sea palaces rising to meet him. Each of them written in a word in his mind, a piece of verse destroyed, concentrated in the wind, concentrated by the motion of the sea. His head is full of warmth, the nausea hot like brandy in his throat.

At last they are to be together again. His body soothed by the pungency of oil and milk. There is a longing in his eyes, a searching of intent. His brow stroked by the waters, sliding like a sail, irresistible, terrible.

'Amber!' he cries. It is Ralph's voice that returns his call.

They are all three silent together in the waves. He has left a bundle of letters on the shore behind him, wrapped in string, the name of his past written in faint ink on the surface of the package. His full confession to the niece he betrayed.

'Again they come!' and mutter'd as he died.